HIS
DARK
CLAIM

ISBN: 979-8-9996850-1-8

Published by Trifold Publishing
A Division of Eratu LLC
Pennsylvania, USA
info@trifoldpublishing.com

Dedication

To the women who crave chains more than flowers.
This is your altar. This is your surrender. This is *your* world.
Live in it.

Content Warning

Kidnapping and captivity
Forced marriage / Coercion
Graphic violence and murder (on-page)
Gun violence
Psychological manipulation
Obsession and possession
Non-traditional power dynamics
References of trauma
Profanity and explicit language
Dubious Consent
Mentions of abuse

This story is a work of dark romance. It contains morally grey characters, toxic dynamics, and situations that are not to be emulated in real life. Reader discretion is strongly advised.

HIS
DARK
CLAIM

LUNA SADS

TRIFOLD PUBLISHING

E nchanting.
　　　　And delicate. She wasn't the prettiest woman he had seen, nor was her body curvaceous.

No, she was uniquely peculiar. A dangerous kind of seduction. And his addiction.

She was like a flushed glow with her fair skin. Wavy and wild chestnut hair swayed from her slim shoulders to rest on her small waist and plump breasts he dreamt of every night. Petite, that little thing was barely five-three, yet she was a fevered dream he couldn't escape. From where he sat gazing at his little doll, he had the perfect view.

His dirty secret was smiling and giggling over the compliments she had been receiving all night long from filthy rich men who eyed her. His blood boiled. Just a few more minutes. Her hands moved as she explained the painting of her own creation on the wall.

He knew she could feel his gaze on her, and that satisfied his soul. He knew she was an anxious one, pretending to be calm. He knew that no one noticed the slight shiver of her fingers and the occasional bead of sweat glistening on the back of her neck. Slender and slim. He wanted to wrap his hand around it and know if his hold would choke her. Last night was not enough, and his beast was running wild, growling to claim the vixen.

She was talented, really talented.

She sold three of her masterpieces for more than fifty thousand in her first bidding. Would she notice that all three of her paintings were bought by the same person?

He wondered if she'd appreciate the special present he had planned for her that night.

A motion of his hand, and the man standing just behind him handed over an empty check and a pen.

He signed the check and kept the amount unfilled. He watched as the assistant walked the check to the woman in the center of the crowd. That would be one of his gifts to his little vixen.

After tonight, he wouldn't return here, nor would she.

After tonight, she would be dead to the world, relying and depending solely on him. Only him. He felt himself getting hard and reached for a sip of champagne.

Soon. In a couple of hours, she would be under him, in his darkness, in his mansion. Caged and protected, just like a secret.

His dirty little secret.

CHAPTER ONE
His Claim

My fingers trembled as I held the check, and the smooth paper almost slipped from my grip.

One hundred thousand.

More than I'd made that night.

It was definitely mine. I checked the immaculate writing showing my name again: Celestine Devereaux.

Tearing my gaze from the check, I glanced around the room. All my eyes caught were fancy-dressed people, chatting and laughing. Faces blurred together—some familiar, others strangers. A woman smiled at me warmly, and a man raised his glass in a passing greeting.

I forced a small smile.

But none of them seemed to claim ownership of this... odd gesture.

My chest tightened. I'd already sold three of the pieces I'd brought here, so why would someone pay me extra? And no name on the check.

I clutched the check closer to my chest, and a flush crept up my neck as I felt eyes on me. My eyes darted from face to face.

"Celestine!" A familiar voice broke through my racing thoughts.

I turned to see Grace. My insides uncurled at the sight of one of the few people here who felt like a friend.

"Look at you!" Her emerald dress shimmered, catching the light in her eyes. "You've outdone yourself tonight. Everyone's talking about your work."

∞

By the time I got to my car, I was half-convinced Grace would follow me into the parking lot. She had this uncanny ability to appear whenever I least expected it, usually with a cup of coffee and an opinion about my life choices, especially about Adrian. Especially about how I shouldn't leave my own exhibit to celebrate an anniversary.

Sliding into the driver's seat, I glanced at the check again, tucked safely in my bag. My thoughts wandered as I started the engine.

Was Grace right, and some mysterious benefactor had decided to fund me?

Years in art school hadn't been wasted after all. Maybe it was time to set up my own studio. I couldn't keep leaning on Grace and Adrian forever.

A strained sigh left my lips.

Maybe I should talk to him tonight. He'd definitely... have opinions. Adrian always had opinions, unhurried and practical. But I didn't mind. He had a way of making sense of my chaos, even if it sometimes felt like he was trying to fix me.

He had carried me through darker days without ever mentioning it. Paid my loans and supported our family when we almost became bankrupt.

The parking lot of our familiar building was half-full when

I parked and turned off the engine. I smiled faintly, imagining him in the kitchen, engrossed in dinner prep. Adrian liked to cook, especially on nights like this. And tonight was special.

Four years. Four years of support, of quiet smiles and steady hands. I'd planned to surprise him with something small, maybe a new watch or a book he'd been mentioning, but now, with the check burning a hole in my bag, I wanted to do more.

The familiar scent of lavender and faint cooking spices greeted me.

"Adrian?"

No response.

I slipped off my shoes and wandered toward the kitchen, and the faint sound of steak being roasted in a pan filtered through my ears. The stove lights were on, but he wasn't there.

I turned off the stove and turned to the dining room, grinning like an idiot at the sight of a neatly set table. Candles lit, wine glasses waiting.

"Adrian!" I called out louder this time. A faint shuffle of movement from the bedroom. "You're going all out tonight, aren't you?" I started, stepping toward the sound.

A strange scent hung in the air, and I told myself it was nothing.

The door slid open silently showing me what was now in our bedroom... and I froze.

He stood with his back to me. His silhouette broad and disturbingly still. The faint light from the bedside lamp cast long shadows, but it was his hand that drew my eyes.

Time slowed as my breath caught in my throat and the room narrowed to that single detail: the gun held loosely at his side. My stomach churned, bile rising as my gaze shifted, drawn unwillingly to the floor.

The metallic tang of blood hit me first, and then my eyes wandered to the dark pool seeping into the fibres of the grey carpet. My knees buckled.

This wasn't real. It couldn't be real.

Move. Run. Do something!

Adrian lay crumpled on the floor, his limbs twisted unnaturally. His shirt was soaked, the pristine white now a horrifying crimson. His eyes—those warm, familiar eyes—were open, but there was nothing in them.

"No." The sound didn't come out of my mouth.

I should've run. Every instinct screamed at me to bolt for the doors, but love was the cruelest liar, a rope that bound even as it strangled.

My gaze locked on the figure standing over Adrian's body.

A man. Broad-shouldered, his back to me.

As I took a step back, the floor creaked beneath me, and I stiffened.

He turned.

The light danced across his features. I'd never forget that face. A scar carved down his cheek, pulling his lip into a permanent frown that twisted with something unspeakable. His eyes—wild, unhinged—glistened with evil.

He didn't say a word.

But the silence did.

Something in me broke, and I spun on my heel and ran. My bare feet pounded against the threadbare carpet, my breath coming in panicked gasps. Behind me, I heard him move.

I didn't dare look back. I threw myself into the foyer as my fingers grazed the walls for balance.

The door…. My fingers wrapped around the handle, and I twisted it. I was about to open it when a hand clamped over my knuckles.

I screamed, but my body was slammed against the door, cutting me off. His strength was overwhelming, and then a second later, both my wrists were pinned to my sides. I thrashed, kicked, anything to get free, but he was formidable.

Tears blurred his face, his breath was hot against my skin, and I yelled.

Steel grey eyes penetrated me.

My mouth was dry and I couldn't gather saliva to talk. But the more I looked at him, the more I hated him. He just stood there, knee pressing between my legs, eyes watching, and hands pinning me down.

I opened my mouth to curse at him, but before I could speak, something sharp pricked my neck. My vision blurred. His hands loosened their hold, and I thumped to the ground on my knees in front of him.

The last thing I saw was his face—twisted in chaos, but utterly, terrifyingly silent.

Then, oblivion.

CHAPTER TWO
Dolcezza

I could hear myself breathing slowly and deeply. My body was tied to something I assumed to be a chair. I couldn't move, and it crept more and more into my senses than it should. My eyelids twitched, and after several attempts, I managed to force them open. I was in a dim room, barely recognisable. Concrete with no windows, just a metal door.

The events of last night came rushing in. I remembered looking... Adrian. My chest tightened before a sob broke through.

The man. The gun. Blood. And the needle.

How did... everything crash in just one night? Why?

Where was I? Why was I here? How did I get here? I wanted to scream, but my throat was dry and sore, like my limbs. And this alien feeling frightened me more – a lack of control over my body such that I could only gasp for air.

I screamed, and this time, though guttural and strained, it was audible. I shifted, moving my limbs, only to realise the ropes were tight. Tears came unrequited to my eyes, streaming down my cheeks in cold rivers.

My movements were clumsy and unnatural. I managed to unbalance the chair, and fall to the ground, still bound. The armrest broke, and my limbs came free.

I crawled away from the broken chair while ripping the ropes off of me, half-tripping over the long pale blue fabric of a long dress I never remembered putting on. I began sprinting as fast as I could towards the metal door when something yanked me back, slamming me forward, scraping my chin and knees on the floor. My instincts had been too slow, not allowing me enough time to balance myself.

Tugging, I was met with hard metal chains bound at one end to my right ankle and the other to the metal ring, which was bolted to the floor. Oh god…

Kidnapped. The realisation harassed my thoughts.

Someone kidnapped me. But that didn't halt my struggles. I wiped the tears off my cheeks praying that all this would turn out to be one of my nightmares. I wasn't rich or valuable, so why did someone kidnap me? Why did they… kill Adrian? And even if someone wished to use me to their advantage, no one would care if I was abducted or not. My thoughts wandered to the darkest reality.

I was probably taken by some sick predator who meets women and rapes them, and then kills them in such a way that no one could recognise their mutilated bodies. Shivers ran uncontrollably up and down my spine.

The metal door creaked, jerking my head up.

A soft light infiltrated first. Even though it was not bright, I was blinded for a moment.

Then I saw him.

He stood in the doorway like a bringer of death. His hair fell over his forehead, dark and slightly messy.

Last night, I'd been too panicked to look at him, but now… The way he was dressed and carried himself, he hadn't broken into our apartment to steal.

Lethal and terrifying.

"Hello, Dolcezza," he said softly, stepping into the room.

I scrambled off my arse as he stalked towards me like a hungry tiger circling the rabbit. Something in his eyes glinted, and I noticed the wildness too quickly.

I was going to scratch his face if he touched me.

A step closer from him, a step back from me. Then another and another, until I was pressed against the wall, the chain tight around my ankle, dragging me down to sit.

His shiny, polished shoes blocked my vision, and I craned my neck to look at him. He tilted his head, and my eyes caught the scar that ran down his cheek. It was faint, yet not something you could miss. Unhinged stormy grey eyes trained on my face, dragging down my body, lowering to my bleeding knee. His lips twisted.

"Who... who are you?"

He lowered himself, and I flinched as he knelt in front of me. I stared at him, wanting to ask him so many questions, but couldn't with my heart hammering in my throat.

He patiently watched me, observing my shaky limbs and trembling lips.

I made myself stay still when his hand was raised to touch my face. I just sat there. This murderer's fingers were gentle on my skin, almost tender. For a moment I was disoriented.

"Who am I?" he repeated my words. "Who do you think I am, Dolcezza?"

My ankles ached against the chains, and I knew I was bleeding, yet I couldn't stop pulling. Futile, useless, desperate. My body fought for freedom even as my mind sank deeper into the hole.

"Why?" I spat, my voice trembling but firm. "Why did you kill him? Why are you doing this to me?"

His lips twitched—a ghost of a smirk that never reached his eyes. He tilted his head, studying me like a puzzle he had all the time in the world to solve.

"Knowing why will not make this hurt any less."

This time I flinched when his hand trailed down my cheek, deceptively tender, until it gripped my jaw with bruising force. My teeth clenched under the pressure, and I whimpered, hating the sound that escaped me.

"You want to know why I killed him?" he continued, and I glared at him with hatred burning in my eyes. "Because he was in my way."

Tears burned my eyes, but I refused to let them fall. He didn't deserve to see me break. My throat ached as I swallowed down the sob clawing its way up. Adrian was gone. His laughter, his warmth—stolen by this monster that now crouched before me.

"You're sick," I hissed, my voice cracking.

His grip tightened, forcing my head back against the cold wall. His face was calm, unnervingly so, like my words did not have any impact on him.

"I've been called worse."

I thrashed, trying to pull away, but he held me easily, his strength a cruel reminder of how hopeless this was. My wrists burned, and I felt the sticky warmth of blood pooling beneath the chains.

"What are you going to do to me? Kill me?" I hated how he scared me.

He chuckled as if my trembling voice amused him.

"I find you worth keeping, Dolcezza."

His words sank into me like knives, and all I could do was shatter more and more.

"Why… why did you do this? What have we ever done to you? What do you want from me?"

11

For a moment, his jaw tightened and a faint tick betrayed an otherwise eerily calm demeanor. Then he chuckled, sending a chill down my spine.

"What do I want?" he echoed, his tone deceptively soft. His storm-grey eyes bored into mine before raking over my body. "What any man wants—sex."

My heart thundered in my chest as I struggled back.

"Let me go!" I screamed, and the chains rattled against my frantic movements. "I'll call the cops!"

His lips moved into something between a smirk and a sneer.

"And what would the police do? Rescue you from a man they'll never find?" He leaned closer.

"Stop it, please!" I begged, tears blurring my vision as I pressed myself tighter into the wall. "Don't you understand that this is wrong?"

His head tilted slightly, as though considering my words. "What is not right? A man wanting to have sex?"

I thrashed against the chains, panic coursing through my veins. He was disgusting. "This is kidnapping me and caging me against my will. Threatening to rape me and-"

"Threatening?" his chuckle was darker this time. He reached out, gripping my chin with one hand and forcing my gaze to meet his. "You're using some heavy words, Dolcezza. I just want to fuck you, hard and raw, so that every breath leaving your body ends on me. I want to see your swollen red cunt after I'm done fucking you, the sounds you make while my cock slams into your-"

"Stop it!"

He pulled back just enough to look at me. Then, without warning, he grabbed my arm and yanked me forward, dragging me to my feet. I stumbled, barely catching myself.

"Why? You asked what I wanted, so I'm telling you. This

will be the last time I'm explaining this. Next time, I show you."

"Let me go-" I thrashed as he gripped my dress and pulled me to his chest. My head was pulled back harshly. His eyes penetrated through my soul, the scar glistening.

"No can do. Not till I have my fill and you're fucked loose for any other man out there."

I shut my eyes. My head hurt. My body did too. And everything else.

"You're insane!"

He chuckled. "You didn't like it when I was gentle, so I figured you'd like the hard way better."

I sobbed.

I heard him take a deep breath before his grip on my hair loosened, and he released me. My body crumpled to the floor, gasping for breath as his words settled over me.

"Twenty minutes. Wash up, change, and clean the mess you made. Talk back and I'll cut out your tongue. Run, and I'll break your legs. Disobey me in any way, and you'll wish you hadn't."

I didn't respond. Couldn't. My mind reeled, trapped in a storm of grief, fear, and rage. Adrian was gone. The life I'd known was gone. All that was left was this—chains, blood, and the man who had destroyed everything.

I would fight even if it broke me, even if it killed me. I would not let him win.

CHAPTER THREE
Ruins

When he left, I broke down into gut-wrenching sobs. Nothing made sense. I should have fought harder. I should have run. But I didn't. It wasn't logic that held me still or fear of what he might do. It was something darker, something I couldn't name. Something I hated myself for.

I was scared of him.

And I was scared of myself.

The door opened again, and a woman walked in. Middle-aged, grey hair, and lips pulled in a straight line. She didn't say anything. Just stood there with what seemed to be clothes in her hands.

"Who are you?" I hated how my voice trembled. She stepped closer, and I flinched as she knelt beside me and grabbed my ankle. I went to pull away but stopped when she started un-cuffing the cuffs.

My skin was raw beneath the metal. I pulled my legs toward me, curling them, but the ache was still there.

She didn't meet my eyes. Not once. Her expression was carved from stone, just like the man she worked for. The silence stretched between us, and coated my skin.

"Who are you?" I tried again, the tremor in my voice betraying the anger.

Still, she said nothing. Instead, she held out the bundle of clothes, her hand steady.

"I'm not putting that on." It wasn't disobedience, it was desperation. She didn't flinch, didn't even react. Just waited.

Her silence was worse than any threat. It filled my chest with something I couldn't fight.

"You'll want to wear them. He doesn't like waiting."

Ice flooded my veins, and I shook my head. "No," I whispered. "No, I'm not—"

Her gaze snapped to mine then. "You don't have a choice, Miss."

My fists clenched, and all I could do was stare at her, the clothes in her hands, the door still slightly ajar behind her. But there was no running, no escaping that bastard.

With trembling hands, I reached out and took the bundle.

"The bathroom's that way."

I moved toward the bathroom like a marionette, the bundle of clothes hung heavy in my arms. My bare feet scraped against the cold floor, and the door clicked shut behind me, closing me in a hollow space that reeked of bleach and despair.

The mirror was right above the sink. For a long moment, I couldn't look. My hands gripped the edge of the counter, knuckles turning white, as I willed myself to breathe.

When I finally dared to lift my gaze, the reflection staring back at me wasn't mine. It couldn't be.

The girl in the mirror was hollow, her eyes rimmed red and swollen. Her lips quivered, her face—my face—was streaked with the tracks of tears that had long since dried. There was no fight left in her. Only a shadow of the person she used to be.

I hated her.

An ugly sob tore from my throat, and I clapped a hand over my mouth to stifle it. Adrian should've been beside me, laughing, loving, and… alive.

If I stayed here, I'd die. Maybe not today, but soon.

I dragged my gaze back to the mirror. My fingers twitched as I grabbed the cloth from the bundle, wrapping it around my hand. The mirror trembled under my fist before shattering into a spider web of jagged pieces. The sound was muffled.

I fished out the largest shard. Its edge was sharp enough to bite into my skin.

I quickly slipped into the purple dress and tore the remains of my old dress into strips, wrapping the shard in the largest piece and shoving it against my chest.

My heart thundered against it.

I just needed to act my part. He wouldn't trample over my life without me fighting back.

The purple dress fit too well. Too perfect, as if it had been made for me.

I bit the inside of my cheek hard until I tasted blood. Pain stranded me.

Hiding my shaking hands behind my back, I took a breath and left the bathroom. The woman was not there. The cuffs lay on the floor. I clenched my jaw before walking to the metal door. My fingers hovered over the handle, and I forced myself to take a deep breath.

She was waiting. Her eyes swept over me and without a word, she simply turned and gestured for me to follow.

If I couldn't escape, then I'd make him regret ever touching my life.

She led me down a narrow, dimly lit hallway. It was a basement, I realised. Grey and black walls and a concrete floor. Yellow bulbs and a stench… which I didn't want to decipher.

There was a door at the end of the staircase, and somehow I knew where it led. The moment I stepped onto it, my breath hitched. The door opened into a grand room, and my eyes widened, momentarily forgetting to breathe.

What... what place was this?

My moist eyes took in the cold marbled floor stretching underneath the high ceiling. Everything gleamed with wealth, like the house didn't know how to be lived in.

The witch tugged me forward, snapping me out of my trance. My feet faltered as my mind raced. Whoever this man was, he wasn't just rich—he was powerful. The kind of power that made people disappear without a trace.

What could he possibly want from us? From me?

The maid led me through an arched doorway into what appeared to be a dining room.

There he sat at the head of the table, his back to me, his fingers curling around the stem of a wine glass, the liquid inside catching the light like blood.

I thought I knew fear, but this man redefined it.

He didn't look at me right away, but somehow I felt his sentience.

The shadows played tricks on his face until he looked more like a nightmare than a man.

I stopped in the doorway, my fists clenched at my sides.

Hot anger and hatred surged through me. It was so volatile that I nearly pulled out the glass and plunged it into his neck.

Instead, I forced myself to breathe.

CHAPTER FOUR
A Little Death

The woman pushed me toward the table. I resisted the urge to glare at her, watching the way her fingers trembled as she tried to guide me. Still, it didn't make me hate her any less.

He hadn't looked at me since she brought me here, but I knew he was aware of my every move.

A few slow steps and I was just behind him. My heart hammered against my ribs as I imagined pulling the broken glass from my dress. It would be so simple. One quick thrust into the artery of his neck.

My fingers twitched.

"Don't."

His deep voice made my hand fall limp at my side, my fingers trembling.

There was no way he could see me—no way he could read the thoughts raging in my head.

Chaos, he infiltrated inside me. I'd never felt such strong emotions for anyone, not even love, until this hatred. Disgust. Loathing.

The moment stretched into another, and I only released

the captive breath when he motioned with the wine glass in his hand.

"Sit," he commanded.

The woman behind me stiffened and stepped away quickly.

I clenched my fists as I reluctantly obeyed, lowering myself into the chair across from him. The table was an untouched expanse of white cloth, the kind you'd see in a fine dining restaurant, not a prison.

Food was placed in front of me—lavish and warm, the kind of meal meant for celebration. My stomach churned at the sight.

He finally looked at me and gestured toward the plate. "Eat."

I stared at him, bile rising in my throat.

"Eat?" I repeated. "You think I'm going to sit here and eat after you—" My voice cracked, and I swallowed hard. "After you killed Adrian?"

His gaze didn't falter, didn't even flicker. He just sipped the wine as if I'd trust him with the food. It could be poisoned or drugged for all I knew.

"You must be hungry," he said simply, ignoring the venom in my tone.

I shoved the plate away. "Don't pretend you care," I spat and glared at him. "You're just a cold-blooded murderer."

He tilted his head at me, and I almost winced. He didn't say anything even though I was expecting much worse. Then, he leaned forward—just a fraction. It wasn't dramatic, but the shift made him look dangerous. Instinctively, I leaned back, barely registering it.

"If I wanted you dead, you wouldn't be sitting here," he murmured, so calmly I felt his words touching skin like wildfire. His eyes bored into mine, piercing grey like a storm cloud.

I had no reply.

The silence that followed was suffocating. He leaned back, not taking his eyes off me, and for a moment, I thought I saw something flicker in his expression. A crack in the ice.

"Eat," he repeated, softer this time.

I wanted to disobey him, to throw the plate across the room, and scream in his face. But I could feel the glass pressing against my ribs.

This wasn't the time. Not yet.

I couldn't breathe without tasting the bitterness of my own helplessness. I couldn't think without shattering.

He was a puzzle I couldn't solve. The fork trembled in my grip.

"Why?" The word slipped out, barely audible, and I knew if I stared at him anymore, I'd definitely lose myself. I blinked back the tears that burned, refusing to let him see. "Why are you doing this?"

He didn't answer. His eyes were like ice. So damn cold I could feel the frost on my skin. They dissected me and peeled me apart layer by layer until I felt naked, exposed.

How could someone so beautiful, so composed, hold so much cruelty?

Something in me cracked. A sob clawed at my throat, but I swallowed it down. He wasn't going to answer.

"I don't understand!" I slammed my palms against the table, the pain reverberating up my arms. "You killed him! You took everything from me, and now you sit there, ordering me to eat?" The tears fell down aggressively. "Do you want me to beg? Is that it? Do you want to see me crawl? Because I don't—I can't—"

Still, he just stared, wearing that cold mask.

"Say something!" I screamed. "Anything, you fucking psycho!"

He put the glass of wine on the table, unfolded his legs, spreading them wide and leaning back.

"If you're going to beg, do it properly, Dolcezza. On your knees."

I sat as if I hadn't heard him correctly. But the look in his eyes told me I had.

My pride rebelled, screaming at me to stand, to spit in his face, and throw his plate to the ground. But the weight of grief and fear crushed me, dragging me down. And in the next second, I fell to my knees, tears spilling down my face as I pressed my palms to the cold floor.

"There," he murmured. "Better. Now, pray."

I blinked through the tears. "What?"

His lips curved into the faintest shadow of a smile. "Pray. At my feet."

My chest tightened, my humiliation choking me as I lowered my head.

A deep breath. I had to act. Now. I was close enough to attack him.

Slowly reaching into my dress, my fingers wrapped around the glass. With a yell, I lunged at him, aiming for his throat, so ready to feel his blood on my hands.

Everything happened too fast. His hand shot out, catching my wrist in a vice-like grip. The shard clattered to the floor, my arm wrenched behind my back. Pain shot through my shoulder, as he twisted my other arm and slammed me against the cold surface of the table.

I gasped, struggling against him, his weight pinning me down. My breath came in short, panicked bursts.

What... what just happened?

Then I felt it: something sharp against my throat, and my eyes widened.

"Let go!" The sharp bite of the glass stole my breath, momentarily freezing me in place.

"You're braver than I thought," he mused. "Dolcezza."

I tried to shake my head, to speak.

"You want to kill me?" He leaned closer as his breath brushed against my ear. "Go ahead. Try again."

My lips trembled as terror took hold. I had underestimated him. Whatever he was, whoever he was, he was far more dangerous than I could have imagined.

"Next time, don't miss."

CHAPTER FIVE
Fear and Flesh

The moment his hands left me, I collapsed into the chair like a rag doll, my limbs trembling and my breathing uneven. He stood tall and unbothered beside me.

How do you name a reality that feels wrong in its existence?

I heard him exhaling sharply. I dared to sneak a glance at him as his jaw tightened and his gaze burned into me. The faint scar slashing across his cheek twitched when his lips curled into a sneer. My heartbeat thundered in my ears as he bent down, his hand gripping the armrest of my chair.

A single sob escaped me.

"Get up," he whispered through clenched teeth. When I didn't move fast enough, he grabbed my wrist in a bruising grip and yanked me to my feet like I weighed nothing. My legs buckled, but he forced me upright.

"I don't repeat myself, Dolcezza," he growled, shaking me as if I were just a toy. "You don't want to test my patience. Trust me on that."

My lips parted, but no sound came out—not an apology,

not a protest, not even a plea.

His eyes dropped to my mouth, lingering there for a moment. He slowly lifted his hand to my face and brushed his thumb over my trembling bottom lip making panic course through me, my body tensing.

"Stop shaking." His brows narrowed as if he couldn't understand my reaction to him. "What are you so afraid of?"

I wanted to disappear, and never face the smirk tugging at his scarred mouth. My knees threatened to give out again, but his body forced me to stay up.

I felt like glass under his touch.

Breathe. Just breathe.

His hand on my arm was fire and ice. Burning. Freezing. Both. Neither.

I stared at the floor, desperate for it to swallow me whole. Vanish. Disappear. Cease to exist.

"Look at me," he grumbled.

I couldn't.

"I won't ask again," he repeated. Deadly this time.

Tears wouldn't stop falling. I was pathetic. Weak. A rag doll in his hands.

If only I could numb myself.

I flinched, feeling his fingers brushing my jaw, and forced my face up. "There it is," he murmured, his piercing grey eyes locking onto mine.

It wasn't just terror. It was misery. And he saw it. Drank it in.

I was drowning in the depths of his stare, and he knew he was crushing my soul.

Just as I thought I couldn't take any more, the sound of approaching footsteps cut through the suffocating silence. Before I could see, I heard him. "Mr. Vitale?"

I nearly sobbed in relief. Someone else was here. Someone

who might stop him, save me from whatever nightmare he was about to drag me deeper into.

But he didn't look away. Instead, he just tightened his hold on my jaw, making me wince. My breathing hitched, and I cursed the involuntary shiver that wracked my body.

The man stepped into the room, and from the corner of my eyes, I saw his polished shoes. He was tall, dressed in a crisp black suit that fit him like a second skin, adjusting his glasses, not even sparing me a glance.

The nightmare towering over me looked at me one last time before forcing me into the chair. I thought he'd go back to his chair, but he just stood behind me. I could't help fidgeting with my fingers, hyper-aware of his eyes on me.

The monster behind me put his hand on my shoulder, making my hands freeze.

Somehow, I knew I would be killed before I could speak a word.

It almost felt like he was warning me to stay quiet or he'd remind me of my place again.

I clamped my mouth shut, and swallowed down every word that was on my tongue.

My head lowered instinctively, my shoulders curling in as I tried to make myself smaller.

The other man placed a sleek black bag on the table after clearing his throat. The sound of the zipper tore through me. From inside, he pulled out a thin black file, setting it on the surface with an almost reverent care.

"The papers are ready."

"Explain them to her." His hand on my shoulder stayed there, pinning me down.

The man nodded and flipped open the file as he began to speak. "This document outlines the terms of a legally binding agreement between Party A and Party B. Party A, as outlined here"—he gestured vaguely behind me—"will assume full legal authority and control over Party B, who agrees to comply with the conditions set forth herein without contest."

My frown deepened. What the hell did that even mean?

"The contract includes stipulations regarding personal conduct, residency, and obligations of loyalty." The man's tone was clinical, almost bored, as he continued. "Party B"—he glanced at me briefly—"will forfeit any previous claims to property, finances, or legal autonomy. In return, Party A guarantees…"

I barely heard the rest. My pulse roared in my ears as I struggled to understand what I was hearing.

"What… what is this?"

The man didn't answer. He simply looked behind me, and only then added, "It's a marriage contract."

The floor dropped out from beneath me. My breath hitched, my chest tightening until I thought I might suffocate.

I felt him leaning down till his face was close enough that I could feel the heat of his breath against my skin.

"You're going to marry me, Dolcezza. Whether you like it or not."

CHAPTER SIX
Disobedience

I felt like a caged bird, and he held the key—but instead of setting me free, he seemed to tighten the bars around me.

Marry him? Marry him?

I blinked at him, waiting for a cruel smirk or hint that he was joking. But his face was as unmoving as stone. No mirth. No mockery. Just that maddening certainty, the kind of confidence that made my stomach churn and pulse race.

He was serious.

"Dolcezza." The word rolled off his tongue like smoke, sweet and suffocating, curling around my ribs and squeezing until I couldn't breathe. Sweetheart. He said it like I was something fragile, but nothing was fragile or pure about the storm bubbling inside me.

The audacity. The arrogance. The absolute nerve.

As if… it was the most natural thing in the world. As though my life was his to rewrite, my choices his to command. He didn't ask. He declared.

"This can't be…" I swayed in the seat, my hands shook, and my eyes tried to adjust. This had to be some kind of twisted joke because no way… he was asking me to marry him.

"You're wasting my time, Dolcezza," he murmured, and I felt his voice striking me across the face.

My throat burned with words I couldn't force out. Marry the bastard of a man who killed a man, kidnapped me, ruined my life, and now wants me bound to him for some unknown reason?

I hated him. For making me feel this way. Furious and lost all at once. And yet, something about him made my knees weak. No amount of protest could change my fate. My fate. My goddamn fate. My freedom had been stripped from me before I even realized it, and now this man was here to seal my fate with his name on a contract I didn't understand.

"I can't do this," I whispered, ready to bolt. But where could I go?

The man sitting in front of me again adjusted his glasses, understanding the tension and feeling uncomfortable. I was also aware of the woman standing in the corner of the room. But none of them terrified me more than the man standing behind me.

He didn't do anything, but I felt it, the way his hand curled around my shoulder. "This isn't a negotiation. You'll do as I say."

Tears pricked my eyes, blurring the ink on the page in front of me. I couldn't think, couldn't breathe. "You're… you're taking everything from me."

He chuckled. "Everything? No, Dolcezza. I'm giving you something. A purpose. A place. Protection."

"Protection?" I spat and whipped around to face him, ignoring the ugly anger on his face. "You're not protecting me. You're imprisoning me, you bastard!"

A part of me wanted to take a step back, to put distance between us, but I stood my ground. I refused to let him see me falter. I was panting now, too angry to care if he'd kill me. That was better than marrying him.

I glared at him. The stormy-greys narrowed, and a tint of anger flashed in his eyes. "Prisoners don't get silk sheets and diamonds."

The audacity made me sick, but the way he said it—so casually, like my life was just another transaction to him—froze me in place.

I turned back to the paper, my hands shaking violently. My vision tunnelled. "You can't... You can't make me do this..."

What was happening anymore, I couldn't decipher.

"You have ten seconds," he said softly, and it was worse than if he'd yelled.

I bit my lip, hard enough to taste blood. My mind raced, desperate to find a way out of this nightmare. What could I do? Run? Stab him with the pen? How far could I go? What would happen to me after that? Would I ever be able to leave? Everything agitated me.

Every second I wasted thinking was another second closer to the point of no return.

He trapped me in every sense of the word. And if I asked why, I knew he wouldn't tell me. Tears burned my eyes. I felt so frustrated. Oh dear lord... show me some way. I couldn't stay here and let him ruin me.

I was so engrossed in my thoughts that I didn't feel him move. One moment I was standing, and the other, he placed his hand on my back and leaned. "Five."

My lips trembled as I tried to make sense of it all.

"Please," I choked out.

"Four."

I turned to him, tears streaming down my face, hoping—praying—that he might show some shred of humanity.

"Three."

His gaze bore into mine.

"Two."

I couldn't do this. I couldn't—

"One."

The pen was in his hand before I could react. He grabbed my wrist and slammed it down on the table, forcing the pen into my trembling fingers. His grip was bruising.

"Sign it," he snarled. "Or I'll show you what it means to have no choices."

I thought fear had a limit—until he found new ways to unravel me.

"You know," he started, his tone turning deceptively calm, "I didn't think it would take this much effort to get you to co-operate. But I suppose you like being difficult."

I didn't respond. My body was too drained to fight him verbally, but my silence didn't deter him. Instead, it seemed to amuse him.

"You're afraid," he continued, his voice dropping to a near whisper as he leaned closer. "Afraid of me. Afraid of what I can do. And you should be."

I swallowed hard, refusing to meet his eyes.

"You've already lost, Dolcezza. It's time to stop pretending you have a choice."

He moved behind me, his hands gripping the back of the chair. I felt his breath against my hair, making my stomach churn.

"Your father's in the hospital, isn't he?"

My heart stopped.

I turned to look at him, my eyes wide with shock. "What did you just say?"

He smirked. "A man his age, in his condition, shouldn't be left alone for long. Would be a shame if... something happened to him."

My mouth parted, and I stared dumbfounded at him. How... how did he even... know about this?

"Your friend... what's her name? Her business isn't doing so well, is it? Those loans are piling up, and the banks are starting to circle."

I gasped this time, my knees nearly buckling, but his hand on my waist balanced me. "How... how do you know that?"

He chuckled. "You think I don't know everything about you, Dolcezza?"

My chest heaved as panic clawed its way up my throat. "You're lying. You don't know anything about me."

His eyes darkened, the amusement vanishing in an instant. "Don't I?"

He took a step closer, and I instinctively stepped back, my spine hitting the edge of the table.

"Your mother used to braid your hair every morning before school," he said, his voice low and deliberate. "She'd hum that awful lullaby to keep you calm when you cried. What was it again? Oh, right. La Luna Triste."

I froze, my blood turning cold.

"Stop it!" I screamed, shoving him with all the strength I had left. "How do you know these things? How?!"

He barely moved under my assault, his expression unchanging. "I told you. I know everything about you."

"Why?!" I cried, my voice cracking. "Why are you doing this to me?!"

He grabbed my wrists, his grip like iron as he pulled me close. "Because I can," he growled. "And because I want to."

I struggled against him, thrashing and kicking, but it was useless. He was too strong, too damn dominating.

"You're a monster," I spat, my voice trembling with rage and fear.

His lips twisted into a cold smile. "Disobey me again, and

I'll make sure you see the monster I am."

Before I could respond, he released one of my wrists and pulled out his phone. He dialled a number, his eyes never leaving mine.

"Make the arrangements," he said into the phone. "Start with her friend. Bankrupt her."

My eyes widened in horror. "No! Please, no!" I screamed, tears streaming down my face.

He hung up without another word, his gaze hard and unrelenting as he watched me crumble.

"How could you?" I sobbed, my voice breaking. "How could you do this?"

"Because you need to understand, Dolcezza," he said coldly, his grip tightening. "There's no part of your life I can't control. No one I can't touch. If you think you can fight me, think again."

CHAPTER SEVEN
Wife

My hands were shaking as I signed the papers. The pen slipped slightly when I finished writing my name. My vision was blurred from tears, my chest tight with a mixture of rage, humiliation, and despair.

The moment I finished, he snatched the papers away without a word. His cold eyes scanned my signature as if ensuring I hadn't made some last act of defiance.

He didn't respond, didn't even look at me. Instead, he turned his head slightly, his voice sharp and commanding. "Elena."

The young maid, who'd been standing silently near the doorway, stepped forward. She kept her eyes downcast, her body rigid, as though afraid to even exist in his presence.

"Take her to the room," he ordered emotionlessly. "She'll be staying there as my wife."

Wife. The word stung. I wanted to scream at him, to throw something, to rip those papers apart, but I couldn't even move. I was frozen in place, drowning in the reality of what I'd just done.

"Yes, sir." She nodded.

Without so much as a glance at me, he turned to the man, the lawyer, I guess.

"Please, come with me, miss," the maid muttered.

I followed her silently, my legs weak and unsteady, my body moving as if on autopilot.

She led me to the stairs and then a sleek hallway. It was endless and inescapable.

The maid glanced back at me a few times. "This way," she murmured, opening a large wooden door at the end of the hall.

I stepped inside, and my stomach churned. The room was enormous, bigger than any space I'd ever lived in. The bed was massive, draped in luxurious fabrics that screamed wealth and power. The walls were adorned with expensive art, and the windows were so tall they nearly touched the ceiling.

"This will be your room."

My room. Not our room. Not his room. Mine. That should've been a relief. This wasn't a sanctuary. It was another prison, gilded and opulent but suffocating all the same.

"Does he... does he always get what he wants?" I asked bitterly.

The maid hesitated, her expression conflicted for a second before she masked her emotions. "He... he's not someone who's used to hearing no."

I let out a hollow laugh, more a broken sound than anything resembling humour. "I gathered that."

She fidgeted with her hands, her gaze darting to the floor. "I'll bring up your things," she said softly, as if trying to ease the tension.

I turned away from her, unable to look at her pitying expression any longer. "Don't bother," I muttered. "None of it matters anymore."

The door closed behind her, leaving me alone in the silence of the room. I stood there, staring at the bed, my fists clenched so tightly that my nails dug into my palms.

I walked to the window, my breath hitching as I stared out at the sprawling estate. It was on the edge of a cliff. The view from the window was cruel. The endless waves hurled themselves against the jagged rocks as if wanting to wash me along. Beyond them, the horizon stretched infinitely. My lids broadened as I looked at the back to find the forest. Even the sky was grey and brooding.

Beauty, I realized, could be a far greater prison than these walls.

This wasn't an island, but it wasn't Italy either. I swallowed hard, staggering back, and my reflection stared back at me in the glass. Of a woman I barely recognized. Swollen eyes and face, pale and drawn. I looked defeated.

And in some sense, I was.

Because he had won. The man I didn't even know the name of. The nightmare I was fucking married to. He had stripped me of every ounce of power, every piece of control I thought I had. He knew things about me I hadn't even told the people I loved. He knew me better than I knew myself.

I slammed my fist against the window, hoping for pain to take him away from my thoughts.

I hated him. God, I hated him.

But what scared me most wasn't the hatred.

It was the part of me that feared I would never escape him.

A sharp, bitter laugh escaped my lips, cracking halfway through as it dissolved into a sob. This couldn't be real. But it was.

I turned away from the window, pacing the room like a caged animal, my breath coming in sharp, erratic gasps. My chest ached.

I needed to feel something, anything, other than the crushing despair suffocating me.

My gaze darted to the bedside table, where an ornate vase filled with fresh flowers sat like a cruel mockery of beauty. Without thinking, I grabbed it, the delicate porcelain cool against my trembling hands as I slammed it on the floor with a gut-wrenching scream.

But even that wasn't enough.

I moved to the vanity, sweeping everything off with one violent motion. Perfume bottles, jewellery boxes, and trinkets clattered to the floor, some breaking, others rolling away into the corners of the room. My reflection in the mirror taunted me, the twisted face of a woman who had nothing left to lose.

"You ruined me!" I screamed again as I shredded everything I could get my hands on. "You ruined everything, you fucking monster!"

When my energy drained, my knees buckled, and I sank to the floor amidst the wreckage, the cold shards of porcelain and glass biting into my skin. But I didn't care. The physical pain was nothing compared to the storm raging inside me.

I wrapped my arms around myself, rocking back and forth as sobs wracked my body. I felt like I was falling apart, piece by piece, and there was no one to catch me.

He knew everything. My father. My childhood. My friends. My fears. He had peeled me open like a book, reading every hidden chapter, every secret I thought was buried deep. How could someone know so much and still be so cruel?

I buried my face in my hands. There was no escape. No way out. He had trapped me in his web, and now, all I could do was wait for him to pull the strings tighter.

I cried for what felt like hours. I didn't even realise when I lost consciousness, but when I felt the cold seeping into my veins and stiffness in my body, I stirred.

CHAPTER EIGHT
Punishment

I pried open my eyes with difficulty. The window was open, no curtains draped, and the warm sun rays fell upon my face. I groaned and looked around. The room was a mess as far as I remembered. My throat was raw from crying, and my eyes were puffy and burning. I felt hollow, like the shell of someone I used to be. But even in the stillness, I could feel him.

My gaze flickered to the door, half-expecting him to storm in at any moment, to continue his twisted game.

I sat up slowly, wincing as pain shot through my stiff body. My muscles ached from how tightly I had curled in on myself the night before.

A knock at the door shattered my thoughts, making me jump. My heart slammed against my ribs as the door creaked open.

Elena stepped in. I swallowed hard as she took in the scene. Her eyes widened slightly before she put on her stoic expression. "Mr. Vitale requests your presence in the dining room."

"Requests?" I muttered bitterly. "He's not actually asking."

She didn't reply, keeping her eyes trained on the floor. Of course, she wouldn't. She worked for him. They all did.

"I'll be there," I muttered, forcing myself to stand.

Her gaze flicked up to me briefly, pity shining before she nodded and disappeared through the door.

I glanced at the clock. It was barely eight in the morning. Too early to face him. Too early to stomach whatever new torment he had planned.

But I didn't have a choice.

I brushed my teeth, surprised at finding all the necessities in the bathroom. And took a shower I needed desperately. The dress I wore was ruined now, so I covered myself with a robe. When I returned to the room, Elena was there, holding a broom and a bucket, cleaning the mess I created. I felt bad for her.

Feeling pathetic, I cleared my throat. "Can I… have something to wear?"

She looked up and placed the broom down before disappearing through the door adjacent to the vanity I destroyed. After a minute or two, she came back with three pieces on hangers and placed them neatly on the bed.

"Here, you can choose." She resumed her work, and I stared at the clothes, more like dresses. I'd be lying if I said they were ugly. No, definitely not. However, they were not to my taste. I picked a dress and inspected it. Emerald, long and revealing. The other two were no better. One was deep purple, equally revealing yet decently articulated.

I didn't even want to look at the third one. It already looked short enough not to cover my behind, though the neckline was elegant.

My blood boiled. Was he expecting me to wear this? For him? He seriously was making this marriage a reality? I threw the dresses on the bed. "I'm not wearing any of these."

Elena sighed. "They were the more modest of them. You wouldn't like to anger him, Mrs. Vitale."

My jaw clenched tight. "I'm not his wife. Don't call me that."

"He's not a man you'd want to provoke. You've seen what he's capable of, what he did to your lover. He wouldn't hesitate to repeat it." She paused, tilting her head and motioning at the dresses. "The only reason you're breathing is because he wants you to. Don't mistake that for kindness."

My chest felt like a stone sinking in water. I swallowed hard. I didn't want to listen, didn't want her to be right. But the image of Adrian... his hands red. My hands trembled as I stared at the dresses. He wanted to parade me around like some trophy for him? Like this marriage was real?

"It's not fair," I whispered breathlessly, slumping on the bed. "Why is this happening to me?"

Elena remained silent. I gritted my teeth. I wouldn't win this fight like this. She was right. He was capable of far worse. My father, my friends, even Adrian's family... what if this unhinged man decides to do something to them? I didn't know if he was bluffing or not, but the madness in his eyes stated what I feared.

Taking another defeated breath, I grabbed the emerald dress and, with a heavy heart, changed into it.

It gleamed like liquid silk. Flowed and hugged my curves with effortless grace; it startled me. The high-slit tease was too much. Minimal, modern, and utterly revealing.

"Come, I'll style your hair."

I clenched my jaw. "He wants a wife or a trophy?" She grabbed my arm and escorted me to the vanity I remembered destroying, but somehow, Elena managed to tidy it up.

"Men... tend to... be distracted by captivating things. The prettier they are, the tamer they will be."

I scoffed as she gathered all my hair behind me and secured it with several pins. "I wonder if we're talking about the same man. He's more like an animal than a human being."

I saw a faint smile crossing her face. "With that I can't disagree."

She seemed like a kind woman, despite the occasional glares she offered. I wondered how she ended up working for a monster like him. By the time she was done, she applied some blush and tint to my lips. Though I looked decent, I hated that he was going to see me dolled up for him.

∞

When I entered the dining room, he was already there, sitting at the head of the table like a king on his throne. His dark suit was immaculate today; this time, he wore a navy blue one with a white shirt peeking out. His posture was relaxed, but his eyes... damn those stormy eyes.

I slowly walked to the dining table, trying to make my presence as small as possible.

"Good morning, Dolcezza." He noticed, of course.

I clenched my jaw, refusing to respond as I sat down at the far end of the table. He was having coffee, and a black file was sitting beside his plate.

"Silent treatment already? We're not even a full day into our marriage."

I shot him a glare, my stomach churning at the word marriage.

"Eat," he commanded, gesturing to the elaborate spread of food on the table.

"I'm not hungry."

He leaned back in his chair, his eyes travelling the dip of my breasts, and a slow smirk played on his lips. "I wasn't asking, Dolcezza."

He waited until I was halfway through the food. My fork scraped against the plate, and I could feel his eyes on me. The silence was suffocating, but I refused to look at him. Not until he cleared his throat.

It stopped just short of my plate.

He slid the file I was eyeing earlier towards me.

I froze, my stomach twisting into knots. I hated that file. Ninety-nine percent of the time, it carried nothing but pain—contracts, threats, ultimatums. My fingers trembled as I reached for it, the words 'Agreement of Conduct' stamped boldly on the front.

"What is this?" I could already feel that this was another prison sentence for me.

He leaned back in his chair and sipped his coffee leisurely. "Rules," he said simply. "Rules you'll follow as my wife."

I snapped the file shut and pushed it away. "I'm not your puppet."

"No, you're my wife," he replied, visibly not liking what I just did. "And as my wife, I expect three things from you: obedience, loyalty, and respect. Fail to give me any of those, and you will face the consequences."

I clenched my fists under the table. "Consequences?" I hissed. "What are you going to do? Lock me up? Hurt me?"

He chuckled darkly, which made the hair on my neck stand on end. "Locking you up wouldn't be necessary. But if you test me…" His stormy eyes locked onto mine, and I momentarily ceased breathing. "You won't like the result."

My teeth ground together. What did he think of himself? "You can't control me like this."

He leaned forward this time, and the scar on his fucking face gleamed. His voice dropped dangerously. "But I already do."

The file remained on the table between us. My chest

heaved with the effort of suppressing the scream clawing at my throat.

"Read it," he commanded. "And don't waste my time."

My fingers trembled as I opened it, dread pooling in my stomach. The text stared back at me, bold, black, and damning. I scanned the first line, and my chest tightened with every line.

I felt my stomach twist as bile rose to my throat. The words blurred as my hands trembled. He was insane. A monster.

"You've read enough." His voice startled me.

I looked up to see him looking at me. He was calm, too calm, and that terrified me more than any display of anger.

"This is…" My voice cracked. I swallowed hard and tried again. "This is ridiculous."

"Is it?" he asked, crossing his arms across his chest and widening his legs. "It's what I call necessary."

"Necessary?" I muttered. "This is slavery, not a marriage."

Anger burned hot in my chest, but fear shadowed it, cooling the flames before they could fully ignite. I couldn't let him win, couldn't let him see how deeply he rattled me. "And what if I don't obey?"

His smirk disappeared, replaced by a deadly calm. "Then I'll ensure you regret it."

My fingers itched to crumple the paper, to throw it back in his face, but the weight of his gaze pinned me down. I pushed the file back toward him. "I won't sign it," I kept my voice firm. "You can't take my basic human rights."

He didn't flinch, didn't react. That was somehow worse.

Instead, he shrugged as if he expected it. I watched as he slowly pushed back the chair, and the sound scraped against my chest. My head tilted back as I watched him standing up. He looked larger than life, standing there, unbuttoning the buttons of his navy blazer and draping it elegantly over the back of the chair. "Brave words, but bravery has its limits." He uncuffed his cuffs and rolled the sleeves of his white shirt, exposing the veiny and muscular tattooed forearms. I swallowed hard as his stormy greys collided with mine. "Congratulations, you just earned your first punishment."

My stomach twisted at his words, and in terror, I pushed back my chair and stood on my shaky legs. "What... are you talking about?"

He didn't stop prancing until he was standing just in front of me, towering over my petite frame. I could already feel the intimidating aura of his, like a rabbit caught in a lion's hands. I waited for him to strike me, slap me, or grab my hair and slam my head against the table. But the more I stared at him, the deadlier he looked.

His hand rose. I flinched instinctively. His eyes darkened, and I was suddenly aware of the way his eyes were touching me with his intense gaze, moving from my exposed breasts to the slit on my thigh. Feeling conscious, I quickly covered my chest with my hands. He smirked. "Foolish too."

I didn't have time to react, or even run, before his hand was moving to my arm and I was harshly pinned against the table. Second time in two days. Air knocked out of my lungs, and my arms were held above my head. "What-"

"Keep moving your mouth; it only gets me excited."

His grip on my wrists tightened, pressing me harder against the table, and the edge dug into my stomach. My pulse thundered in my ears as his body hovered over mine. The heat of his suffocating breath ghosted over my face. Stormy eyes hardened.

I struggled, the fight instinctive, but the brute seemed unbothered. "Let go."

He snickered. "You don't give orders here, Dolcezza," a gravelly voice scraped against my back.

I sucked in a breath as his free hand trailed down my side. The fabric of my dress bunched in his fist, sliding higher and higher until I felt the cool air hit the bare skin of my thighs. My body jolted in panic. A strangled gasp left my lips, and shame curled around my spine.

"Stop, please," the words trembled on my lips.

I tried to twist away. Another futile attempt. His fingers brushed against the bare skin of my thigh, the heat of his touch leaving a burning trail. My muscles tensed.

"Look at you," his lips so close they brushed the shell of my ear. Molten voice grated, and terror intensified. "Trembling like a leaf."

I flinched as his fingers tapped against the curve of my ass.

"What-" I started, but the words cut off with a sharp gasp as his palm landed on me. A sharp crack echoed through the room.

He palmed the middle of my back and pinned me down. My cheek met the cold wood, and I tried not to hyperventilate. I briefly closed my eyes when I realised I was not going to get away. I wouldn't give him the satisfaction to see me plead. He could hurt me all he wanted; I'd rather die than beg a monster like him.

Pain bloomed hot.

I gasped, half-choked, and my lungs refused to cooperate.

On the second slap, my entire body reeled forward on the wooden surface. I gripped the edge of the table. His hand was merciless and hard, with the sole intention of hurting me. I wondered if he had a heart. Of course, he didn't. If he did, he wouldn't be humiliating me this way.

I bit my lips hard, almost tasting blood on my tongue, but it was hard. Too hard to suppress the sound that escaped me. I wished it hadn't. Because he palmed my behind. "That's better," his tone dripped with satisfaction. "Now you're paying attention."

I turned my head, glaring at him over my shoulder through my teary eyes. His lips curled in a smirk as his gaze roamed over me. "Keep looking at me like that. Those pretty eyes are just making me hard."

"You're sick…" I mumbled through the pain, and he just chuckled before he grabbed my hair and yanked me up. My back arched.

"Respect, obedience, and loyalty." I pursed my lips together as he slapped my arse again. "Etch those fucking words in your head. Provoke me again, and your flesh will pay." Slap. "You will know your place." Slap. "You will be the perfect little wife for me. Is that clear?" Slap.

The pain was too much. I choked out, "Please… stop…" I sobbed. My legs were trembling, and so was my whole body.

"Words, Dolcezza." I shut my eyes.

"Yes…"

"Yes, what?"

"Yes, I will… obey."

He paused; instead, his hand cupped my red arse. I thought he'd let me go, but then I felt his cupping my womanhood. My head snapped back to stare at him at the same time, and a wicked smirk tinted his lips. It made him look like a reaper ready to take a soul with him.

I tried to wrench my head to the side, desperate to reclaim even a shred of dignity, but his grip on my hair was instant. "You're being difficult again."

The pad of his fingers teased my neck, but I bit down on my lips so hard I tasted copper. His eyes darkened, simultaneously pushing aside my panties, and I felt his fingers against my bare core. "This time, you'll use your words. Next time, your cunt will pay the price."

CHAPTER NINE
Lethal

I'd somehow made it through the embarrassment. Whatever he thought he was doing, pretending to play house with me, appointing rules as if I was a prisoner and not a human. The damn emotions he made me feel all at once: ashamed, enraged, and pathetically scared.

I was not one to get intimidated by men easily. But him… he had this superior aura, something that wrapped around my neck and choked me. I couldn't breathe in his presence, I couldn't fucking think. It was like he could read me like an open book, solve every damn puzzle in my head, and then leave me panting and squirming under his stormy gaze. Nothing about him was human. Not the way he assessed me, or the way he looked down on me as if I were just an insignificant creature.

I finally stood, wobbling slightly on my feet as the chair screeched against the floor. The sound echoed. My knees buckled, but I caught myself on the edge of the table, glaring at the dark wood as if it were the source of my humiliation. The reality of my situation felt surreal—like a nightmare I couldn't wake up from, no matter how hard I tried.

Adrian was gone. Dead. The man who had once held my heart in his hands had been ripped away from me in the cruellest of ways. And now, I was tied to his murderer, bound by law and circumstance to the man who had stolen not only my love but every shred of control I'd ever possessed.

The burn on my ass was nothing compared to the fire raging in my chest. A storm brewed beneath my skin, the combination of anger, pain, and a humiliating pull I couldn't shake. I could still feel the ghost of his touch on me like a brand.

Obey me.

My fists clenched, nails digging into my palms hard enough to draw blood. I hated him. I hated the way his presence hovered over me even in his absence. And most of all, I hated myself for the way my body betrayed me—for the way it burned and tingled in places I didn't want to acknowledge.

I limped toward the window, needing air but finding none. The view outside the mansion was bleak, the roaring waves reminding me of the prison I was trapped in. I leaned against the cold glass, hoping it might numb me, but it did nothing to dull the heat that simmered beneath my skin.

Why me? Why did he have to choose me? I wasn't strong enough for this. I wasn't strong enough to endure his torment, to face the darkness that seemed to consume him. Adrian had been light, hopeful, and loving. And now I was shackled to the opposite—his killer, a man who seemed to delight in stripping me bare of every defence, every ounce of dignity.

But why? What did he want from me? Why did he go out of his way to break me? Was it revenge for something I didn't understand? Or was this simply who he was—a killer toying with his victim?

I pressed my forehead against the glass, closing my eyes against the overwhelming swirl of emotions. Tears threatened to spill, but I bit them back, refusing to give him the satisfaction of breaking me completely. He might have power over my body, but he wouldn't have my soul.

He might have taken everything from me, but he wouldn't take me—not fully, not completely. Somewhere deep inside, beneath the shame and the fear, a small flicker of defiance still burned. It wasn't much, but it was enough to remind me that I was still here, still fighting. And no matter how much it hurt, no matter how much he tried to destroy me, I wouldn't let that fire go out.

Not yet. Not ever. Not in this lifetime, at least.

It wasn't just hate. No, that would have been easy. Clean. This was messier. This was the shameful flicker of warmth that accompanied his gaze, the traitorous pull of my body toward his, the unbearable recognition that even as he crushed me, I burned in the presence of him. And that made me hate him—and myself—even more.

I buried my face in my hands, fingers curling into my scalp as I tried to silence the war raging inside me. But my thoughts were relentless, unravelling me thread by thread. How had this happened? How had my life been reduced to this? A puppet to a man with darkness in his eyes and cruelty in his hands? I was suffocating under the lethality of it all.

I needed to get out. I had to escape.

There was no future for me here, no version of this life where I came out whole. Every moment I spent under his roof, under his control, chipped away at me. The longer I stayed, the more I'd lose—pieces of myself, my dignity, my sanity. And eventually, I would lose all of it.

Escape. It sounded so simple, but I knew it would be anything but. This house was a fortress. And him… he was always there, always watching as if he could see every thought I tried to hide.

But I couldn't let the fear stop me. If I didn't act, if I

didn't find a way out, I would drown here. He would consume me, body and soul, until there was nothing left of the woman I used to be.

I thought of Adrian again, of the life we'd dreamed of together. I thought of the promises we'd made, the love we'd shared. And then I thought of him—of the monster who had stolen that future from me.

I swallowed hard.

I didn't have a plan yet. I didn't know how or when, but one thing was certain—I wouldn't stay here. I wouldn't let him win. No matter how tightly he tried to hold me, no matter how deeply he tried to carve himself into my soul, I would find a way out.

And when I did, I would make sure he regretted ever thinking he could break me.

CHAPTER TEN
Red

I shouldn't be here.

Not in this house. Not in this situation. And definitely not standing behind a damn pillar, heart pounding like a caged bird while I watched him.

The man of my nightmares. The man who killed Adrian.

He stood in the centre of the foyer as he barked into his phone. Twenty minutes. That's how long he'd been pacing, threatening whoever was on the other end. His posture was rigid, his fingers clenched around the device as if he could crush it. The way his jaw ticked, the sharpness in his tone—it was almost hypnotizing.

Almost.

Then, with a final, growled command, he ended the call. His expression remained unreadable, but the tension in his body told me enough. Someone had pissed him off.

Good.

I held my breath as he strode toward the front doors, his long, deep brown trench coat swaying with each step. Two men flanked him—tall, broad, armed. Bodyguards. Just like I suspected.

The door opened. A rush of cold air slipped inside. He didn't even glance back before stepping out.

Then came the sound I'd been waiting for.

The deep, guttural roar of his car.

I counted the seconds, pulse drumming in my ears. Ten… fifteen… twenty…

Gone.

I exhaled sharply, my grip loosening on the smooth stone pillar. My legs felt shaky, but I forced myself to move. One cautious step after another, I crept toward the grand staircase, my bare feet soundless against the marble.

The front door loomed ahead.

I knew better than to think escape would be easy. This place was a fortress, trapped between an unforgiving sea and a dense, endless forest. He wasn't stupid. He wouldn't keep me here without precautions.

Still, I had to try.

I reached for the handle, fingers grazing the cool metal—

Locked.

Of course.

I swallowed the curse burning in my throat. This wasn't unexpected. I just needed a new plan.

Think.

I was running on scraps of information. Last night, I'd slept—no, hidden—through dinner just to avoid him. Elena had brought me food, even though I'd pretended to be lost in sleep. This morning, when she'd come to wake me, I'd faked it again. She bought it.

I'd spent hours holed up in my room, trying to figure out my next move.

And now, here I was. Dressed in yet another ridiculous excuse for clothing, creeping around like some pathetic little prisoner.

My fists clenched.

I was a prisoner.

No more playing the terrified captive. If I wanted out of here, I needed to be smart.

And that meant understanding him.

Where did he go when he wasn't here, making my life hell? What kind of business required those hushed, brutal conversations? Who was afraid of him enough to tremble at the other end of a phone line?

Answers were in this house.

His bedroom. His office. His secrets.

I pivoted on my heel, turning away from the door. My heart pounded as I moved deeper into the mansion, the eerie silence wrapping around me like a second skin.

I needed to be quick.

And unseen.

My nerves thrummed, every hair on my body standing on edge as I passed room after room, my gaze darting to every shadow, every darkened corner.

This place wasn't just a house. It was a lair.

And I was trapped inside it.

The house was too quiet.

Not the peaceful kind, but the wrong kind. The kind that made my skin crawl like I was being watched, even when no one was there.

My bare feet whispered against the marble as I moved, slipping past dimly lit hallways and cold, lifeless rooms. There weren't many people here. Just Elena, a few maids I hadn't even seen properly, and the guards who lingered in the darkness.

For a man who acted like he owned the world, this place was unnervingly empty.

No, this wasn't home. It was a prison. A well designed one.

I swallowed and pushed down the uneasy feeling clawing at my chest. I didn't have time for this. I needed to find his room, his office… something that could tell me who the hell he really was.

My gaze flickered between the doors lining the corridor. Heavy. Solid. Expensive.

I pressed a hand against one, testing it.

Locked.

I moved to the next.

Locked.

Of course, the bastard wouldn't make this easy.

I exhaled sharply, frustration simmering under my skin. I didn't know how long he'd gone, but if he caught me snooping, I doubted I'd get away with just a warning.

I groaned in frustration and pushed until I reached the end of the hall.

Then I saw it.

A door unlike the others.

Bigger. Heavier. The kind that belonged to someone who had something to protect.

Bingo.

I reached for the handle and—

It turned.

Not locked.

Adrenaline spiked through me as I eased it open, slipping inside before I could second-guess myself.

The scent hit me first.

Dark, woodsy. A mix of leather, expensive cologne, and something deeper – something him. It wrapped around me like a rope. Scratching against my insides and killing me.

I swallowed down the shudder crawling up my spine and forced myself to move.

The room was massive, but not grand, the way I expected.

No vanity, no pretentious decorations. Just dark walls, heavy curtains, and sleek functional furniture. A king-sized bed in the middle, black sheets rumpled, like he didn't sleep much, or when he did, it was violent.

To the right, there was a fireplace. To the left was a bookshelf lined with titles I didn't have time to care about. Against the far wall, there was a desk.

My heart slammed against my ribs.

I didn't waste time. I hurried across the room, fingers grazing the surface, searching for anything—notes, documents, a laptop—anything that could tell me what kind of monster I was dealing with.

Nothing.

I yanked open a drawer.

Empty.

Another.

Papers. Plain white sheets. Useless.

Damn it.

I turned toward the bookshelf, skimming over the spines. Nothing unusual. Nothing screamed hidden secrets. But something – a feeling, a sixth sense, or maybe just my damn gut warning me – told me there was something off.

I stopped. My gaze lingered on one book. It was out of place. Too new. The edges weren't torn, and the cover was metallic. It looked untouched. Why would someone have a metallic book? Was it just for decoration? He didn't seem like a man who would do something without a reason.

I hesitated. My pulse quickened, and I slowly reached for it. My fingers just brushed over the metallic book, and the second I pulled it from the shelf, a soft click echoed through the room.

I froze.

A chill ran down my spine.

A hidden door.

My pulse skyrocketed.

The bookshelf groaned as it shifted. The entire structure moved, and I yelped and jumped back, watching with wide eyes.

I stared.

What. The. Hell.

I should've backed away. Should've left, pretended I saw nothing, and continued my pathetic excuse of an escape plan.

But I didn't.

Because this bastard had secrets, and if there was one thing I hated more than him, it was being left in the dark.

I inhaled sharply, forcing my feet forward. The hidden doorway was narrow, but enough to accommodate a person or two. I stepped through even though every nerve in my body screamed at me to stop.

The moment I turned the corner, my breath caught.

A red room.

Not just red—crimson. Dark. Sinister. Like a warning carved into the walls themselves.

Leather straps. Chains. Cuffs hanging from the ceiling. A sleek black table lined with polished instruments that gleamed under the soft light. Some familiar. Some... horrifyingly foreign.

A whip coiled neatly at the centre. A bench with restraints. A cage.

A fucking cage.

A sick feeling curled in my stomach.

This wasn't just some rich man's indulgence.

This was control. This was discipline. This was power, wielded by a man who enjoyed watching people squirm.

I swallowed, forcing my legs to move as I stepped closer, as if some invisible force dared me to understand what kind of monster I was dealing with.

Why wasn't I surprised?

Of course he had a fucking torture chamber in his house. Of course he had an entire room dedicated to breaking people, bending them, and moulding them into whatever he wanted.

I should've expected this.

My stomach twisted.

I could picture it too easily—the way his stormy gaze would darken with something unreadable, the way his voice would drop to that terrifyingly low register, murmuring commands that no one dared to disobey.

Had he brought people here? Women?

I squeezed my eyes shut, bile rising in my throat.

The worst part?

I didn't know what unsettled me more. The fact that he had this room.

Or the fact that I wasn't entirely shocked.

Because deep down, I already knew he was the kind of man who enjoyed taking, owning, and controlling.

But now, I had proof.

And if I wasn't careful, I'd be next.

CHAPTER ELEVEN
Mine or His

Secrets have a scent. And his smelled like leather, whiskey, and blood. Sinfully dark.

The bookshelf slid back into place with a muffled click, but the sound shattered the silence as if I'd just been shot in the chest.

My fingers trembled as I wiped them against my dress. As if they could erase what I had just touched, what I had just seen.

The room still existed behind that wall, even if I pretended it didn't.

And I had left the papers untouched, yet I knew too much. Too much to sleep. Too much to breathe properly.

Like a loaded gun. And the worst part?

I wasn't sure whether it was aimed at him… or me.

Shit. What more was he hiding? How many of these… terrifying secrets did he have?

I ran a shaky hand through my hair. Knees threatening to collapse.

Then I heard it.

Approaching footsteps.

I quickly shut the door to the red room and turned just in time, when a shadow stretched along the dimly lit corridor outside the library.

My breath hitched. Still in the wrong place. Still too close to the truth.

I turned just as the heavy door creaked open.

Elena.

Her wide brown eyes flickered between me and the bookshelf, but she didn't speak right away. The silence carried its own accusations.

What did you see?

Do you know what happens to people who dig too deep?

But she didn't say any of that. Instead, her voice was a breath above a whisper, "Miss… you should return to your room."

Not 'What are you doing here?' Not 'Should I call for help?'

Just that.

And that's when I realised—Elena was neither friend nor enemy. She was something worse.

A bystander.

She knew exactly what kind of man he was. And she did nothing.

"Is he looking for me?" I asked, my voice even despite the chill creeping up my spine. I damn well knew he wasn't at home, so whatever kept my skin attached.

Her fingers tightened around the fabric of her apron.

For a moment—just a moment—I saw something flicker across her expression. Regret? Pity? Fear?

"Not yet." A pause. Then, even softer, "But he will once he's back."

A shiver slithered down my spine.

He will.

∞

Elena was right.

By the time the summons arrived, I had already been waiting for it. It didn't make sense, how I'd been messed up throughout the day, thinking about the inevitable. I wonder if Elena snitched. Knowing her loyalty to him, she would. She should.

Yet only a few words left her mouth. "He wants you in his office."

I should've run. I should've burned this house down.

Instead, I rose from my chair, exhaling slowly.

Into the lion's den, then.

The air smelled like fresh-cut roses and wealth when I made my way downstairs, and it made me sick. The walls were lined with the kind of artwork people killed for. The chandeliers dripped with more money than most would make in a lifetime.

And the man who owned it all?

A monster wearing a tailored suit.

∞

The study was warm, dimly lit, thick with the scent of leather and whiskey—like power wrapped in something deceptively soft. It smelled like him. Strangely his. Unmistakably his.

He was sitting behind the massive wooden desk, sleeves rolled up, exposing forearms lined with veins and… scars. Scars that didn't look like accidents.

His whiskey glass sat untouched beside him, the ice melting into golden ruin. How long had he been sitting there, waiting? Thinking? Deciding what to do with me?

And then there was him.

Terrifyingly beautiful in the way only monsters could be.

It was strange that his face wasn't just striking—it was sculpted by something cruel, something that had no interest in kindness. A brutal kind of beauty, too sharp to admire without bleeding for it. The scar that slashed across his cheekbone didn't take away from it. It cemented it. Made him something carved from war and wrapped in tailored silk.

A predator in his den.

A god on his throne.

And me?

Just a little thing, trespassing in his kingdom.

His eyes lifted.

The warm room suddenly turned cold, and I unconsciously tugged at the edges of my dress. His gaze pinned me in place, slowly travelled from my feet to my legs, and then settled over my face. Unhurried. Gauging. As if he were deciding not whether to kill me, but how.

And I realized something.

Men like him didn't raise their voices to scare you. They lowered them.

And right now? He wasn't saying a damn thing.

And somehow, that was worse.

"You're late," he murmured, not even bothering to hide the hunger in his eyes.

I wasn't. I had arrived exactly on time. But I knew this game. Knew what he was trying to do.

I still had doubts about whether Elena had told him something, but if she hadn't, I couldn't risk getting caught.

I swallowed the sharp reply that burned my tongue. "You didn't specify a time."

His gaze narrowed. Sharpened like a knife, he wanted to stab me in my chest.

"I didn't think I had to."

Something cold slithered down my spine. But another

part of me—one I didn't recognize—rose. Fuck that.

"Maybe next time, be more specific," I muttered, hoping he wouldn't hear, but he did. "It'll save us both the confusion."

For a second—just a second—something flickered in his eyes.

Amusement. Interest. A lion humouring a rabbit, letting it think it had room to run.

Then, in the space of a breath, he stood.

The chair scraped against the floor as he rounded the desk. Not hesitant—never hesitant. He moved like a man who had never been denied anything, a man who had never learned what it meant to ask.

And then he was in front of me.

Close.

Too close.

My lungs forgot how to function.

The air shrank to nothing. Collapsing in on itself like a dying star, pulling me into its gravity before I even had a chance to resist.

Heat licked up the back of my neck.

I felt it everywhere—the sheer force of him, the quiet dominance in the way he took up space as if even the walls bent to his presence. My stomach tightened. My fingers twitched at my sides, desperate for something to hold on to, something to keep me tethered.

Leather and spice— invaded my senses.

My knees locked.

But still—I didn't move.

Didn't step back.

Didn't flinch.

Even as he raised his hand and his fingers brushed my chin, tilting it up with a touch that was both lazy and possessive, like he had all the time in the world to undo me.

Even as his thumb ghosted along my jaw, his skin was impossibly warm against mine.

Even as my body—traitorous, foolish—shivered beneath his touch.

"You've been restless today," he mused, his thumb skimming along my jaw, leaving a trail of fire in its wake.

I forced my features into something close to boredom. "Maybe I just don't like being locked in a mansion with a man who refuses to use words when he has them," I murmured.

His lips curled in a sharp real smile.

And it was the most dangerous thing I had seen all night. Or my life. It was the first time I'd seen him showing this kind of emotion.

"Careful." His thumb traced the curve of my lower lip, lingering just enough to make my pulse slam against my ribs. "You're starting to sound brave."

I met his gaze, refusing to look away. "And that would be a problem because...?"

His fingers flexed against my skin. Just slightly. Just enough to remind me who was in control here.

Then, just as suddenly, he let go.

Stepped back.

And smiled.

"Because, Dolcezza," he murmured in sin and leather, "bravery is such a fragile thing in the wrong hands."

Mine, or his.

I didn't want to find out. Cause in the end, some women collect memories. Others collect scars. And I was about to collect both.

CHAPTER TWELVE
The Devil's Gift

Some men use words as weapons. He used silence—and it was far deadlier.

The intensity of his gaze pinned me to the chair. It wasn't just a look; it was a goddamn assertion of his dominance like he was sizing me up, deciding whether I was worth breaking or keeping.

I curled my fingers against my lap, pressing my nails deeper into my palm. Anything to keep my expression blank. To keep my pulse from betraying me.

He was now sitting behind his desk, and I was sitting just opposite him. I didn't know why he called me here, but whatever the reason was, I wanted to leave. A lion studying an outsmarted mouse.

Then, finally—finally—he spoke.

"What were you doing in the library?"

My heart slammed against my ribs. Fuck.

No. No, no, no. He knew.

I felt the blood drain from my face, my stomach twisting so hard I thought I might be sick. Stay calm. Stay—Did Elena tell him? Did someone see me? Oh my god. He must have had cameras around. I wouldn't be surprised if he did. He was testing me all this time, then? Wanting me to tell him myself?

I gripped the armrest of the chair as my nails dug into the leather. I needed to think. One wrong word and I was done.

"I was looking for something to read," I forced my voice to remain calm.

He didn't move. Didn't even blink. Just watched me like a predator watches a wounded animal—knowing it was only a matter of time before it collapsed. I swallowed hard.

He assessed me with that sharp steel gaze of his, and I forgot to even think. He'd make me speak anyway.

"And you found it… behind the hidden door?"

I stopped breathing. I should react—deny, lie, or run. But my body had locked up, frozen in some kind of sinful way. I was hyper-aware of his gaze. That steely grey piercing gaze. Threatening to rip me alive.

Shit. Shit. How did he know?

"I—I got lost," I tried, visibly shaking.

He let out a low chuckle. The kind that sent more ice down my spine.

"Lost?" He casually tilted his head, leaning onto his elbows and meeting my nervous eyes.

The way he said it made my pulse stutter.

"It's a big house," I muttered.

"It is," he agreed, nodding. "Plenty of places to get lost. Plenty of places to hide things."

I swallowed hard.

He didn't break eye contact. He didn't need to.

Oh god.

I clenched my fists, forcing myself to hold his gaze. If I cracked now, I was as good as dead.

But then… he smirked. A slow, knowing curve of his lips.

"Did you like what you saw?"

My stomach dropped. My breath caught in my throat.

The red room.

Leather. Steel. Restraints bolted to the walls. Silk ropes, whips, clamps—things I didn't even have the words for.

Heat licked up my neck. Not the good kind. The terrifying kind.

"You went through my things, Dolcezza, you saw what was there," he mused, rounding the desk like he had all the time in the world to play with his prey. "Curiosity is such a dangerous thing. Especially when it leads to places you don't belong."

I gripped the edges of my dress, trying to keep my hands from shaking.

"I didn't touch anything."

"Ah, but you wanted to."

My throat tightened. No.

He took another step. I took one back. A mistake.

His hand shot out, gripping my jaw. Fingers pressed into my skin, forcing my head back so I had no choice but to meet his gaze.

"Tell me, Dolcezza," he murmured with dark amusement. "Which one fascinated you the most?"

My pulse slammed against my ribs.

"The cuffs?" His thumb dragged over my lower lip. "The blindfolds?" His grip tightened, making my breath hitch. "Or was it something else? Something hard?"

I let out a shaky breath, but it barely made it past his fingers.

"None of them," I forced out, my voice barely above a whisper. "I wasn't—"

"Lying doesn't suit you."

His thumb dipped into my mouth, pressing down against

my tongue.

I went rigid.

Heat. Shame. Fear. It all crashed into me at once. My body locked up, my nails digging into his wrist, but he didn't let go.

"You should've asked if you wanted a demonstration," he murmured, voice nothing but silk and sin.

I yanked my head back, and he let me go. A slow retreat. A calculated one. He was toying with me, and we both knew it.

I swallowed hard, my throat raw.

"You think this is funny?" I bit out, trying to steady my breath.

He just smiled.

"No," he said. "I think it's cute."

My stomach twisted. He was enjoying this. My fear. My helplessness. The way he could bend me without lifting a single finger.

Then, as if he hadn't just spent the last minute making me question every choice I'd ever made, he reached into his pocket and pulled something out.

A small, black velvet box.

I stared at it.

"A gift."

I didn't move.

"Take it."

My fingers trembled as I reached for it, the velvet soft against my skin. I flipped the lid open— and froze.

It was an anklet.

Delicate, shimmering under the low light. Diamonds woven into thin platinum links, gleaming like something stolen from royalty. Too expensive. Too beautiful.

And too intimate.

"Why?" My voice was barely above a whisper.

His head tilted, watching me like I was something fragile.

Breakable.

"Because I like seeing pretty things in places only I can touch."

I sucked in a breath.

"Put it on."

I hesitated. His gaze sharpened. "Do it, or I'll do it for you."

I shook my head, my fingers tightening around the box. "No."

His smile didn't falter, but something dark flickered in his gaze. So dangerously amused it terrified me. Like I'd just told him something utterly ridiculous.

"That wasn't a request."

I turned to move, to put space between us, but he was faster. His fingers clamped around my wrist, yanking me forward so fast I barely had time to gasp before I was against him, his body a wall of heat and dominance.

"Stubborn little thing," he murmured. "Should I punish you for making me work so hard?"

I opened my mouth, but the next second, I was airborne—lifted like I weighed nothing and dumped onto the desk. A sharp yelp escaped me as papers and pens scattered to the floor.

He caught my ankle before I could kick him, fingers wrapping around the delicate bone. His grip was firm, unrelenting, as he dragged my leg up—higher, higher—until my calf was slung over his shoulder.

"Let me go," I gritted out, shoving at him, but he didn't budge.

"Shh." He stroked his thumb over my ankle like mocking me with tenderness. "You should be thanking me. Not every girl gets jewellery on her pretty little feet."

I gasped as I felt the cold metal brush against my skin.

He was slipping the anklet on, slow, methodical, like he was savouring every second. The clasp clicked into place, locking me in.

And then—

His lips grazed my ankle.

I sucked in a breath, my entire body tensing as his mouth lingered, warm and wet, tongue flicking out to taste the anklet.

"Perfect," he murmured, breath ghosting over my skin. His voice dripped with satisfaction. "Now every step you take, you'll feel it. My mark on you."

I shuddered, torn between fury and something else. Something that made my stomach tighten and my skin burn.

He lifted his head, eyes gleaming. "I wonder…" His fingers trailed up my calf, lazy, teasing. "Should I put something else on you? Something only I can take off?"

My pulse stuttered.

His smirk deepened. "Say no again. I dare you."

CHAPTER THIRTEEN
A Reason She Can't Refuse

Monsters don't always look like nightmares. Sometimes, they wear expensive suits and sit behind mahogany desks, watching you shatter piece by piece. He was just like that. Cruelly handsome and sinfully arrogant.

I could still feel the anklet biting into my skin.

I should never have walked into this room.

I should have never stepped into his world.

But now, I was trapped.

He casually pushed himself off me and sat in his chair like he owned the universe, one arm draped over the leather rest, fingers idly tapping against the dark wood. The scar on his face only made him look intensely ruthless, scheming as if he was already planning my demise. I would've punched him, but looking at him, I felt like he knew more about me than anyone else. This man was so much worse.

The rhythm was slow, unhurried—like a clock counting down the seconds to my annihilation.

"Take a seat," he said.

I didn't move. But I did slip from his desk and grabbed the

chair to steady my trembling legs.

His lips twitched. Not in amusement. Not in frustration. Just... something cold. Detached. "Suit yourself."

He reached into a drawer, and then with a sharp thud, he pulled out something.

I flinched.

A stack of papers lay in front of me, bound together in a way that made my stomach twist.

"Read it."

I didn't reach for it. My hands curled into fists at my sides. It must be some other contract he must have fished out for me. "What is it?"

He tilted his head like he was indulging a particularly slow child. "A contract."

The word sent a chill through me. Fuck him and his contracts.

His gaze was steady, and his tone awfully flat. "You'll obey. You'll submit. You'll belong to me. I don't have to say it twice." He gestured at the papers like they were nothing more than a routine business deal. "Sign, and I'll make sure you never have to wonder about her again."

I swallowed hard. "Who?"

His fingers tapped the desk again. Tap. Tap. Tap. Then he said it. "Your mother."

The world tipped sideways.

My breath hitched. My heart twisted violently inside my chest.

"You're lying." The words scraped my throat.

His expression didn't change, and my stomach dropped. "Am I?"

A muscle in my jaw twitched. "She's dead."

"Yes," he murmured. "But you don't even know why, do you?"

My stomach clenched. I felt sick. He didn't know anything. He couldn't. No one did.

His voice dropped lower. "Or should I say, you don't know who she really was?"

The floor beneath me might as well have disappeared.

My body locked up. My fingers dug into my palms. "You're bluffing."

He leaned forward, forearms resting on the desk. "Sign, and I'll tell you everything."

A sharp, hysterical laugh burst from my throat before I could stop it. "Do you think I'm stupid? You'll say anything to get what you want."

He sighed, slow and measured, like I was testing his patience. "Do you want proof?"

I stayed silent.

His fingers found the chain around my ankle. A reminder. He tapped it once, then again—like I wasn't a person, just another object in his possession.

"Listen closely, Stina."

My entire body stiffened.

That name. Stina.

That fucking name.

No one knew. No one.

My mother was the only person who ever called me that. And she hadn't spoken it since— My legs gave out before I could stop them.

The floor met my knees in a harsh collision, but I barely felt it. My breath came fast, shallow, and uneven.

How?

I forced myself to look up at him, searching for something—anything—that made sense.

Nothing did.

His expression remained unreadable, but his voice was

merciless. "Do you believe me now?"

I shook my head. I wanted to scream. To demand how he knew. To claw the answer out of him.

But my voice failed me.

I swallowed back the bile rising in my throat. "How do I know you won't lie to me?"

Something flickered in his eyes—something dark. Dangerous.

He leaned down, fingers grazing my jaw. Not gentle. Not cruel. Just... possessive.

"Every time you let me play with you, let me fuck you," he murmured, "I'll give you another piece of the truth."

The room spun.

This wasn't happening.

This couldn't be happening.

No, this wasn't happening.

He couldn't just... he had no right to...

But deep down, I knew he did. He had every right when he held all the cards, when he was the only one who could give me what I had spent my whole life chasing.

Answers.

"What the fuck do you even want from me?" I whispered.

His slow smile sent chills down my spine.

"I want you on your knees."

My breath hitched.

His fingers traced the curve of his lips as he looked lewdly at me, and I resisted the urge to cover myself. "I want you at my feet, plaint, obedient, fucking mine." His voice dropped, taking a deeper edge. "Every time you let me have you, Dolcezza, I'll make sure you know what your mother was. I'll feed you what you crave. Until you beg for the next."

Heat coiled low in my stomach. Not the good kind.

The terrifying kind.

"The fuck is wrong with you? You're sick!"

I shoved the chair back so fast it scraped against the floor. "You're insane if you think I'm going to…"

"Dinner."

I froze.

He smiled. "You have until dinner to decide. I'll be waiting in the library. Or," he glanced at the contract, tapping it with a single finger, "you can walk away. But I promise you if you do…" His voice dropped to something lethal. "You'll never find out what happened to her."

Terror curled around my throat.

He wasn't bluffing.

And that was the worst fucking part and feeling.

I turned on my heel and stormed out, but my hands wouldn't stop shaking. Because no matter how much I told myself I could fight this…

I already knew what my choice would be.

CHAPTER FOURTEEN
Storm

The anklet burned against my skin.

Not in a literal sense, but in a way that made my skin crawl with disgust, like it was searing my existence into this place, this goddamn prison disguised as luxury.

I sat on the cold tile floor of the bathroom, knees pulled to my chest, arms wrapped around them like they could somehow hold me together. My throat was raw, my breath coming in sharp, uneven gasps, and I hated myself for the tears. For how fucking weak I was.

It couldn't be happening.

Yet the cold bite of metal around my ankle told me otherwise. It was there, constantly mocking me that he owned me.

I pressed my hands to my face, trying to steady the hurricane in my chest. My mind was a mess, tangled with too many thoughts, too many questions that seemed to be piling up with each encounter with him.

How did he know about my family?

Who even was he?

Did I even know his name?

A cruel, hollow laugh bubbled in my throat. No. I didn't. A man had stepped out of nowhere, killed my fiancé, and now I was here, trapped, blackmailed, with nothing but my body as collateral.

It was humiliating.

But the worst part? I knew there was nothing I could do.

Because he had threatened me. Not just with answers but with my father, with Grace.

I clenched my jaw, gripping my hair in my hands. Fuck.

I hated him. I hated him more than I intended to. And yet... If anything happened to my father, if anything happened to Grace...

I squeezed my eyes shut. Aunt Brenda would take care of my father. She wouldn't let anything happen. But how long before she'd realise I was gone? How long before she'd notice I had disappeared without a trace? And Adrian...

My stomach lurched as red danced in front of my eyes. His soulless eyes. Had anyone found him yet? Did they know? Or was his body still in that apartment, cold and alone, the way I had left him?

A sob ripped through me.

Adrian.

God, Adrian.

I clutched my chest, gasping as grief twisted violently inside me. I missed him. I missed him so much it made me sick. I could still feel his touch, still hear the way he said my name, still remember the warmth of his laugh.

And now he was gone.

Taken away from me like my mother.

Just like that.

I choked on breath, my fingers trembling as I dragged them over my face. My mother. He had spoken about her like he knew her, like he had some secret truth locked away, waiting for me to beg for it.

A part of me wanted to believe it was a lie, that he was just another powerful bastard who liked to play with his victim first.

But…

Something about him told me he was beyond that.

I shuddered at the memory of how I had almost run from his office. And the shameless part, he wasn't even ashamed.

I was six when she had called me Stina, with that soft voice of hers, and warm hands cradling my cheeks. And the next year, she was gone. Like everyone else I had ever loved.

My chest ached and my breathing hitched. I couldn't do this.

I didn't want to sleep with him.

But if I refused? I'd never know the truth.

A bitter laugh bubbled in my chest as my head thudded back against the wall.

What was my body even worth anymore?

At least, if I obeyed, it would be my choice. At least, if I let him take me, it wouldn't be by force.

Would it?

Or was I just convincing myself this was control when it was nothing but another form of surrender?

Tears slid down my cheeks. I wanted to believe there was another way, but deep down, I already knew my choice.

I had no choice.

If I wanted the truth, if I wanted to protect the only people I had left, I would have to give him everything.

Even if it shattered me.

A sudden, sharp knock on the door startled me, snapping me out of daze.

I sucked in a breath as I froze on the cold floor. My head was pounding as another knock came, and I panicked.

Was it him? No. If it were him, he wouldn't knock twice.

"Mrs. Vitale?" Elena's familiar voice echoed, and I sucked in a sharp breath. "It's time for dinner. Mr. Vitale is waiting."

My stomach twisted.

I wet my lips, staring at the locked door like I could keep reality out for just a little longer. I had lost track of time, lost myself in my grief, my panic, my anger. Now, reality was here to collect me.

I swallowed hard. "What time is it?"

A pause. "It's past eight."

Shit. I pushed myself up too fast; my legs trembled beneath me. Had I really been here for hours? How did I let time slip away like that?

Before I could think or speak, the door handle rattled. "I'm coming in."

I barely had time to back away before the door opened, and Elena stepped in. Her black hair was pinned into a sleek bun as her sharp eyes assessed me.

She was holding something draped over her arm. A dress.

"Put this on," she said, stepping inside.

I didn't take it. My body refused to move.

She sighed, unimpressed. "You don't want to keep him waiting."

A fresh wave of nausea crashed over me.

"I…" My voice cracked.

She looked me up and down and handed the dress to me. It was… breathtaking. Deep crimson, the kind that belonged to candlelit sins and whispered confessions. It had a plunging neckline that would expose more of my chest than I was comfortable with, the delicate straps thin enough to snap under pressure. The silk clung in all the right places, dipping low in the back, the hem flowing in a way that made it both elegant and dangerously seductive.

Yet, I felt sick.

My grip on the fabric tightened. "Why… why is he doing this?"

Elena tilted her head. 'Because that's what he wants."

My stomach clenched.

"You…" My breath hitched. "You know what he's doing, don't you? You know he's forcing me into this."

Something flickered in her eyes. "Yes."

I stared at her. "And you're okay with that?"

Elena exhaled through her nose. "Okay with it?" She let out a humourless laugh. "Tell me when this world started caring about your consent?"

I flinched.

"Do you think power cares?" She was right. "Do you think men like him lose sleep over morality? Over right and wrong?"

I was speechless. "That's not-"

She cut me off. "You're looking for justice in a place where justice does not exist."

The words hit like a slap.

"You think you have a choice? No, Celestine. He is your choice. You can fight it. You can scream and cry and resist all you want, but in the end, you will still be his because that's what happens when men like him decide to claim something. And you? You were claimed earlier than you realised."

My heart slammed against my ribs.

She took a step back. "So go ahead. Do what you want."

Silence stretched between us. Something cracked inside me. Not just fear. Not even helplessness. But something deeper. Something that had been breaking since the moment I stepped into this world.

Because I knew, in the end, she was right.

And that was the worst part.

CHAPTER FIFTEEN
Shackled in Sin and Silk

The walls felt tighter here. They felt like they were closing in, like they could hear my thoughts, feel my panic, and taste the fear curling around my throat like an invisible noose.

My heels clicked against the marble floor as I followed Elena down the long corridor. Walking felt heavier, and breathing like a luxury I couldn't afford. My stomach was twisting with something violent. Dread, maybe. Or the sickening weight of inevitability.

Run.

My subconscious reminded me again. Run. As if I could. As if there was anywhere to go.

I clenched my fists, my nails digging into my palms. I was trapped. I knew that. And yet, my mind kept trying to map out an escape route, grasping for possibilities that didn't exist. A window I could jump from? A door that his guards did not guard? A weapon that would most definitely be useless against him?

The world inside this place was solely crafted for me. With illusions. And me? Just another pawn caught in its web.

Elena stopped in front of his office. I swallowed hard, my pulse hammering against my skin as I stared at it.

This was it.

She turned to me with the same unreadable expression she bore earlier. "Knock. He'll let you in."

I hesitated. My fingers curled around the fabric of my dress, the silk smooth and cool beneath my clammy hands.

Elena exhaled sharply. "You'll be fine." And then, just like that, she walked away, leaving me alone in front of the lion's den.

I swallowed again. This time with utter difficulty. My throat was dry. My body was at war with itself... one half frozen in fear, the other itching to run. I raised my fist, hesitated again, then finally knocked.

Silence.

For a moment, I thought maybe he hadn't heard. Maybe he was making me wait on purpose, just to toy with me.

"Come in."

My breath hitched. A shiver ran down my spine, but I reached for the handle anyway. The door creaked open, revealing the room beyond.

It was exactly as I had left it. And yet... it wasn't.

The seating area had been rearranged, the dark leather couches now facing the massive floor-to-ceiling windows. Beyond them, the sky bled in hues of pink and gold, the sea stretching endlessly below, waves crashing like whispered secrets against the shore.

Candles flickered on the low table between the couches, their soft glow cast elongated shadows across the room. A table, set for two, stood nearby, covered dishes waiting beneath the silver lids.

For a moment, just for a slight second, I forgot why I was here. Only when shadows in my periphery moved, I saw him.

There he was.

I gasped, my fingers automatically tightening around the doorframe.

He was leaning against his desk, arms crossed over his broad chest, ankles crossed at the boots. His head tilted slightly like he was assessing me silently, and those stormy grey eyes raked over me, drinking in every inch.

The scar.

I had never looked at it properly, nor purposely tried to ignore it. It ran from his temple to the edge of his cheekbone, jagged and cruel like a mark that told stories without ever needing words. It should have ruined him. It didn't though. If anything, it made him more terrifying. More real. Like a wolf marked by wars and still standing. Still dangerous.

I forced myself to meet his gaze. A mistake.

His eyes were just like the sea outside… violent, endless, and swallowing. Aa depth that shouldn't exist, a darkness that knew no bottom. The kind of eyes that made you forget to breathe, that stripped you bare without ever laying a hand.

And then his gaze dipped, just for a second, lingering at my ankle. At the thin band of metal locked around it.

The smirk that curved his lips sent ice through my veins. He was amused. Of course he was. He enjoyed this. My misery. My helplessness and the way I squirmed beneath his scrutiny.

I clenched my jaw, heat flooding my face. I wanted to scream. I wanted to throw something at him. I wanted to wipe that smirk off his face, carve it off if I had to. But I knew better.

I was here.

Standing in front of him. And that meant only one thing.

I was going to trade my body for the answers only he had. And the worst part? He knew it.

The silence between us became thicker with passing seconds. My heartbeat pounded against my ribs, loud enough that I was sure he could hear it. He still hadn't spoken, still hadn't moved. Just watching.

I hated that look in his eyes, the way it stripped me bare, peeled me apart, exposed every inch of my hesitation. He knew exactly what he was doing.

Smirking to himself, he moved like he had all the time in the world. One step, then another, until he was close enough that I had to tilt my head back to keep eye contact. My breath caught in my throat as he lifted his hand, his cruel fingers brushing a loose strand of my hair. The touch was deceptively light. But then he tugged, enough to tilt my chin.

"Scared, Dolcezza?" he rumbled lowly.

I clenched my fists. "No."

Liar.

His smirk deepened as his thumb slowly traced my lower lip, staying there for a second too long before he let go. He stepped back just enough to stretch out an arm and point to the couch near the windows.

"Sit."

The word dropped like a command. I hesitated, shifting on my feet. His expression didn't change, but something in the air did. The temperature. The intensity of his presence. It pressed down on me, making my skin prickle.

"Unless," he drawled, "you were thinking of running?"

My throat dried up. The way he said it... so casually, like the idea of me running amused him. Like he wanted me to try. Like he was already picturing exactly what he'd do when he caught me.

He took another step closer.

"You run, and I'll make sure you can't fucking walk for a week." His voice dropped lower. "And not in the way that'll make you beg for more."

My stomach flipped. And I moved before I could think, practically stumbling onto the couch.

He chuckled before sinking onto the opposite side. Unlike me… who was sitting with legs pressed tightly and hands curled into the fabric of the dress, he spread out, arms draped lazily over the back of the couch, one ankle resting over his knee.

I didn't know what to do now.

Should I eat? Wait for him to tell me to eat? Serve him?

I swallowed hard, staring at the untouched dishes between us. My fingers twitched with hesitancy.

"Go on, Dolcezza." His voice was velvet and steel. "Eat."

I picked up a fork, my hand shaking slightly as I lifted the lid off one of the plates. The scent of something warm and rich filled the air. My stomach grumbled, part with nausea and part with hunger.

I took a decent portion on one plate and took a small bite. All while he watched me. That made me cautious and insecure.

It made me swallow the bite, almost choking.

"Relax." He chuckled again. "You look like you're about to pass out."

I gritted my teeth, forcing myself to take another bite. But the smirk on his face told me one thing. This wasn't just about dinner.

This was about control.

And he had all of it.

CHAPTER SIXTEEN
Burning

I barely ate anything, barely tasted a single bite. My stomach was already full for some reason. The suffocating tension and sinful way he was analysing me was tremendously nerve-racking. I already felt like I was losing my mind. Like he wasn't just closing in but swallowing me whole, leaving nothing behind.

He hadn't touched his plate yet. Not even the salad. Not the main course. Nothing. Just the wine. Deep red, rich and smooth liquid he sipped nonchalantly. This was definitely an effortless game for him. I could tell the way he was so confident and shameless while being a pervert. I didn't miss when he tilted the glass against his lips deliberately before lowering again.

It was getting on my nerves for all the bad reasons.

On another note, his eyes never left me. Not even for a second.

I swallowed hard, slowly putting the fork down. My throat was too tight and dry, while my clammy hands shook. I felt exposed and watched. Like a deer in a hunter's sights, the bow was already drawn and the arrow pointed straight at my heart.

He casually leaned back, exhaling softly as his fingers lazily ran over the rim of the glass before setting it down. A quiet hum left his lips, dragging over my skin like silk and sin.

"Are you done?"

I didn't trust my voice, so I just nodded.

He hummed again, deeper this time, slithering down my spine and wrapping around my lungs, squeezing the breath out of me.

I peeked at him through my lashes, wondering what was going on in his head. He was unpredictable to the point I couldn't trust my own thoughts with him. He had this strange control and way to make me obey him, no matter what.

The monster in front of me set his glass on the table and shifted. I shifted with him unconsciously. With his same unbothered grace, he uncrossed his legs, spreading them wide.

My stomach bottomed out.

My breath hitched as he ran his thumb over his lower lip as if he was deep in thought. His stormy grey eyes darkened, taking me in, devouring me piece by piece until I was sure he'd burned me into his memory, and I didn't want to know how I appeared in his eyes.

I was so ready to beg him to give me some more time to prepare myself, both mentally and physically. I was ready to crush my self-respect and plead with whatever I had left in me. Hell, I was even ready to trade anything to have some more time. But he seemed to read my thoughts. The slow smile turned into a malicious grin as he drawled. "Crawl."

I blinked. Wondering if I heard him right. Or even if I heard him at all. I did hear him though. I knew I did. But...

"Pardon?"

His expression didn't change; if anything, his smirk deepened. Lazily, he patted his thigh once. "Crawl to my lap."

My stomach twisted violently with the same intensity his eyes were raking over me with. My skin scorched, and I felt my face burning with shame. Was he serious? Yes. Yes, he was.

He leaned forward just a fraction, enough that I could see the way the candlelight carved out the sharp angles of his face. That jagged scar and that sinfully filthy mouth. Those goddamn eyes that held nothing but amusement laced with darkness.

He was enjoying my panic.

Enjoying the way I stared dumbfounded at him, wide-eyed with my breath uneven and my hands gripping the fabric of my dress so tight my knuckles ached.

I opened my mouth, ready to refuse, but his expression stopped me cold.

This wasn't a request.

My pulse pounded as he tilted his head, running his tongue along his bottom lip like he had all the time in the world to see me unravel and get on all fours.

Lies. He didn't have any patience. I knew it. The only reason he was being patient right now was because he knew I'd do it. One way or another. Even if it ended up with me being on the ground with his hand in my hair, forcefully or willingly, he was giving me a choice here. His way, or mine, which in reality was his way also.

"Dolcezza," he murmured, voice like a dark promise. "Don't make me repeat myself."

I could feel it. The shift. The thin line I was forcing him to cross. One that wouldn't end well for me.

Something in me screamed to run. Another part? The traitorous part? It shivered. With anticipation, fear and dread. I knew if I made a run for it, my legs would give up on me.

His patience was wearing thin. I could see it as his fingers tapped against the armrest. Tick. Tick. Tick.

I was playing with fire. And he was the fucking inferno.

Obedience.

The word tasted bitter on my tongue. Every part of me rejected it. I didn't want to do this. I shouldn't, but there was no other way.

None.

He was the immovable force. The unshakable pillar. The lion watched its prey thrash in the trap, knowing full well there was no escape.

I was cornered completely. My mind ran through every possibility, every alternative. Could I say no? Would he let me leave? Would he let me breathe, exist without any consequences?

No.

I knew that already. I'd always known.

A sharp pang hit my chest as my fists curled. It wasn't fair. It wasn't fair. And yet, my body moved before my pride could stop it.

Slowly and painfully, I uncurled my fingers, letting go of the last shreds of my resistance tangled in the silk. Shaky breaths shuddered out of me as I slowly lowered myself.

The wooden floor was cold beneath my palms as I pressed them down, my knees following next. Shame burned through me. I could feel the heat crawling up my throat, sinking its claws into my chest and ripping out the flesh.

I kept my gaze low, refusing to see the satisfaction I knew would be painted all over his face.

My insides churned as I shifted onto my knees completely. Humiliation curled, and I suddenly couldn't breathe. This was what he wanted. To break me. To strip me down until I was the perfect submissive woman in his eyes.

My spine straightened even as my body trembled while I crawled to him.

I crawled until I reached him, everything in me breaking with each second. I wanted to hide away from him. This man was crazy, insanely horrifying.

Just when I was close enough, I stopped.

"Look at me," he ordered, and even with no heart to obey him, I did it.

The look on my face pleased him, and he cradled my cheek with his large palm. There was no other physical contact, but still, it was enough to unravel me. He leaned, invading my personal space until his mouth was barely an inch away from my earlobe.

"That's my good girl."

My face turned red. All I could do was flutter my lashes as he caressed my ear.

"Come closer."

I was already between his legs, on the verge of touching his thighs, so when he slightly nudged me to his body, I shivered in response before my hands involuntarily landed on his muscular thighs for balance.

The moment my hands touched him, I was taken aback by the solid muscles under my palms. It was laughable how my entire palm was barely half the width of his thigh. He was tall, broad-shouldered and muscular, but I never imagined him to be rock solid.

That only heightened my terror. This man could crush my skull with his one hand.

As I lifted my eyes, I was suddenly hit by the realisation of where my mouth was. I yelped in fright, trying to back away when his hand moved from my earlobe to the back of my neck, keeping me in place, closer to his crotch as he shifted the side of my face to nuzzle the tent between his thighs.

Laughter bubbled from above, and I instinctively clutched onto his thighs. My chin was lifted as rough fingers on his other hand angled my face upward. The hand on my neck loosened its grip as he reached between us, and I heard the unmistakable clink of a belt followed by the sound of a zipper.

And I couldn't take my eyes off him. Either I'd lost my mind, or he simply had the magnetic presence that was daring me to break eye contact. And trust me, there was nothing but unbridled lust and something wild in his gaze.

"Take out my cock."

CHAPTER SEVENTEEN
Her Heart

N°. The word rang like a gunshot in my head, loud, desperate, but it never reached my lips.

"Take out my cock."

My skin burned. My fingers twitched where they still clung to the fabric of my dress, wriggling it, strangling it, as if it could somehow anchor me to reality. But there was no reality here. Only him. Only this moment. This trap I had willingly walked into.

I wished I could laugh, scoff and scream. Something. Anything to push against the brutal force of his command. But I didn't.

Because I knew.

Knew that resistance would only make him hungry. My defiance would only make this worse. His fingers flexed in my hair, almost lazy, but the gravity of them was crushing. He had all the time in the world to watch me fall apart.

"Come on, Dolcezza. I'm waiting."

The humiliation was worse than anything. I squeezed my

eyes shut, willing my body to move, to respond, but all I could do was sit there, frozen in place as shame hollowed me out from the inside.

His patience snapped like the courage inside me. The fingers threaded my hair, fisting it, and a yelp died in my throat as I was forced to meet his stormy gaze. "Now."

My stomach lurched. My nails dug into his thighs, desperate to hold onto anything, to slow this down, to stop this from happening. But it was already too late. I knew it. He knew it. And that cruel smirk told me he was enjoying every second of my downfall.

His free hand moved between us, tugging at his slacks, parting them just enough to make me see how serious he was.

My throat closed as I struggled to breathe. I could feel him. The heat. The danger.

His grip on my hair loosened, fingers tracing down to cradle my cheek. His thumb dragged over my parted lips, teasing and claiming.

"Open," he ordered. And I did. Because we both knew how this would end. He did not give me time; instead, he was unzipping his slacks. The fear in my eyes brought a smile to his face as he pulled out his enormous member.

The size and girth of it had me panic. He wasn't fully hard, yet it made me want to run for the hills. My throat went dry suddenly, and before I knew it, I was pushing at his thighs, trying to get away. No. I couldn't do this.

But this unpredictable man had some other plans. He fisted my hair, pulled my mouth close to his rod. My lips met flesh, forcing me to open my mouth as he slowly pushed himself inside, resting it on my tongue as he waited for me to adjust to his size. "Bite, and I'll make you regret having a mouth."

The threat was clear. His thumb traced over my cheek, deceptively gentle, but his stormy gaze held no mercy. I knew he wasn't bluffing. My fingers curled against his slacks, but it was already too late. It had been from the moment he laid his claim.

A slow, satisfied grin spread across his lips as he bit them. "Good girl," he murmured, tilting my chin. "Now, suck it."

My lips parted, but not out of obedience—out of sheer, breathless fear. I had never done this. Even with Adrian, we had normal sex, vanilla even. He never asked me to give him a blowjob. Now, kneeling in front of this man, I realised how dark this world truly was.

The weight of his manhood rested on my tongue, and it felt so foreign, intrusive and unrelentingly hot. The taste of salt, of power, of inevitability, bled into my senses, drowning me in a moment I wished I could escape.

I wanted to scream. To bite down. To remind him I wasn't something to be conquered. But his grip on my hair was mercilessly malicious.

He owned this moment. Owned me.

A choked whimper betrayed me, and his grin deepened, sin incarnate, carved in arrogance. His thumb smoothed over my cheek. "Look at you," he breathed, tilting his hips just enough to make my lips stretch wider, to make me feel the slow, merciless pulse of him against my tongue. "So fucking pretty when you're dripping with my seed."

Shame curled in my gut like venom that burned through my veins. My fingers tightened in his slacks, knuckles white, nails pressing deep enough to leave crescent moons in the fabric.

I could hear my pulse.

"Breathe," he murmured. "Relax that pretty little throat for me, Dolcezza. It's going to be a long night."

He didn't wait. He never did.

With a slow push, he claimed the rest of me.

And I shattered.

CHAPTER EIGHTEEN
Sins and Desires

My jaw ached. My tongue burned. My throat clenched around the sheer impossibility of him. He was too thick, too big, too much for my body to take, and yet—he wasn't stopping. And he didn't seem like the type of man to stop either.

Tears pricked the corners of my eyes as I forced myself to breathe, to adjust and survive this moment without breaking. His fingers flexed in my hair, controlling every motion, every breath, every inch I took as he forced his manhood into my mouth. As if he didn't know or didn't care if my throat was burning like crazy.

"Come on, Dolcezza." I hated how his voice was getting raspier and heavier. The sheer lust and desire in his eyes had me pinned in place and kept my head moving back and forth. "You can take it."

No, I couldn't. I knew it. He knew it. But that wasn't the point.

The point was watching me try. Watching me struggle. Watching me mould myself into something he could ruin.

Something entirely his.

My throat convulsed as he pressed deeper, the blunt, throbbing heat of him pushing past the tight resistance. My fingers scrambled against his thighs, not to stop him—there was no stopping this—but to anchor myself to something solid so that I wouldn't end up passing out.

His free hand tilted my chin, forcing me to look up. His stormy gaze burned with possession, with cruelty, with something far more dangerous than lust, and he was still inside my mouth. I bet I looked obscenely lewd in his eyes; that image of me was evident in his eyes. And he loved that more than anything. "There you go," he praised, dragging his thumb over the corner of my mouth, smearing the moisture that gathered there and pushing the girth of his cock further in. It didn't make sense how he was still only halfway. "So fucking beautiful when you're choking on my cock."

Humiliation licked up my spine, like a slow, searing crawl of fire and shame. I wanted to disappear, to sink into the floor and never return. But he wouldn't allow that. He demanded presence. He demanded my submission in every way that mattered.

I struggled to take more of him, my throat constricting as my breath stuttered, but he gave no reprieve. Just a slow, steady push that stole the air from my lungs.

"Relax," he ordered, his grip tightening as he guided my movements again. Slower this time, giving me more time to adjust to his length and controlling the rhythm with devastating care. "You'll learn. I'll make you learn."

I didn't want to learn. Didn't want to be moulded into the perfect little pet who knew exactly how to please him. But my body betrayed me, adjusting inch by inch, stretching to accommodate his brutal demands. If I didn't, he'd probably throw me across the room and force his way in. Like he said, I liked the idea of fake consent rather than being taken by force.

A strangled sound left me as he pressed in further, his fingers flexing, his breath hitching like he could feel every desperate attempt my throat made to reject him.

In and out.

"Good girl," he murmured, voice husky, edged with dark satisfaction. "You're already getting better."

My nails bit into his slacks, my lungs burned, and my dignity lay in pieces at his feet. And yet, there was no escaping the inevitable.

Not when he already owned me. His fingers lightly grazed over the side of my throat, then moved to undo my bun, letting my hair fall all over the sides of my face. I tried my best not to tremble, reminding myself that this would end. The huge thing inside my mouth was far from calming down, and the soreness in my cheeks had started to dull now.

My mind wasn't mine anymore. My breaths weren't mine. Shame, rage and fear. I used to think I was strong. That I had a backbone, a voice, a choice. But here, on my knees, with his fingers in my hair and his cock claiming my mouth, I realized the truth—strength meant nothing in the face of absolute power.

This wasn't just possession. It was obliteration.

To men like him, women weren't humans. We were objects—bought, used, discarded. A toy to be played with. A doll to be posed. Desire didn't soften men like him. He was the fire, and I was destined to burn.

"Breathe." His command came harshly and clearly, laced with lust and something dark. He pulled his manhood out, and I panted, greedily sucking in the air. My chest rose up and down, and I'd lost strength in my body. Through my teary eyes, I dared to look at him and immediately regretted it; he was already staring down at me.

He let out a deep groan, and with an eyebrow arched, he held the back of my neck and forced me to look up at him. My fearful eyes caught the proud satisfaction in his eyes.

His eyes darkened by the second, and he placed his hand on my chin, squeezing tightly. The force exerted was too much, and before I knew it, I was being pushed down on the couch, and he was towering over me.

It all happened in a single second, a rough hand grabbing my arm, pulling me up, and then within the same second, I was being pushed in a way that my head dangled from the couch, and the rest of my body was on the couch as my eyes stared at the ceiling.

It had taken mere seconds.

With a gust of wind, he was hovering over me. My eyes widened as he placed his one knee on the side, leaning down enough to make his manhood slap against my lips. "Open, Dolcezza."

I did, because I had no other choice. As he forced me to swallow his huge rod, my vision began to blur at the edges. His thrusts didn't slow; instead, as if he was possessed by some deep, dark desire, he penetrated further and further. In this position, his manhood reached the depths of my throat.

My thoughts left me, and so did my sanity. I couldn't think of anything, let alone breathe. This man was the epitome of madness. He did not care if I would break this way, if I would never be able to see myself again. All he cared about was his pleasure.

The weak noises of my breathing and the shivers of my coughing merely caused him to swell with blood. Making me feel like I was about to have my throat pierced. I heard him let out a throaty chuckle, and suddenly, an intense pressure was placed between my legs. Startled, the intrusion made me panic, and the maniac took this opportunity to go even deeper.

No. No, please…

But my pleas didn't reach him fully. The dress was shredded, and the remnants clung to my trembling flesh. A yelp bubbled in my throat, swallowed by his manhood as he grabbed the hem of my panties and pulled them aside, gently rubbing his two fingers on my womanhood.

I reached my limit. The sudden invasion made my body feverish. I had never felt this way before, this sense of pain and… something strange. Adrian never treated me this way ever. He was such a caring man, making sure I was comfortable enough for him to have sex with me. Our sex life was all soft and sweet. He'd kiss me, fondle me and make love to me.

But this… this was entirely different.

The man I was about to have sex with, the one who murdered Adrian, the one whose name I still didn't know, had no soft bones in his body.

He didn't kiss, he didn't fondle me… and I knew he wouldn't make love to me.

He'd fuck me, but not before ruining me first, moulding my body to the shape of his fingers.

Tears hadn't stopped flowing; instead, they only made it worse. It didn't make sense. What did he want from me? From a girl so broken she was afraid of gathering her own pieces. He'd left no choice but to turn to him.

"You're wet." I shut my eyes, clenching my thighs together, but he only slapped them open before caressing my folds with tenderness he didn't have. "Your cunt's dripping, Dolcezza."

No.

This was my body's reaction, not my soul's. This was just my body. This was just my body. I reminded myself again and again. But the monster above me had other plans; his hand cupped my core, and his thrusts became slow now, but deeper.

He growled animalistically before pulling his entire manhood out, but I could feel the tip against my lips.

He slapped it against my cheek once, twice, and then ejaculated all over my face. Shame flooded my veins, making me wish for hell. My vision clouded over, and I blinked my eyes rapidly before I saw black dots. I blinked again, and this time it was his satisfied face I saw before I lost consciousness.

CHAPTER NINETEEN
The Art of Breaking

I woke up to a strange scent. A little lost and with throbbing pain in my throat. I felt the softness underneath me and a bubbling sensation of dread. I didn't want to wake up.

Swallowing the thickness with pain, I turned to my side to see an unknown but warm embrace from someone. My chest still had this feeling of stuffiness, even if I remembered passing out. I could feel the corners of my mouth being cracked and stretchy. And even opening it too much was painful.

I twisted, trying to break free when a deep, rough voice grumbled in my ear. "You're awake."

I froze.

Muscles locked as the rough timbre of his voice slithered into my ear. A slow, creeping tremor unfurled within me as if it'd squeeze the air out of my lungs. No. No, no, no.

I tried to pull away, but the arm draped over my waist tightened, yanking me back against the solid heat of his chest. My pulse hammered against my ears, drowning out any other sound but the slow breathing of his against my skin.

"Please…" As if I was once again shoved over the couch,

and violated, I plead. Because that's all I could do. I didn't want him to touch me again after what he did. I never thought he'd be this brutal.

I gasped as he flipped me onto my back. My body hit the mattress, and the sheets tangled around my legs, making me unable to move them. My breath came out in shallow, uneven pants as a violent tremor rippled through my limbs, and the world spun. My head was still foggy from the suffocating darkness I'd woken up in.

My eyes blinked rapidly until I adjusted to the sight of him. Towering over me. Naked.

My stomach lurched. The heat of his skin radiated against mine, a sickening reminder that I was bare too. No barrier, no protection, just my trembling body beneath his.

A raw, desperate panic clawed up my sore throat.

"No!" I thrashed, trying to pull away, but it was futile. The more I struggled, the more brutal the force of his grip was on my wrists.

Large hands pinned my wrists above my head, pressing them deep into the mattress, his calloused fingers wrapping around my delicate bones with ease. His thighs caged mine and forced them apart, restraining me until I had no hope of escaping.

His stormy eyes flickered along the length of my body, making me want to curl up and hide.

"I expected more from you, Dolcezza." He tilted his head as if I were an experiment gone wrong. I hated the shame burning hotter than my fear. How could he look so detached and cold when he almost tore my throat a few hours ago? There was not a single flicker of regret or guilt in his eyes. Those damn stormy eyes I was coming to loathe. Not even an ounce of emotion; if anything, he looked like he'd do it all over again.

What was I even thinking, coming to him and letting him

use me when I knew he had no gentle bone in his body? I was so foolish to even think that if I obeyed, he'd be less cruel. I was wrong, so damn wrong it hurt more than it should.

Feeling bothered and suddenly angry, my body stopped fighting back, and I looked dead in his eyes, matching the coldness. "Fuck you."

I expected a slap, a punch, or even him to force me.

Instead, he chuckled, slightly tightening his grip on my wrists. "You're welcome to try, dear wife."

I recoiled. Wife. Not a prisoner. Not captive. Not even a plaything. But wife. A title that should've meant something sacred. Vows of love, promises and devotion. But with him? It was a leash. A declaration of ownership.

I swallowed hard. Now that he said it, I realised I was bound to him with more than just words and violence. This wasn't a nightmare I could wake up from.

How could he? How could he say it so casually? Did it mean nothing to him? He had no morals, no conscience, and no fucking humanity. A man wouldn't do this. A man wouldn't force a wedding onto someone who wanted nothing to do with him.

No, what held me down wasn't a man.

It was a monster. And I was his bride.

This sudden reality hit harder than it had any business to. He felt it too, 'cause I saw something flickering in his eyes. My throat convulsed as I looked at him.

"You could've had anyone." My voice cracked from the strain of everything he had put me through. "Anyone, willingly. So why me?"

His gaze flickered once again, something there, something gone before I could name it. Like the whisper of a ghost. There but never there. It was tangible and unpredictably unstable.

"Do I even mean anything to you?" My breath hitched,

and I hoped he could feel the pain behind my words. I knew men like him were hard to reach out to, but at least he could see the damage he'd done. "Or am I just... just something to fuck? A sex slave you buy from some brothel?"

His fingers flexed against my skin. And this time, I saw the shift, the momentary lapse where the monster inside him faltered, if only for a breath.

And still, he said nothing. Just looked at me as if he was trying to decode me. Understand me. Understand my irrational words.

"Do you enjoy tormenting me?" Slat and rust rubbed against my sore throat, like all the things I could never take back. "Because that's what this is. Every fucking breath... I feel like dying. I can't escape you. No matter how much I try, how much I bleed."

The silence that followed was dense.

Tears burned, but I refused them and swallowed them like poison. I had nothing left to give him. No more pieces to break, no more screams to steal.

"I am a human," I spoke recklessly, not caring if he'd punish me later. "Not a fucking slave! You can't do this to me. I can't accept this. I won't! It's... It's depressing! Let me go, please! I don't even fucking know your name!"

My chest rose and fell by the time I was done speaking.

He just stared.

Like I was some caged animal throwing itself against the bars, as if my defiance was nothing more than an amusing tantrum.

I wanted to claw at his face, to dig my nails into his skin and rip apart that cold, unfeeling mask he wore so perfectly. Was there even a real person beneath it? Or was he just a hollow thing—one without a soul, without a conscience?

It made me feel small. Insignificant.

Nothing about me mattered to him.

I clenched my fists so tightly my nails bit into my palms.

Did he not understand a single word I said? Was he so far gone in his own twisted world that he saw my resistance as nothing more than a joke?

I felt sick.

A nausea deep in my bones, a sickness that had nothing to do with my body and everything to do with the overwhelming realization that I might never get out of this. Just as I was about to yell at him again, he tilted his head.

Ever so slightly, I almost missed it. His curious eyes followed the path of my tears, and then he met my eyes again. And I flinched because whatever was flickering inside them before was gone, replaced by the cold, detached glint, and he curved his lips.

"Zagreus. Zagreus Vitale."

CHAPTER TWENTY
The Monster

S ome men kill with guns, others with words. But the deadliest of them all? Killing with silence.

Zagreus was one of them.

The room pulsed with heavy and unbearably quiet, thick spaces between heartbeats. A pause before the devastation. I should've feared his anger. But that didn't come, and that was my death sentence.

I tried to push past the suffocating weight of it, twisting and writhing, struggling against his hold, but it was like fighting chains forged in hell. His body remained still, letting me exhaust myself purposely like a trapped little bird slamming against its cage. I fought until my muscles screamed, until my lungs burned and until the tears pricked my eyes in a humiliating display of weakness.

And then, when I had nothing left when my body betrayed me, he slowly moved his fingers, unclasping from my wrists and deliberately finding my throat. My breath hitched, and I looked at him wide-eyed. His grip wasn't fatally choking, but it was enough to send a wave of fear coursing through my veins.

"You can scream," Zagreus murmured, his tempestuous eyes flickering between cold grey and obsidian black as he tilted his head. "Curse it, whisper it in fear." His thumb pressed against my cheek, dragging a lone tear with him, and his grin widened. "But it will be the last name you ever know as your master."

My chest constricted, air catching in my burning lungs.

No. No, no, no...

"You came to me willingly," he continued, tracing my jawline, burning my skin in unholy brand, "offering yourself as my sacrifice."

A cruel smirk tugged his lips as I sucked in a shaky breath. "And now you're backing out?"

The world was a cruel place, but some men were crueller still. Zagreus Vitale was not a man. He was a god carved from violence, his divinity built on the bones of those who dared to defy him. And I wondered if I'd join those dead too. By the look on his eyes, I knew I would. The grey had turned into sharp silver. And I couldn't even breathe properly.

When his hand flexed on my throat, my vision blurred. Tears burned the backs of my eyes, hot and shameful. A song my mother once sang drifted through my mind; the haunting melody and cruel irony startled me. I didn't know the meaning then, but now I was reminiscing about it.

Even the storm bends to love, but love has never bent for me.

Because this wasn't love, it wasn't devotion even. It wasn't passion. It was destruction in its cruelest form.

The way his eyes gleamed mischievously made me realise I was a lost cause from the start. He wouldn't stop, even if he had to force me.

"I stopped last time," he murmured, his fingers tracing my

sternum, lingering over my racing heart. "Not because I had to. Because I wanted you awake for this."

His hand slid lower. My breath caught. His stormy grey eyes darkened with something… cruelly patient.

"I want you to feel everything, Dolcezza. To know it's me. To know you belong to me."

A choked sob escaped me. He caught it… held it.

"Shhh, shhh," he cooed mockingly, his thumb wiping a tear from my cheek. "I hate seeing you cry, Dolcezza. But I love knowing I'm the reason for it."

He tilted my chin up, forcing me to meet his gaze. For the briefest moment, his thumb hovered. A flicker of something almost gentle. But then it was gone. He smirked, the moment shattered, and his grasp became ironclad. "I think I'll make you cry more."

His hand slowly drifted lower until he was close to my forbidden part. And I couldn't even fight. He was not only my captor, he was my grave. And this marriage? A coffin nailed shut.

My lips wobbled and I shut my eyes, letting his words sink into my broken heart. "You're awake, little wife. Shall we continue?"

By the time I realised what he meant, he reached a hand out as he pulled down the sheets covering my lower body. The sudden, frightening struggle and hoarse crying filled the air, and I realised I was on the verge of panicking. "Don't…! Please… don't!"

Knowing my pleas wouldn't work, I wanted him to stop. I wasn't ready, but he didn't listen. Instead, he pulled me to him by my throat, crashing his mouth on mine, devouring my struggles and crying. For some reason, I felt his warmth far more compelling than his coldness. My fingers tightly gripped his biceps, as strong and muscular as the rest of his body, and I

took a deep breath in and stammered into the kiss. "Adrian..."
He stilled against me, and I felt his fury instantly. I knew he
didn't like to hear the name of another man when he was going
to devour me, but I had to do this.

Before he could do something worse, I quickly breathed
out, looking at him with expectant and pleading eyes. "Let
me... see him."

"He's dead," he said monotonously. I could already tell he
was pissed.

I swallowed the grief that came with the realisation. "I
know... I want to know if he's properly buried."

"He is," he muttered, and I felt relieved. At least Adrian
got a proper burial. I couldn't imagine him in that cold apartment. Did his parents find him? Or someone else? Did they
know I was also missing? Did someone report me?

Icy touch clenched around my throat. "Is this your way of
making me mad, Dolcezza?"

"No..." I exhaled shakily, forcing steel into my voice even
as my body trembled beneath him. "Do whatever you want,
like you said. But you want me to be yours, don't you?"

His eyes narrowed. A flicker of something—curiosity,
suspicion—passed through them.

"You think I'm obligated to hear your tantrums?" he
mused, but I heard it—the shift in his tone, the momentary
pause. I had his attention.

I swallowed, gripping onto that sliver of control. "If you
want to break me, do it. But you don't just want my body. You
want all of me, don't you?"

His grip on my throat tightened reflexively, a warning. But
I saw the faint tick in his jaw, the flicker of amusement tainted
with something else.

"I'm not expecting any gentleness from a monster like you
either."

His jaw ticked, and he scoffed.

"Very well then." His rough, big hand landed on my thighs, and I sucked in a sharp breath before I was roughly shoved down. "Spread your legs. Show me how badly you want to see your dead lover."

I glared at him, shame and humiliation coursing through my veins. I wasn't strong enough to fight him.

So, I did the only thing I could to survive. I swallowed my pride, forced my shaking limbs to obey, and parted my thighs.

Once this was all over, I'd show him hell. There was no way I could leave this place on my own. Once I was outside, I'd make a run for it.

I slowly opened my legs, averting my eyes from his sinful face to look at anything but him. "Eyes on me, Dolcezza."

I gritted my teeth and lifted my eyes to him. He was towering over me, pumping his enraged manhood in his palm and biting down on his lips. His eyes focused on me, or my eyes, I could say. He hadn't made any move to touch me, but I knew this relief was short-lived.

He grinned when I spread my legs as wide as I could, exposing myself to his hungry eyes, which only darkened by the second. "Fuck, here you are, dripping wet. Spread your cunt for me, little wife."

CHAPTER TWENTY-ONE
Betrayal of Own

I let out a cry. And it satisfied the extremely pissed man above me. His teasing, rough fingers ran along my inner thighs, burning my skin, but purposely avoiding touching me at the forbidden part. My hazy eyes raked all over him, from his defined collarbones to his exposed manhood. He stopped pumping, yet the organ was alive with life, standing erect, touching his navel.

The more he tormented me this way, the scarier it was getting for me to ready myself. Even though I had convinced myself that this was for my plan. A plan I'd execute once I was out of this goddamn mansion. But looking at him now, I wondered if he was playing with me.

Of course, he was. He always had. There was no doubt about how perverted and unpredictable he was when it came to situations like this, only if he'd get it over with.

My eyelashes trembled as I sucked in another breath. Strangely, my body started heating up for some unknown reason. Knowing human anatomy, I knew this was the response of the mind and my body, not my heart. I didn't want this. I reminded myself again and again.

It was sinful how he seemed to know my body more than I knew myself. Because next moment, he cupped my core, rubbing it with the heel of his palm in tantalising slow circles, making my eyes widen and my fists clenched over his biceps.

Shit. No. I couldn't feel it. I shouldn't.

Yet when he applied a little more pressure, I mewled involuntarily. I closed my eyes as his one hand caressed my breast and rubbed circles on my clitoris with the other. It felt electric, how my body was burning up with his every single touch.

"Don't close your eyes, Dolcezza. Watch as I make you come on my fingers, my tongue and my cock."

I had no choice but to open my eyes. My body was already corrupted, so it didn't matter if I enjoyed this or not. I was breathing rapidly and looked into his eyes.

The bastard smirked, and while looking into my eyes, he covered my core with his hand, slowly putting a finger in. My body jerked, my back arched, and I reached for anything to hold when he pushed deeper, until I was gasping for air.

"You're tight. So fucking tight."

I bit on my lips, preventing anything from slipping out. He could use me however he saw fit, but he would never have my voice, not until I died. That's all he'd get.

But how did I stop the tremors? When his hand on my breast kneaded them, I shivered as he leaned and peppered kisses on the sensitive skin before biting it and sucking on it.

I instinctively tilted my head to the side, still biting on my lips as he nibbled down on the erect nipple, and I gasped.

I didn't know I was this sensitive when it came to sex. Adrian and I had been with each other for four years, yet I'd never felt this way with him. But the way Zagreus feasted on my life essence as if needing to feel it throb beneath his mouth.

I released a shattered breath when his middle finger joined

the index one inside me. "You're wild, for someone who hates me."

I held onto the wrist of his hand, but it was not enough to stop him. "Just… fuck me already."

I gasped as he put more pressure and scoffed. "I decide how to play, not you, wife. I'll fuck you when I want." He was merely fingering me that slowly, and yet I felt like I'd explode. I'd never been so… wanton for male attention, had I?

"Zagreus…" I breathed out.

"Yes, Dolcezza."

"Please…"

I didn't know what I was pleading for, for his fingers to penetrate deeper and give me an orgasm or for his actions to stop. The pressure in my stomach was building with each stroke, and I couldn't rationalise with myself anymore. Something twisted in me, and I was suddenly convulsing all over him. Like I'd just jumped from a cliff with no ground.

When I came down from high, I realised what I had just done and shame bubbled within me. Refusing to look at his grinning face, I panted heavily, trying to catch my breath. But he had other plans; he didn't let me rest. Instead, I was being flipped on my stomach. A gasp left my lips before his arm was wrapped around my mid-section, and my buttocks was lifted in the air.

I was frozen in place, time and everything in between. He looked calm now, but I knew he was still mad about me mentioning Adrian. At least now I knew what ticked him off. And that was a mention of my dead lover. I stared at the metal headboard with its exotic golden motifs, refusing to look at him. Because the more I looked at him, the deeper the darkness sucked me in. I couldn't figure him out, not when he wore his expression with the same ease as he wore his dark suit.

"Part your thighs." He stroked my hair gently.

I slowly repositioned my knees, and the cold air hit my womanhood. I was sensitive there, just after an orgasm, after I came down from high, but the brute hadn't let me breathe yet.

"That's my Dolcezza."

My muscles locked whenever he called me that, and I had no idea whether it was as an endearment or a mocking way to remind me of my misery. Just like most things he did to me, whether he inflicted pain or his dark claim whenever I refused him.

I wondered how many women had become his target. I couldn't be the only one. And I most definitely couldn't be the last either. Men like him loved control, like breathing air. They dwelled in it. Cruel and calloused. Brutal and sadistic. Perverted, too, because he loved seeing me in pain. He wore that quiet, controlled mask like it could hide the monster underneath, but I saw him for what he was… a depraved, perverted fucker who lived to hurt, to take, to own as he saw fit. Twisting cruelty into mercy, making suffering feel like a gift, and now he stood behind me, ready to take another piece of me for his sick pleasure.

Cruel hands parted my buttocks before I felt a gust of wind… or hot breath. My body jerked, and I quickly tried to pull away, only to be held captive by him as his rough hands gripped my waist. "Move, and I'll tie you up."

"What… what are you doing?!"

"What does it look like, little wife? Of course, I wanna enjoy your cunt while it's dripping for me."

"No, it's…" Dirty, disgusting and deviant behaviour. But before I could say anything, his mouth was on me, between my legs, warm tongue penetrating me as his thumb moved to my bundle of nerves. And a strange sensation bubbled inside me as I stuffed my face into my sheets, refusing to moan for him.

Shit. It felt… devastatingly… good. Why?

He had taken everything from me, my freedom, my dignity and the man I loved. Snatched him from my arms, ripped his soul from this world like it meant nothing, and then he turned to me, wiped the blood from his blade like it was an afterthought and told me I was his.

His wife. His property. His plaything.

I should have fought harder. Should have screamed, clawed and torn at him until I had nothing left. But I didn't. Maybe because I knew it would never matter. He would take what he wanted regardless; the monster always wins.

Yet now… now as his tongue wreaked havoc inside me, as he tormented me with slow, languid strokes, unravelling me in ways I didn't understand… my body betrayed me. Welcomed him.

I hated myself for it.

Hated the way my thighs trembled, the heat pooling in my gut, the traitorous pulse of pleasure that coiled tighter, tighter until I wanted to scream, to sob, and to scratch my skin open just to purge the shame from my veins.

"This pussy is mine to fuck, to lick and tame in whatever way I please. When I say bend, you will spread your legs and invite my cock like a good little wife." Every word scraped against my heated core. I saw blur, darkness and everything I was not supposed to. My body had become accustomed to him. Opening for him and inviting him. I'd never felt this way before. Never.

A sharp nip against my sensitive flesh had me jerking, hands gripping the sheets like a lifeline, and I screamed into the pillow. Shit. Shit, shit, shit. It was too much. This pain and pleasure.

Bastard. Sadist. Depraved, insatiable devil.

And yet, as his tongue plunged deeper, forcing another gasp from my lips, I realised something horrible. I wasn't thinking of the man he killed. I wasn't thinking of anything at all. I was drowning in fact... completely, utterly and endlessly like the waves outside. Colliding on the shore, knowing that was the endpoint.

Another electric sensation rippled through me, and before I knew it, I was clutching the sheets tighter, my vision blurred, and I released. It was humiliating how he chuckled and leapt like a hungry animal, licking me down there where Adrian never had.

Tears accumulated in my eyes as the strength in my arms failed and I fell face-first on the bed, panting and trembling. What... what had I just done? I came undone in the hands of my captor.

I wished the earth would split and swallow me whole. I wished I could disappear into the sheets, into the darkness, into nothingness... anything to escape reality and his satisfied grey eyes.

A firm grip tangled in my hair, forcing my head up, making me face the truth I so desperately wanted to deny. His hot breath ghosted over my skin. "That was the sweetest sound you've ever made, Dolcezza."

Shame crawled up my spine, and my lips trembled, parted, but no words came. What was left to say? He had stripped me of everything... my pride, my defiance and my grief... until there was only this unbearable and aching guilt and need.

I hated him for making me crave what should disgust me.

For making my body betray me in the worst way possible.

"You're trembling." He brushed his fingers down my spine, making me arch my back unconsciously. "Was it too much, or not enough?"

The wicked, darkly amused tone irked me.

I clenched my teeth, digging my nails into the sheets. But the sensation of his mouth on me still lingered, burned into my skin, seared into my very bones. My traitorous pulse is still thrumming between my legs.

"Nothing to say?" he murmured, tracing the curve of my hip. "Don't tell me you're feeling guilty now. Because that would be a damn shame, little wife."

I squeezed my eyes. Damn him. I hated how he could read me like an open book while I had to struggle to even know his name. But he didn't stop there; his fingers parted my core, gently running along my parted folds. I could feel the slickness, and that disgusted me.

He chuckled, kissing the back of my neck. "He's dead, Dolcezza. You can mourn him, but he'll never be the one to make you come. That honour belongs to me."

A sob crawled up my throat, but I refused to cry.

CHAPTER TWENTY-TWO
Take Me

Zagreus smirked wickedly, taking in my trembling form and the tears threatening to spill from my eyes. By the sensations of his body against mine, I could tell he saw the internal struggle written all over my face - the guilt, the shame, the confusing mix of revulsion and reluctant desire. It only served to fuel his twisted lust.

I wanted to shove him away. To scream and fight, but my body betrayed me with every shudder and touch.

He leaned in, his lips brushing against the shell of my ear as he spoke in a low, cruelly amused tone. "I can see the wheels turning in that pretty little head of yours, Dolcezza. You're trying to hate me, trying to cling to some semblance of loyalty to that pathetic excuse of a man. But your body... your body knows the truth."

To punctuate his words, he slid a finger inside my slick heat, pumping it slowly, teasingly. A dark chuckle rumbled in his chest as I unknowingly clenched around the intrusion.

My breath stuttered, and shame curled in my gut like a living, breathing thing.

Not like this. No.

"Still so tight, even after coming undone on my tongue," he mused with smug satisfaction. "I wonder how long it will take before you're begging for more, before you're craving the feel of my cock splitting you open, claiming you completely..."

I hated him. I hated the way his words slithered into my mind. I hated the way my own fucking body answered his touch, the way it seemed to respond to him when all I wanted was to fight.

He nipped at my earlobe. "Don't fight it, Dolcezza. Embrace what you are - a vicious little slut, desperate for a real man to fuck you senseless."

His words were venom, seeping under my skin. I wanted to spit in his face, to curse him to hell and back. But when he withdrew his fingers and brought them to his lips, his tongue flicked out to taste me with slow and deliberate cruelty, and my breath hitched in my throat as I stared wide-eyed at him.

His eyes never left mine, watching my every reaction with that sadistic glee.

"Now, be a good wife and get on your knees. It's time for your next lesson in obedience." He commanded coldly, one hand already working between us, unleashing his throbbing erection.

A strangled noise left my lips as I lowered myself.

I squeezed my eyes shut. No. No. I'm not. This isn't me.

But the truth was as ruthless as him. And Zagreus? Zagreus lived to strip me of it.

Desire was such a traitorous beat, licking at my skin with molten hunger, and even as my mind clawed for escape, I knew I was gone. He was the knife pressed to my throat. Dark abyss whispering sweet nothings, the devil in a silk-lined coffin, grinning as he buried me alive.

I should hate him. I did. But hate was a fickle thing. A

blade with two edges, and one of them was carving my ruin with every breathless second. My body betrayed me.

They said a woman's virtue was a fortress, but what was a fortress against a siege that was over before it began?

His cock head teased my slick folds, the thick girth parting the lips, not yet pushing inside but hovering maddeningly at my entrance. His eyes, dark and hungry, raked over my trembling form kneeling before him. A cruel smirk played on his lips as he drank in the sight.

"Look at you, Dolcezza, so wet and ready for me already," he taunted, rolling his hips to grind his cock against my slit, not entering me but painting my folds with my own arousal mixed with his leaking pre-cum. "Your cunt is practically begging to be stuffed full of my dick, isn't it?"

One large hand gripped my chin, forcing me to meet his smug, arrogant gaze. The other hand gripped my hip hard enough to bruise, holding me in place as he continued his filthy torment.

"I bet that pathetic little prick you called a fiancé never made you this desperate, this hungry for cock." Zagreus sneered, punctuating his words with a sharp thrust against my core, the head of his dick catching on my entrance but not pushing inside. "He could never fill you like I can, never fuck you like you need to be fucked."

He leaned in closer, his breath hot and heavy against my face. "Tell me, little wife, don't you want to feel my cock stretching you wide, claiming every inch of your greedy little cunt? Don't you want to scream my name as I ruin you for any other man?"

His voice dripped with cruel, arrogant amusement, relishing the power he held over me at that moment. His cock continued to tease my entrance, and my insides twitched. "Beg for it, Dolcezza. Beg for my cock like the desperate slut you are. Maybe if you ask nicely enough, I'll give you what you're craving..."

He wanted me to beg. To be unravelled by him. To fold like paper beneath his grasp. And the most terrifying part? I thought I just might.

With a harsh, animalistic grunt, he finally plunged his thick manhood deep into my core, not giving me any time to adjust as he began to ram into me with brutal, punishing strokes. My back arched, a scream tearing from my throat at the sudden, rough invasion stretching me wide.

I had always thought pain and pleasure were two separate spectrums. That pleasure and pain existed as two different things, never meant to intertwine. But Zagreus was both, like a cruel alchemist who turned suffering into seduction, pain into poetry.

And I was the ink bleeding onto his pages.

I wanted to believe I still had a choice, that my body was mine to govern, that the trembling in my limbs was fear alone and not something far more damning. But the truth was bitter. I had lost this battle long before it began. He saw it, felt it and relished in it.

Shame curled in my stomach as his thrusts became violent, shaking me, shaking the bed we were on, and my world at the same time.

It wasn't real, I told myself. It was just biology, just nerve endings firing against my will.

But no lie, no desperate justification could erase the way I clenched around him, the way his voice dripped into my ears like candle wax, hot and slow, searing through my dignity.

"Fuck, your cunt feels even better than I imagined," he growled, one hand fisting in my hair, yanking my head back as he pounded into me mercilessly. "So goddamn tight and hot, like it was made to milk my cock."

I wanted to weep, but my body had already answered him in ways my lips never would.

He flipped me onto my hands and knees, my arse high in the air, and drove into me even harder from behind. The new angle allowed him to plunge impossibly deep, his heavy balls slapping obscenely against my clit with each brutal thrust.

"That's it, take my cock like the filthy slut you are," Zagreus snarled, giving my arse a harsh smack that must have left a handprint on my skin. "I'm going to ruin this pussy, ruin it so good that you'll never forget who it belongs to."

I could only sob and wail as he used me, my fingers scrabbling at the sheets, knuckles white with the force of his fucking. He pulled my hips back to meet his every thrust, and my body jolted with the impact as my breasts bounced.

My world tilted on its axis. Every thrust sent shockwaves through me, and I found myself floating somewhere between agony and something far worse... acceptance.

He changed angles and suddenly, he flipped me onto my back, spreading my legs wide and driving back inside me, looming over me with a dark, sadistic grin. "I want to watch your face when I split you open on my dick," he rumbled, pounding into me with deep, powerful strokes that seemed to reach my womb.

"Scream for me, little wife. Let the whole damn island hear who's fucking you, who's claiming this sweet cunt as his own," he commanded, hammering relentlessly, the obscene sound of flesh slapping against flesh filling the room and making my insides churn.

Through the haze of pain and reluctant pleasure, I could only clench around him, feeling every ridge and vein of his thickness dragging along my sensitive walls. Tears streamed down my face as he used me, and my body no longer was my own as he fucked me raw and ruthlessly.

CHAPTER TWENTY-THREE
Never Be His

Zagreus's cock pistoned in and out of me with each forceful thrust, driving the air from my lungs in ragged gasps and desperate moans. Driving me closer to something I couldn't name. A breaking point, probably, a reckoning or a place where my body was no longer my own.

I wanted to resist, but everything in me betrayed me. The sound and moans of surrender just made him more animalistic. He could feel my velvet walls fluttering and clenching around his thick shaft, gripping him like a vice as he stretched me wider than I'd ever been before.

"Fuck, I knew this pussy was meant to be mine from the moment I saw you," he grunted, hammering with brutal, merciless strokes. His balls slapped lewdly against my arse with every pump of his hips, the obscene sound mixing with the creaking of the bed frame beneath us. "Your cunt is sucking me in, begging me to fill it up, to pump it full of my seed until it overflows."

A shaky breath left my lips as he hooked my legs over his elbows, bending me nearly in half as he loomed over me, his muscular body blanketing mine. The new position allowed him to plunge impossibly deeper, his cock kissing my cervix with every thrust as he fucked me with a wild, animalistic abandon.

No. No, it wasn't right.

Yet I felt so starved for touch. So easily manipulated by sensations. I could feel it reacting, hips tilting, walls tightening as if the same primal part of me believed him.

His shaft stretched me wider than I should allow, more expansive than I thought was possible until it felt like he was fucking his way into the very fabric of my existence.

A body learns its master even if the mind struggles.

Tears stung my eyes. Not from pain anymore. Not even from pleasure. But from the realisation that I could no longer tell the difference.

"This is what you needed, isn't it, Dolcezza?" his voice lowered. "To be split open on my cock, a pretty little cunt to ruin. A set of holes for me to ruin," Zagreus taunted, his voice a dark, cruel rasp in my ear.

His words scraped something against my skull, digging into places I could not afford to let them take root. I wanted to tell him he was wrong, that I would never be his.

Suddenly, he flipped me back again, shoving a pillow under my hips to tilt my arse up higher. He knelt behind me, gripping my hips bruisingly as he slammed back into me with a guttural groan.

"Scream for me, fucking scream!" He roared, spanking me hard as he jackhammered into me, the obscene slap of flesh on flesh echoing through the room. "Let everyone know who this cunt belongs to now, who's ruining it for anyone else!"

Tears poured down my face, my body no longer felt my own as he claimed me, conquered me, and owned me completely. I could only sob and wail, feeling my orgasm building, my body betraying me as it raced towards a shattering climax.

"That's it, fuck, milk my cock, take every fucking inch."

My body tensed, and I clamped down around his piston-ing cock like a silken vice as my climax approached. He fucked into me even harder, spurred on by the knowledge that he was pushing me to my limits, wrecking me utterly.

"Yes, that's it, fucking come on my cock!" he snarled. I knew he could feel my upcoming orgasm.

But as my vision began to swim and darken at the edges, Zagreus didn't let up. He fucked me through my climax, using my fluttering core, his cock grinding against my G-spot with every thrust as he chased his own release.

"Fuck, I'm going to pump you full, fucking breed this pussy," he growled, his hips stuttering, his balls drawing up tight. With one final, savage thrust, he buried himself balls-deep inside me and came, his hot seed erupting from his cock to paint my insides white.

As his scalding essence flooded my womb, my eyes rolled back in my head, and everything went black. My body went limp beneath him, and my breathing grew shallow and slow as I slipped into unconsciousness, completely fucked out and claimed.

Still, then, I endured.

Because I refused to give him the satisfaction of seeing me battered, even if my body betrayed me, even as my walls fluttered and gripped, even as pleasure poisoned my veins, I swore to whatever gods were listening… I would never be his.

∞

The first sensation that crawled through my body was the dull, persistent soreness between my thighs. A lingering echo of his brutality. My hamstrings burned with the sweet ache of overuse and stretched past their limits, cramped in protest. Even as I lay still, wrapped in warmth. My body recalled every thrust.

I didn't know when I lost consciousness. But I was grateful I did.

I ceased to be a person and became something else entirely. A plaything. A possession. A body without a soul.

The sheets were soft against my skin, velvety and warm like a cocoon. But the wreckage inside me was anything but. There was something else, something foreign against my body.

That felt like lace.

The moment my fingers brushed over the delicate fabric, a cold rage settled in my chest. My jaw clenched so tightly I swore my teeth would crack.

Soft pink lace lingerie.

I breathed in through my nose, out through my mouth, fighting the scream clawing up my throat. So he had the decency to clean me up? To wash away the evidence of his sins and dress me like a doll, ready for display again? Or was it Elena? Did she pull the ruined sheets from beneath my body, wipe the dried tears from my cheeks and whisper apologies I didn't want to hear?

I didn't care. I hated everyone, including her.

My stomach churned, nausea curling at the back of my throat. It wasn't kindness. It was control. He didn't leave me in my filth because he wanted to remind me I wasn't even allowed to carry my own shame. He stripped me even of that.

My fingers curled into fists and I swung my legs over the edge of the bed, but the moment my feet touched the cold floor, a sharp pain shot through my core, tearing through my thighs, my abdomen and then my chest. My knees buckled.

A hollow laugh escaped my lips.

Look at me.

A woman dragging herself across the floor, she did not recognise because this wasn't my room.

No.

This was his.

I could tell by the oppressive weight of darkness from every corner. Black sheets matched the darkness outside. Dark walls. Minimalist space stripped of warmth, stripped of life, much like the man who owned it. Cold. Gloomy and devoid of anything soft, anything human.

Like his ugly fucking soul.

He wasn't here.

I exhaled. I didn't even realise I was holding it in, as relief and resentment warred within me. He was gone. But he'd be back. That was the problem with monsters. You couldn't wish them away. They always returned to finish what they started.

With slow agonising steps, I dragged myself to what appeared to be the bathroom. The pain worsened as I pressed my hand to my lower stomach as though I could hold myself together, and keep my insides from unravelling completely.

The bathroom was magnificent. Marbled floors, sleek counters, and a sprawling Jacuzzi that could drown me with ease. Wealth. Power. Luxury.

But luxury meant nothing when you were drowning.

And then I saw her.

The girl in the mirror.

I stopped breathing for a moment.

Bruises bloomed across her skin like ink bleeding through parchment, smudges along her throat, her collarbones, and her wrists. Lips swollen, parted in a silent plea, a scream never released. Hair tangled around her shoulders, and the soft pink lace mocked her.

A breath shuddered from my lips.

It was me.

He did this.

He took away everything. Ruined me, not just for anyone

else, but for myself.

I could never touch my skin again without remembering the way his hands defiled it. Could never wear lace without the feel of his touch. Could never look into a mirror again without seeing him behind me.

But this girl? She was shattered.

Tears burned my eyes, but I bit them back.

CHAPTER TWENTY-FOUR
The Devil at the Dinner Table

Regret is a funny thing. It doesn't come knocking like guilt or creeping like shame. It stands in the corner of the room silently, watching and waiting for you to acknowledge it.

But I couldn't.

Every time I looked at myself, I regretted not fighting harder. I regretted not screaming louder or clawing at his face or making him bleed the way he had bled me dry. But instead, I gave in. I didn't want him, not because the thought of his hands around my throat thrilled me, but it was for the answers I desperately craved. A bargain. My body for the truth. And yet, I had nothing to show for it but the phantom press of his fingers branding my skin.

A sharp knock on the door yanked me back to reality.

"Coming," I mumbled, knowing it was Elena. 'Cause knowing that pervert, he'd never knock.

"Dinner is ready, Mrs. Vitale." Her voice was gentle, strangely, and there was something else, too; pity maybe.

I wanted to tell her I wasn't hungry, that I couldn't possibly stomach sitting across from him after what happened between us. But my silence wouldn't change a thing. Zagreus would come for me himself if I refused. And I refused to give him the satisfaction.

So I did as I was told.

Dressing mechanically in another violet-ruffled dress, combing my hair, smoothing my expressions, and ensuring not a single trace of him remained on me. But I knew I would still feel raw, exposed like an open wound.

I descended the stairs slowly, my hands clenched into fists at my sides. It felt like I was at war with myself. I wanted to hide and to disappear, to fold into a forgotten letter.

But like I said, I needed answers as soon as I entered the dining room, and I found him sitting at the table. There were no candles like the ones in his office, no dim lighting meant to lull me into some false sense of intimacy. The dining room was simply elegantly set. Silver gleamed under the chandelier's soft ambient light, and the scent of rich cuisine curled in the air, teasing my empty stomach.

I didn't look at him.

I couldn't.

Not after the last time we were together.

But I felt him.

His gaze followed me as I rounded the table with unsteady steps and settled on the chair opposite him. He was a man who devoured with his eyes alone, before his hands ever touched.

I sat, suddenly hyper-aware of everything around me. Even with a huge gap between us, even without looking at him, I knew he was watching me like a creep. He always did that. Observed how I acted around him, how I ate, how I behaved in general.

The steady tap of his fingers against the table sent something crawling up my spine. A slow but predatory rhythm.

I chanced a glance through my lashes.

And there he was. Zagreus Vitale. The man who broke me, and yet, he looked… pleased. Satisfied in a way that made my stomach tighten with something unnameable. His cold eyes held a strange kind of glow, something darkly dangerous. Like a sculpture gazing at his masterpiece of ruin. A poet savouring the gravity of a tragic verse. Like fire finding beauty in what it consumes.

His beauty was the kind that made fools out of saints, that lured the lost and the lonely into his den. It was a lie so sweet, so perfectly woven, that even I, broken and knowing, still ached for that trap.

I averted my eyes.

All that just made him a pervert and a serial killer.

Picking up my fork, I dug into the food without waiting or acknowledging him. To my surprise, there was red wine too. He watched me with immense interest as I poured the drink for myself and gulped it down. If I were to talk to him, I couldn't do it sober.

He hadn't touched his food yet, and even though I was halfway done, there was no sign of Elena. It took me several deep breaths, five glasses of wine, and five mini panic attacks to push the plate away and part my lips.

"How do you know about my mother?"

My voice cut through the steel. And I was ready for him to laugh in my face. But he just shifted slightly, leaning back and tilting his head as if he was peering into my soul. And my insides shuddered at the intensity of his stormy eyes.

It took everything in me not to flinch and get under the table; as if there was a big enough table to save me from him.

"The way a man knows the bones of his own hands."

I frowned, my fingers unknowingly tightened around the stem of my glass as I resisted the urge to throw the wine at his face. "That's not an answer."

His lips curled into a slow and lazy smile. "It is. You're simply too dumb to understand it."

Frustration flared in my chest. "Stop talking in riddles. Tell me the truth."

He tilted his head to the other side. "Would you believe if I did?"

Something about the way he said it sent unease slithering down my spine. He knew something. Something about me that I didn't even know myself. Like a marionette tangled with strings. Sand slipped through my hands, no matter how hard I tried to clutch it.

It wasn't fair. I gave him my body, and he was supposed to be true to his words. Rage bloomed restlessly as I glared at him, ignoring how intimidating he looked.

"You're a liar," I accused, pushing the chair back sharply. His stormy eyes followed me as I slammed my hands on the table. "You used me."

His expression remained unreadable, but something flickered in those steel eyes. The glint from earlier was replaced with something sinister. Amusement? Or was it disappointment?

"You used yourself, Dolcezza." He leaned back, fingers tapping the armrest, his voice maddeningly calm. "I only gave you the opportunity."

The words hit harder than any slap could. I felt like a fool. A pathetic, desperate fool who bargained with the devil and expected mercy. Was he even listening to himself? How could he? How could he go back on his word?

Tears burned at the back of my throat. "I wish I'd never crossed paths with you."

And that was when I saw it. The shift. The amusement was gone. The creeping funny bled into his features. Jaw tightened, and the muscle there twitched. I watched fearfully as his fingers curled into a fist against the table. The storm was brewing.

My breath hitched, and my neck craned as I watched him push the chair back and stand to his full height. Time stilled for me. Even for a moment, but that took everything in me not to get on my knees and beg for his mercy. My leftover pride didn't let me. The food in my stomach threatened to make a reappearance, and the wine I drank sobered me up instantly.

The gigantic dining room became too small. I was still contemplating running. How long would it take me to make a run for my life? Before I could shift, he was across the room as his presence swallowed me whole.

"You wish you'd never met me?" He repeated my words as if he was giving me a chance to take them back.

I opened my mouth, but no words came. Because the next second, his hand was on my throat. The heel I wore did nothing to match his height as I was pulled up on my toes, and instinctively, my hands flew to his wrist. His grip was suffocating, too tight, making me see black dots.

"P-please…"

The plea escaped like a prayer.

I trembled not only from fear but something worse.

I thrashed like a leaf as he pulled me to his mouth. I felt his hot, angry breath hitting my face. "You don't get to erase me from your life, Dolcezza." His voice lowered an octave. "You don't get to wish me away just because it's convenient for you."

From the way my body trembled when I caught the unhinged gleam in his eyes, I wished I could reverse time and take my words back. I hated it. This feeling of patheticity and vulnerability. The way he held all the cards.

His hand moved from my throat to the cup around my jaw, forcing my gaze to his. "Shall I remind you?" he murmured, stepping into my vicinity and forcing me to back against the table. I was shoved back till I was half straddling the table and half his thigh. "Last night wasn't enough for you?"

I quickly shook my head. It was enough. I couldn't take any more. I was scared that I would again lose myself.

But the gleam in his eyes said he didn't believe me.

His fingers flexed against my jaw possessively, his touch feather-light yet immovable, as if he were savouring the way I trembled beneath him.

"No?" His lips barely moved, the syllable like a phantom against my skin.

I swallowed hard. My throat felt raw, tight, and stretched thin over the weight of unspoken things.

His other hand slid to my waist, gripping, anchoring, and I realized—too late—that retreat wasn't an option. Not when his thigh was already wedged between mine, not when the table's edge dug into my spine, not when he was everywhere, everything, swallowing me whole.

As much as I wanted to deny it, to scream at him, I knew deep down, in the marrow of my bones, that he was right.

His hand tugged at the rims of my dress, fisting it and bunching it in his palms. My panic flared, but his free hand gripped my wrists and pinned them above my head. I pleaded with my eyes, but he seemed to ignore them.

My pulse skittered when his gaze dragged over me, undressing me without shame. I knew that look. I'd seen it before.

Not like this.

Heat crept up my neck, pooling low in my stomach as he gathered the dress at my waist, exposing my legs to the cold night air, and pulled me closer. When his fingers brushed my cheek, tilting my chin up, I forgot how to breathe.

"You provoke me on purpose, don't you?"

His voice was rough, frayed with something wild, something barely restrained. My thighs clenched as his words slid over my skin like smoke.

"Let me go." That was all I could muster.

"No." His voice sharpened as his fingers dug into my waist. "You are Celestine Vitale," he murmured, pressing his knees deeper, and I bit my lips.

"No," I whispered.

He bit my jaw. "Yes."

His fingers trailed lower, burning a path down my stomach and into my panties, and I shivered. "You live with my name. You will die with my name."

His teeth grazed the side of my throat where he held me earlier, just over my pulse as his voice dropped. "You will scream with my name on your lips."

A broken whimper slipped from me before I could stop it, my breath stuttered as his hands finally... finally... reached where I didn't want him to touch. Between my legs. No. Please, not there.

He laughed softly, almost pleased. "Ah, there it is. The truth your mouth won't admit."

I arched against him, hatred and desire warring inside me, but he was relentless, refusing to let me slip into either entirely. He kept me balanced on the edge of the blade, right where he wanted. And I was... lost.

CHAPTER TWENTY-FIVE
The Devil's Game

I'd never felt pain. Not like this at least. Truth is an assassin. It kills you every time it's spoken.

Zagreus knew this. He wielded truth like a blade, pressing it against my throat every time I disobeyed him. And I slumped in the chair as he pulled away from me. My skin burned where his hands had been. He cornered me against this very table a moment ago, and let his mouth trace over my jaw in a cruel mimicry of tenderness. And then, as if he hadn't just tossed my world upside down, set fire to my bones, he stepped back, straightening his shirt, dusted off invisible specks from his sleeves, and took a seat.

"Finish eating." His voice was smooth, dispassionate as he picked up his fork. "You're turning skin and bones."

I reached for my fork, hoping he would leave it at that. But he didn't.

"I don't fuck skinny women."

The bite of food turned to ash in my mouth.

There was nothing accidental about the way he said it. Zagreus spoke like a man who knew exactly where the landmines were buried, who enjoyed watching people step on them just to hear the explosion. I could feel his eyes on me as I chewed, forcing it all down without reacting.

I didn't want him on me again. I didn't want his rough hands tracing my flesh, his sinful tongue into my throat, or his filthy words unnerving me.

He lived for the reactions.

I learned that once before… with Adrian.

He had been the first to teach me that silence was a currency. That restraint was a weapon, and some men only enjoy the things they can break. Not in the obvious way. Adrian never raised his hand at me, never locked me away, or forced me into submission. No, he had been smarter than that. He loved me. Though there were times, he indirectly demanded surrender. And I, young and naive as I had been, had given it to him without realising the cost.

We were… not passionate… but compatible with each other.

I don't think Zagreus and Adrian were the same kind of men, but they were made of the same material. While Adrian always prioritised me physically, I was coming to realise I was too dependent on him. Wasn't this why I started painting in the first place? I was so dedicated to making my own money that I didn't realise he didn't want me to work.

Just for my sake, I reminded myself.

But Zagreus, he didn't even want me to breathe without him. Celestine Vitale.

I forced another bite into my mouth, swallowing it down with a sip of wine, ignoring the burn.

Zagreus watched me all the while. "What do you want to know?"

I paused. Zagreus never gave anything away for free. If he was offering me answers now, it was because he had already decided how much I was allowed to have.

A sick realisation curled in my stomach.

"You were playing with me, weren't you?" I murmured, feeling stupid. "It's all a game to you."

His lips tilted, and I clenched my thighs tight. "Wouldn't it be boring if it weren't? We play games to pass the time, don't we?"

I exhaled slowly, setting my fork down. "What happened to my mother?"

The amusement in his eyes didn't disappear, but it cooled. He casually leaned back, swirling the wine in his glass, watching me through the red liquid. "She made a deal."

The words landed like a fist on my ribs. *A deal.* "What kind of a deal?"

"The kind you don't walk away from."

Still not an answer. He liked talking in riddles. What was he, a poet of some kind? "And?"

"And," he grinned, "that's all you get for your performance last night."

I went still. My skin felt too tight, and my pulse was loud in my ears. Emotions were expensive, and I had no intention of paying the price tonight.

Zagreus exhaled, setting the glass down. "You wanted to see your lover's grave, didn't you?"

The words hit me worse than a bullet. I almost forgot about that. I wasn't expecting him to bring up the topic. Though I did ask him to, I didn't think he'd actually let me see him. Judging by the madness he showed last night, I was certain I'd never bring up Adrian again to provoke him.

But he seemed to know how to read people in almost unnatural ways.

The lights flickered over his face, casting deep shadows over the sharp edges of his cheekbones, the sharp line of his jaw, and the wicked slash of his mouth. And then there was that scar. Making him look devastatingly lethal.

He was too composed for the man who looked possessive and viciously insane.

I could feel the heat climbing my throat. Adrian. My pulse hammered. I hated how aware I was of him. Of the way his dress shirt stretched over his broad shoulders, the way his fingers toyed with the rim of his wine glass.

"You will let me see him?"

He leaned forward and curled his lips. "I think I will. Would you like to see him now?"

The words crashed into me like a wrecking ball. The room tilted, my stomach twisting into knots. My fingers clenched around the stem of my wine glass, tight enough that a little more pressure might shatter it. Adrian.

The name was a wound, raw and festering, torn open with a single flick of Zagreus's tongue. My breath hitched, the phantom weight of Adrian's hands brushing over my skin—a memory, a ghost, a curse. I swallowed hard, but it did nothing to dislodge the lump in my throat.

Zagreus watched me, waiting, a predator enjoying the way his prey struggled against the inevitable.

I forced myself to meet his gaze, but my voice had abandoned me. My throat was tight, my body stiff, and yet my traitorous heart pounded at the mere thought of Adrian's grave.

Would I find closure there? Or just another grave to bury myself in?

Zagreus's fingers drummed against the table, slow, deliberate. "Well?"

I exhaled sharply, setting my glass down before I really did break it.

And then, in a voice I barely recognized, I whispered, "Take me to him."

CHAPTER TWENTY-SIX
Ghost of Your Name

"No," he whispered darkly, and something inside me roared.

What did he think of himself? I had played his games far too many times to even consider killing him. Though I was not capable or had the heart to harm anyone with that sort of intention, he made me feral like himself.

I didn't care what consequences I'd face or how much I'd suffer; all I wanted was for him to disappear.

But knowing my luck and my fate in his hands, I resorted to the less violent path.

"You're disgusting."

Like insulting him would change anything. And like I predicted, it didn't cause the germ of the devil to even shift with the force of my push, but something flickered behind his eyes. Something dangerous. His lips curved.

He leaned down, his breath brushing over the shell of my ear. "And yet... you still haven't run."

"I should," I whispered.

"But you won't," he said, his lips ghosting along my cheekbone. "Not until you see him."

That shattered everything. The name was unspoken between us. Adrian.

I stilled, my entire body going rigid in his hold. Zagreus felt it. His fingers loosened, and finally, mercifully, he let me go.

But not before he whispered, "Don't mistake your grief for hatred, Dolcezza. Sometimes the lines blur."

I stepped back so fast I nearly stumbled, dragging my arm to my chest as if I could wipe him off me. My voice cracked. "You don't know anything about my grief."

He didn't reply. Just turned and began walking toward the grave.

And even though every cell in my body screamed to leave—to run—I followed. Because somewhere in the sea of tombstones, Adrian waited. And this… this was the last piece of him I had left to face.

The graveyard was too quiet. Not the kind of quiet that felt peaceful, but the kind that clawed at your throat, thick and heavy like the sky before a storm. And I was walking into it with him.

Zagreus.

The name tasted like a curse. Like ash and blood on a bitten tongue.

I hated that I flinched at the shadows now.

Gravel crunched beneath my heels the more we walked. My pulse was stuttering, wild and rabbit-fast in my chest, but I didn't stop. The scent of damp earth and rotting lilies filled the air, and somewhere in the distance, a wind chime clattered like brittle bones.

He walked ahead, coat trailing behind him like the shadow of a darker thing, shoulders carved out of war and arrogance. His back to me. His hand was no longer on my arm. But I still felt it. The phantom imprint of his fingers branded into my skin. Adrian's grave waited.

My knees wanted to buckle.

Please... please let it be untrue. Let this be a cruel trick. Let him be angry at me for believing it. Let him scream at me for showing up like this. Let him breathe—

But no. This was the kind of pain that was too still, too quiet. The kind of pain that didn't blink. And Zagreus... he just stood there, hands in his pockets like we were visiting some fucking museum and not a field of the dead. His jaw ticked once. No words.

Then I saw it. The stone. His name was carved into cold granite. Adrian Valente. Born. Died. Buried.

No.

My breath strangled itself. My knees caved. I folded, graceless and broken, onto the earth in front of the grave as if my body had been waiting to fall. This was real. This was final. I pressed my palms to the soil. It wasn't warm. It wasn't him.

And then I heard it. The drag of leather boots behind me. A presence. A pause. Zagreus stood a few feet back, watching me with that same dead calm he wore like skin.

"You did this," I whispered.

A laugh. Low. Hollow. "I buried him, Dolcezza."

I looked over my shoulder, and the fury that surged up from the pit of my grief wasn't something I'd prepared for. "You didn't have to kill him to destroy him."

His eyes narrowed, head tilting just slightly, the shadows under his lashes deepening. "Careful, Dolcezza."

"Or what?" I spat. "You'll kill me too?"

"You're not that special," he replied. But something inside him twitched.

I pushed myself up from the grave, dirt clinging to my palms, my chest rising and falling in a rhythm I couldn't control. "You think this makes you powerful? This... killing? This silence?" I laughed bitterly, stepping toward him. "All this death you carry—you'll face it one day too."

He moved closer.

"I'll tell you what I see," I whispered. "I see a man who's going to die alone. And no one's going to cry over your grave, Zagreus. Not one soul."

His jaw tightened.

"You'll rot somewhere just like this. But the difference is—" I stepped into him, my chest brushing his coat, "—you won't have a name etched in stone. You'll vanish. Forgotten. No one will light candles. No one will miss the monster."

The air changed.

Something inside him snapped.

The next second happened like a thunderclap. His hand shot out, curled tight around my throat—not choking, but holding. Owning. The breath stalled in my lungs.

"You talk like you know me," he said, voice low, rasping, barely human. "But you don't. You see the mask. You kiss the devil's teeth and think you know his hunger."

I clawed at his wrist. "Let—go—"

But he wasn't listening.

His other hand fisted the front of my dress and shoved me back with brute, calculated force. My spine slammed into the cold marble of Adrian's grave. A gasp tore out of me. The stone bit into my skin.

Zagreus pressed in, body a wall of fury, lips close enough to graze mine if he leaned just a breath forward. "You think I haven't felt love?" he whispered, and this time there was something else—something raw, ugly, broken in the way his voice trembled at the edges. "I have. I killed it. I buried it. I slit its fucking throat because it made me weak."

He laughed. One short, bitter sound. "And look at you, trying to tell me what I'll never have. Like you've seen the ending to a story I'm still writing."

"I have," I whispered, gasping. "It ends with you—alone, bitter, with nothing but a name carved in a stone no one visits."

That broke him.

His hand slammed beside my head on the grave. The marble cracked beneath the force. Dust and splinters of stone trembled into the night air.

His eyes—God—his eyes weren't human anymore. There was violence there. A storm that hadn't broken yet.

His voice dropped, dark and dangerous. "Keep talking, Dolcezza. Let's see how many pieces I have to break you into before you stop."

I stared at him, trembling. Not from fear. From the sheer weight of everything I was trying to hold in. The grief. The rage. The loss. But I didn't look away. Not this time.

Because maybe I wanted to be broken. Maybe then, I'd finally stop feeling.

And maybe… just maybe… he would, too.

But reality didn't work like that. It never did.

Grief doesn't soften a monster's heart.

Zagreus's breath ghosted over my skin with that unholy intention. I could feel Adrian's grave pressing into my skin. But the one looming over me had my full attention.

"You think I'm afraid of dying alone?" he slowly asked. I caught a faint sense of emotion in his tone before it was gone. "I was born alone, Dolcezza. I live in solitude and I rule it well."

"You don't rule it," I said. "You survive it. Barely. But deep down…"

I saw it then. A flicker in his brow. "…you wish someone would choose you. But no one will because you're a monster!"

I spat viciously. Not afraid of what he might do to me. I was so consumed by my grief and pain, I wanted something else to hurt. Maybe physical pain. But not this gut-wrenching suffering. I wouldn't survive it.

Instead of punishing me, the monster smiled. I thought he might let go and slap me, or worse, kill me too. But when he moved, fingers dragged down the front of my bodice with deceptive calm, and I panicked. "What…"

His gaze didn't leave mine, even when the sound of fabric ripping filled the chilled silence of the graveyard. The fabric split under his fist like paper, and I gasped at the audacity of it.

"You want to see the monster?" he asked. "You want to peel back the skin and stare into the pit?"

Hand curled around my jaw, tilting my face up until I could see him, his fury, his hunger, and the graveyard of emotions he'd buried beneath that deadpan cruelty.

"I'll show you, Dolcezza," he rasped, staring down at the partially covered chest. "I'll ruin your idea of monsters."

I stared at him wide-eyed, chest heaving. "Adrian would've never touched me like this."

I regretted it the moment the words left my mouth, 'cause in a blink, a feral primal sound came from his throat as he fisted what was left of my dress, yanking it harder until the fabric gave way completely. I cried out, one hand flying to shield myself, but he didn't stop.

"Stop, please!"

He didn't. If anything, he manhandled me under him.

"I'm going to fuck you," he growled, grabbing my waist and pulling me flush against him, "I'm going to fuck you right here, on the grave of the man I killed for you. I'm going to make you scream so loud, everyone for miles will know you're mine."

He crashed his lips against mine, kissing hard and rough. His hands roamed my body, squeezing every inch as if I solely belonged to him, my chest, my thighs. He wanted to mark me, to claim me, to make me forget that I ever loved anyone but him.

"You're mine," he growled against my lips. "You've always been mine. I'm going to fuck you until you can't remember your own name, let alone his. I'm going to make you crave my cock, need it, fucking worship it."

"I'll kill him again if I have to," he snarled. "I'll kill him a thousand times if it means you'll be mine..."

He attacked my neck with bites and kisses, sucking dark marks into my skin. His hand slid down the back, cupping my arse, squeezing it hard.

And there was this thing about monsters, they never know when to stop. They didn't draw lines. They didn't ask for consent. They took.

Because somewhere along the way, someone taught them love was a war and they were forged to win, no matter the cost.

Zagreus wasn't a man. He was the war itself. And the way he looked at me now, he wasn't seeing a woman. He was looking at a toy to be owned.

CHAPTER TWENTY-SEVEN
Grief Meets Skin

"Do your worst," I choked, glaring up at him through the blur of my tears.

I didn't flinch, and I wouldn't.

If I were going to shatter, I'd make sure he felt every goddamn crack.

His face didn't change. No twist of surprise or anger, just that infuriating calm that made it feel like I was drowning alone, like he'd always be the one above water, watching.

His thumb dragged across my cheek, smearing the tear that dared to fall.

"Careful what you ask for, Dolcezza," he murmured, and the rasp of it made something coil inside me, something I hated. "I never do anything half-hearted."

He leaned in, close enough for our breaths to tangle. And I hated that I felt it again, the spark that lit behind my ribs when he touched me; that slow, traitorous way my body reacted even when my soul recoiled in disgust.

Why did he always feel like fire and gasoline?

No. Not fire. Fire warned you as it crackled, blazed, and

screamed its danger into the night.

He was the warmth in a winter cabin, so deceptive and silent it lulled you into dropping your guard, shedding your clothes, letting your fingers inch too deep, too close to the iron stove until skin met heat and pain rattled too late.

He was comforted by cruelty.

The man who made you forget the world was cold until you remembered why you'd built walls in the first place.

And still… Still, my body leaned toward him like frostbite limbs searching for anything that resembled warmth, even if it came with a cost.

It wasn't fire that scared me. It was the undetectable burns.

I shut my eyes as his hand slid over my ribs, up the line of my spine with strange possessiveness like he was trying to lay claim to broken pieces.

He pressed his body against my back, grinding his hard cock against my arse. His hands slid up my sides, roughly palming my breasts through the tattered remains of my dress. He squeezed them hard, pinching my nipples between his fingers.

"You're not the only one grieving," he growled in my ear, his hot breath making me shudder. "Grief doesn't belong to the pure. You forget who taught me loss."

That made me flinch. I blinked at him, stunned. "What…"

Before I could ask, before I could even process what he meant, he pulled me into him with a force that stole the question from my lips. All that remained was the scent of him, smoke and sin, curling around me like the fog in the graveyard.

His lips moved over mine with savagery that scared the death around us like he'd been here before. Like he knew every inch of me more than I did.

The screams stayed lodged in my throat, behind my ribs, as my hands curled into his coat instead of shoving him back.

What was the point anyway?

I was tired. Tired of the pain, the silence, the ache in my chest that never let me breathe. Tired of pretending I was whole and Arian's death hadn't hollowed me out.

So I let him touch me. I let him kiss me like he wanted to erase the man he buried and fill the void with himself.

Maybe I wanted to be ruined.

Maybe I wanted to give in, just once, and make the monster bleed with me.

And maybe... if I surrendered now, I could drag him into the abyss I'd been drowning in for weeks.

He cupped my face again, thumb brushing my jaw, and it angered me more than his brutality. "Get on your knees, Dolcezza."

I didn't want to. I stared at him with every ounce of courage. Hoping he'd see the things swirling in my head.

He stepped back, watching me with a cruel, expectant glare. When I hesitated, he reached out and grabbed a fistful of my hair, yanking my head back.

"Don't make me fucking tell you twice, wife," he growled. "You want to mourn for that bastard? You want to remember his name? Then you fucking do it on my cock."

He let go of my hair, shoving me forward. I stumbled, catching myself on the edge of the tombstone. Zagreus watched me like a hawk as his eyes gleamed with dark pleasure.

"I can't wait to see you swollen with my kids," he groaned, palming himself through his slacks, and I swallowed the lump. "Can't wait to see your belly big and round, full of my cum. You'll look so fucking good, my wife, my woman, carrying my seed."

He reached out, grabbing my chin and forcing me to look at him. His thumb pressed down on my lower lip, pushing it out of my mouth. He leaned in close, his stormy eyes boring into my scared ones.

"Forget him," he rasped. "Forget his name, forget his face. The only name you need to remember is mine. Zagreus Vitale. Say it."

He squeezed my chin harder, his grip turning painful. He was not asking – he was commanding.

My lips trembled. Strangely, it was not the fear; it was long gone. What I felt now was more dangerous. A poison that numbed the pain and warmed the parts of me I thought had died.

His hand hovered by my throat, and I... I let my head fall back. Exposing my neck. My surrender wasn't innocent. It was a deliberate survival instinct.

"Zagreus..." I whispered his name like a sin. Like a spell.

Something primal shifted in him. His lips twitched, and he stared at me before he groaned lowly as he pushed me down, as my back arched over the stone of Adrian's grave.

The grave was cold, but Zagreus's mouth was fire.

He kissed me again, like he hated me this time. Bit down hard on my bottom lip, then sucked it like nectar. Hands tore what little fabric remained between us, and I gasped.

I hated how I'd become this.

Not Adrian's soft-spoken girl. Not the widow. Not the innocent.

But his.

Zagreus Vitale's. The monster who was now my husband.

"Pray to me with that voice," he growled against my throat, dragging his tongue along the vein. "I'll answer every prayer, Dolcezza. I'll give you everything."

His hand slid between my thighs. Roughly parting them and cupping my womanhood, which I swore was still sore. And my body arched.

After a few strokes, I heard the unzipping of his pants, and before I could process, he plunged into me like vengeance.

Like a storm, I had no choice but to encounter it.

And all while my eyes locked on Adrian's name. My heart didn't break. It changed, morphed, and hardened into the same stone.

Because grief wouldn't give me freedom, Zagreus would.

Because survival didn't come clean, it came filthy.

He held me down as I shook. As I cried and came and cursed and forgot who I was.

"Pray at my altar, Dolcezza," he growled, fucking me deeper and choking me as I rocked with his brutal thrusts. "Worship me with your screams."

I tried to hold back. But the way he plunged deeper with every thrust, my insides clenched shamelessly.

I tried to keep Adrian's name on my tongue. But Zagreus didn't fuck like a man.

He fucked like a god starved of worship. Like I was the lamb and the sacrifice, altar, and offering all in one.

And I gave in, body first, mind second, and my soul somewhere far behind.

He licked the sweat from my collarbone, nipping the skin until I gasped. "Is that grief, or pleasure when your cunt clenches when I fuck you?"

My knees scraped the dirt, my nails dug into the grass around the headstone. Adrian was right there. Dead and cold.

But the man above me was alive and warm.

I was pathetic. Depraved and unhinged.

"You don't cry for him," he whispered against my ear, thrusting slower now, but deeper. "You cry for me. Say it. Let the grave hear it."

I choked, swallowed the sob, and moaned instead. A sound, obscene, and unholy.

"Say it."

"I cry for you," I gasped.

"And moan for me too, Dolcezza. Say my fucking name when you come."

"Zagreus!" I whimpered.

He grinned like the devil tasting sin for the first time. "That's it. Bleed my name from your lips like a psalm. Like the only god you'll ever need."

"Stop!" I trembled, coming all over his thick cock, tearing into me. Splitting me open in two.

"Make me," he moaned into my throat, pinching my breasts. He gripped my jaw, forcing my eyes back to the name on the stone. "Look at him when I come inside you."

I whimpered. And he groaned, lowly and viciously as he spilled into me, thrusting deeper and staying there as he dropped his forehead against mine.

"Mine," he said. "Even the dead know it now."

CHAPTER TWENTY-EIGHT
The Cipher

Some wounds whisper louder than screams.

He picked me up like I weighed nothing. Like I was a song he'd already memorised, even if every note of me was a broken melody. I let him, because I couldn't move. Couldn't lift a finger or remember what it felt like to be untouched.

He was right.

Even the dead knew it now, including Adrian.

I was sore in places I didn't want to name.

I thought I might be bleeding down there. I thought I might be cracked open down there. Still dripping, raw and filled with him. His cum slid down the inside of my bruised thighs as he carried me to the car, like proof of his victory. He was calm now. But still brutal.

Like he didn't ruin me on someone else's grave. Like he hadn't just made me forget the only man I ever loved.

The car door opened, and I didn't look at the driver. He settled in the backseat, keeping me on his lap like a child, like a possession, like something he owned before I ever belonged to myself.

He didn't speak, didn't demand anything more. Just wrapped his arms around me, his hand sliding through my hair with infuriating gentleness. His lips brushed the slope of my shoulder, feather-light kisses pressing into skin he had bitten minutes ago.

And I cried harder.

Because this tenderness… it was a lie.

A fucking illusion.

I punched him. Once and then again. My fists were weak, trembling, and pathetically vulnerable. "I hate you," I whispered. "I hate you. I hate you. I hate you…"

His arms only tightened like he knew the rhythm of my rage, as if he had done this before with others. Or maybe just me. In some past life, I didn't remember consenting to.

"I hate you…" I said again. But it came out cracked, wrecked.

I cried into the fabric of his coat, into the scent of him… smoke, sin, and the grave… and I sobbed until the words lost their meaning.

And when I finally stopped, it wasn't because I was done. It was because exhaustion dragged me like waves pulling a corpse out to sea.

My dreams weren't soft. They were full of teeth.

I was running through ash and fire, barefoot and bleeding. The monsters behind me had his face. The monsters ahead whispered Adrian's name. I didn't know who I was running from anymore. Or who I was running to. But either way, I knew the girl who loved the dead boy was gone.

And the woman in his enemy's arms… she was something else entirely.

∞

I woke up to the blinding sun. To the golden light that

spilt across the room and the ocean just outside. Like the night hadn't been violent, and I hadn't been silenced.

I was in a bed, one I didn't recognise. Pillows too soft and sheets too clean. Pristine white. No street noise. No broken pieces. No cold night air around my ankles like chains. However, I was one who was still attached to them.

Just stillness. And his scent.

I wasn't wearing a dress anymore.

A white shirt hung off my frame, too big. It smelled like power and spice and the skin carved from hell.

I was also clean. Washed. It must've been Elena. She would've done it gently, wouldn't she? Would've tried not to look. Would've cried when she saw what her master did to me.

Soreness bloomed between my thighs, across my ribs, and inside my mouth. My body pulsed with phantom pain, some places from the impact and others from the way I let it happen.

Mechanically, I moved. One step at a time. One breath at a time.

I brushed my teeth with a trembling hand, watching the foam bleed pink into the sink.

I bathed. Hot water stung, and the soap slid across bruises I earned. My skin flinched beneath my own touch. But I didn't cry. Not anymore. I was emptied last night.

When I was done, I didn't look in the mirror.

I knew what waited for me there.

The ghost of a woman who lost the war she didn't even know she was fighting. Swollen lips, purple constellations on my neck, and fingerprints pressed into flesh. Dignity buried somewhere between the bed and the floor.

But I dressed anyway.

I found a red dress in the closet, silk, slit high and low neckline, the one he liked on me. The one that made him look at me like a slut. I put it on. Painted my lips red. The same

shade he smeared across my cheek the first time he kissed me.

I curled my hair and left it wild. Let it fall like chaos around my shoulders.

When I was finished, I finally looked in the mirror.

And this time, I smiled.

Because I looked beautiful. Ethereally so.

But inside... inside, I was bleeding. Still drowning. I was still pushed down on the stone and taken like a cheap whore.

And maybe that's what survival is. Looking like heaven while carrying hell inside you.

I didn't know what time it was. Morning? Afternoon? The sun poured through the windows like honey, too sweet for a day like this. But I needed to go downstairs. I needed him to see me. See what he did. See what I made of it.

So I walked. Each step was a small war in itself. Thighs ached, and muscles trembled; it hurt like hell.

And somewhere inside it, buried deep in the bruises and the burn of movement, was that sweet, tangy, regretful feeling.

Not his regret. Mine. For letting it happen. For not stopping it. For some terrible part of me still wanted to be seen by him.

The corridor was long, too quiet as I made my way down the stairs.

I walked into the dining room. And he was there.

Standing with his back to me, shoulders broad and still, staring out the window at the ocean like he hadn't swallowed me whole the night before.

Grey suit, matching slacks. Clean, composed, and unmoved. As if he hadn't bled me last night. As if he hadn't shattered something sacred and stitched it up.

He looked like power. And I hated him for it.

I decided to make my presence known. Though my body shivered at the sight of him. I ignored the rings and let my heels click against the marble. Because I wanted him to see me. I needed him to. So he could hurt me again.

Because hate had become my drug. Hating him. Hating myself more.

But then I stopped when I noticed another presence.

The same man who brought the marriage agreement on the first day. The day Zagreus kidnapped me.

He stood smaller beside Zagreus, shorter and leaner, more human in the presence of a monster. Still in his pressed suit, glasses perched on the bridge of his nose.

The lawyer cleared his throat, adjusting his glasses. "... request your presence, sir." he said stiffly. "Any more delay and the board will proceed without you."

Zagreus didn't move. Didn't even look at him. Just kept staring at the ocean.

It made the room colder than the sea wind ever could.

I stood there, far enough he wouldn't notice yet close enough I could hear them clearly.

Zagreus finally spoke. "I don't care, Jeremy. Let them."

The lawyer stiffened, and so did I.

'I... sir, with respect," he adjusted his glasses again, a nervous flick he couldn't hide, "the Syndicate needs your presence. It's been six months since your last appearance. Questions are being asked and allegiances are fraying."

Zagreus finally turned from the window. And now he was facing the lawyer. "I built the table they sit at," he murmured. "They forget that too often."

He took a slow step toward the lawyer, and the poor man shuddered. "If they need reminding..." A faint, cruel glint tugged at his lips. "Tell Romanovski I'm coming to his party."

The lawyer nodded too quickly, stepping back. Retreated with haste until I heard the door clicking shut behind him.

Zagreus still hadn't turned to me. But something told me

he knew I was here. He knew from the moment I woke up.

"You're not going to look at me?" I hated how soft my voice came out.

Still, nothing.

Only the crash of waves behind the glass. Only the way his shoulders lifted once.

"I looked at you last night," he said quietly. "So closely, I could've painted your soul from memory."

I flinched because I remembered. And because some small, broken part of me wanted him to look at the destruction he'd made.

He turned slowly. And when his eyes met mine, it was like the universe exploded. Hunger. Pride. Possession. All of it coiled behind those stormy-grey eyes.

His eyes were so dark I forgot what the world looked like in the light.

As if he could undo me. Like he was moments away from ripping this dress off of me.

Because his gaze stripped me away anyway. Layer by layer. Until I wasn't the woman, just a toy he could use whenever he wanted.

And somehow… my thighs pressed together.

I hated that too.

His head tilted slightly. "You really like playing the part of my wife, don't you? You like playing with fire."

"You made me that way," I whispered back. "And now you want to be surprised when I burn?"

His lips curled. Not quite a smile. Something deeper and darker. Like pride or even amusement. Maybe he liked it, red on me.

"You only burn when I let you." He turned to the dining table. "As much as I like to entertain you, I don't want you to faint. Come, let's eat."

CHAPTER TWENTY-NINE
The Skin Lies

The dining room was drenched in golden sun and soft, salty breeze. The windows were open and the curtains danced along with the wind's rhythm, unlike my heart, which threatened to leap out of my chest and fall on the silver platter on the table. Elena had dished it out of the cart, followed by a cup of black coffee for him and a crème latte for me.

I'd rate this scenario ten out of ten if the man sitting before me were not as cruel. Even the sunlight couldn't penetrate his darkness. Sitting there like a king with no court. A porcelain plate before him. Cloth napkin on his lap. I'd never seen Zagreus Vitale eat with me, though he was always there, but our every encounter at this table ended with either me bending over and his hand on my ass, or with me crying and him taking his anger out on me.

This time… it was different. He was not angry, but he seemed bothered. Maybe it had something to do with what Jeremy said about the syndicate. I still didn't understand where I fit in all this. I hardly saw him leave this property. Was I the reason? To keep an eye on me?

He rendered me helpless in a way that my every route ended at him. Though I still hadn't formed a plan yet, if I played my pawns right, I might convince him to take me to the party he was talking about.

Yes, I heard that too.

And I also thought that if I left this house, I might be given an opportunity. God wouldn't be so unfair to me, right?

But for that opportunity to arise, I needed to reach that chance first. So, I sat just opposite him, not beside but far away enough to feel like I still had a choice. Close enough for that to be a lie.

Zagreus didn't complain. He cut his food quietly. Just the slow scrape of silver against porcelain. He ate elegantly. And I watched as he brought a grape to his plate. And peeled it.

Slowly, he slid a thumbnail beneath the skin, curling it away like he was undressing it, and last night's flashbacks hit me where my body was still sore. The more he exposed the soft, trembling heart, the tighter I clenched my thighs. I swallowed hard, disgusted at myself.

What was I even thinking? He literally forced me, humiliated me, disrespected the dead, and... made me like it.

I focused on my plate, meticulously cutting the tarts as I watched him place the peeled grapes beside another. And then another. I couldn't look away. I didn't want to ask, but I did.

"Why do you do that?" I asked, hoping my voice was audible over the sound of my own heartbeat.

He didn't glance at me, just kept peeling.

"The skin lies," he muttered as smoothly as the linen beneath our plates. "The sweetness is inside."

I blinked.

He looked up, and those grey eyes met mine with an intimacy that felt like jolted electricity.

I didn't want to know what he meant. So I diverted the

topic.

"When will you tell me about my mother?" I asked.

The silence that followed wasn't quiet, but loud in a deafening way. It screamed behind my rib cage and tasted like iron.

He didn't react like he did last time, didn't even freaking pause, just picked a peeled grape and leaned forward, and held it out between two fingers.

"Eat."

I didn't move; my mouth stayed closed even as my body trembled with hunger that wasn't about food. I hated him for feeding me, I hated the part that obeyed, because I needed him to trust me. I learned my lesson. Meeting violence with violence wouldn't do me any good.

I leaned and watched as his eyes dropped to my chest for a minute or two before meeting mine again with a dark glint. I didn't bother being modest. He made me wear these weird dresses, and even if I hid, he'd make me eat naked if he felt like it, so I didn't bother and opened my lips.

He placed the grape on my tongue, and I bit hard. He chuckled, shaking his head, and leaned back on his seat.

The sweetness exploded into my mouth. So fucking sweet I could've cried.

He watched me chew. And for a moment, he looked... satisfied.

"How do you know I like them peeled?" I whispered. Already knew he was a stalker before kidnapping me.

"I know everything about you, Dolcezza."

The words coiled around my throat like poison, and I swallowed them.

He peeled another and fed me again. I didn't resist this time because I knew what defiance cost.

His gaze drifted to the window, to the horizon where the sea bled into the sky. He took a sip of his coffee.

"Your mother is a beautiful woman."

The sweetness turned bitter, and I whispered, "Was." A correction.

"Your mother is alive."

The words detonated inside me.

My breath caught mid-inhale, and for a terrifying second, I forgot how to exhale. My heart missed a step. Then another. It stumbled like a drunk in a storm.

It felt like someone had cracked my chest open and whispered a lie directly into my lungs.

Alive? Alive... No. No, no, no. It can't be.

I sat frozen. My mouth still tasted of grapes, and now they felt like rot. My fingers curled into the hem of the red dress, crumpling silk like paper, and I let out a disbelieving chuckle.

"You're lying." My voice cracked. "She's dead. She's been dead since I was..."

Was... since when? I have forgotten.

"No," he interrupted, eyes back on mine. "She just left."

And just like that, my body forgot how to hold itself up. My mother. I had glimpses of. All of it... was that a lie? Or was he the lie?

"I don't believe you," I replied frantically. "You're trying to break me again."

He leaned back, a muscle twitched in his jaw, and he looked far too composed for someone who just uprooted my entire foundation. Yet, he peeled another grape and held it out.

I didn't take it.

He arched a brow. "If I wanted to break you, Dolcezza, you'd already be ash. Like I've said before," his eyes narrowed, "I want you."

"Why?" I snapped, trembling like a leaf. "Why would she leave me and not come back? Adrian said she died of heart disease! Why would she fake her death? Why would she..."

"Because she loved something more than you."

My stomach dropped like I'd been pushed off a cliff, and my body hadn't caught up.

"You're lying," I half-chuckled, half-whispered like a mad woman.

He sighed, pushed his chair back, and stood. My head snapped to him, arching, watching as he walked around the table and stopped behind me.

I didn't turn, but my whole body tensed. I felt him leaning before I felt his sinful lips brushing the shell of my ear. "You'll understand soon, Dolcezza. This world doesn't care about you. It doesn't care how you feel, what you want, or if you live. It's not sweet." I stared blankly at where he had previously put the grape skin.

And then, he softly placed the grape on my tongue. "It's rotten."

He stepped back, but the ghost of his cologne refused to leave me. I stared at the table—the silver, the sunlight, the skeletons in the silence. And my heaving chest.

"Get ready for tonight," he murmured, already halfway to the door. "I'll take you to see the dead."

The air stilled. My limbs forgot how to function.

I blinked. Once. Twice. The curtains fluttered behind him like grieving women, mourning something I couldn't name.

The sweetness in my mouth curdled. I swallowed it like a prayer gone stale.

He didn't glance back as he left, and somehow that made it worse.

The grape's skin on the plate caught the light like torn silk— shiny and ruined.

The dead.

Maybe he meant bodies. Maybe he meant memories.

Maybe… he meant me. Or my mother.

CHAPTER THIRTY
Elegy in Ivory

The sun had long since crawled up the sky when I stood again. Or rather, Elena made me.

Her hands were cold as they pressed against my spine, zipping the crimson gown up my back like sealing a wound. I stared into the vanity mirror, but the reflection wasn't mine. It was hers. The girl with bloodless lips, haunted eyes, and a pulse that pulsed too loudly in her ears.

"Sit." Elena pushed me down on the chair, guiding me to the edge of the chaise.

I sat.

She moved around me, quiet except for the occasional clink of a hairpin or snap of a compact case. Her face was blank, carved from stone, not an ounce of sympathy in her eyes. Just like always.

"You look like a ghost," she muttered, tugging a comb through my hair with no gentleness. "Fitting, considering where you're going."

I didn't ask what she meant. I already knew. The dead. That's what he said. He'd take me to see the dead.

My stomach twisted violently, for I lurched forward. My knees hit the floor, and bile burned up my throat and spilt into the porcelain bowl Elena held out just in time. She didn't flinch. She didn't even give me comfort. Just stood there. Watching me unravel.

When I finished, she wiped my mouth with a cold cloth and said, flatly, "It's not weakness to be afraid. It's stupid to let it stop you."

I clutched the edge of the vanity like it could hold me together. My vision spun, dark at the edges, my breath coming too fast. Too shallow. My hands trembled.

"I can't—" I gasped.

"You can." Elena's voice cut clean through the rising panic. "And you will. Because if you don't, someone else will write your ending for you. He already is."

I looked up, locking eyes with her in the mirror. Her gaze was sharp, not cruel but exact like a scalpel.

"Do you want to go?" she asked as something shimmered in her warm eyes. A yes or no.

My lips parted. I didn't know what I was going to say.

The truth?

The lie?

"I'll go," I whispered, because fear didn't excuse ignorance. And if the answers were buried with the dead, I had no choice but to walk among them.

She nodded. "Alright, you can freshen up. I'll fetch your clothes."

My body moved into mechanical mode, walking to the bathroom, and I turned on the shower. I didn't know if I should be shocked that my mother was alive or disappointed that she hid from me all these years. Didn't she miss me? Call for me?

Wouldn't she comfort me, envelop me in her arms, and

tell me she loved me to my face? No flowers bloom without sunlight to raise them; why couldn't she show affection and be my sun amongst this cruel world?

I was wilting from the inside.

The water hit my skin, hot enough to sting, but I barely flinched.

Steam rose, curling around me like the ghosts I never buried—the memories, the questions, the versions of my mother I'd created in her absence. A kind one. A cruel one. A selfish one. A broken one. All of them stood beside me now, watching me fall apart piece by piece.

I pressed my palms against the cold tiles, letting the scalding heat run down my spine. Maybe it was punishment. Maybe it was a rebirth.

The sob crept up my throat, quiet at first. Then louder. Then ragged. I didn't cry like girls in the movies, soft and beautiful and tragic. I cried like I was drowning—choking on grief I didn't know I still carried.

How could she be alive and not come back for me?

I was a child when I stopped celebrating my birthday. Fourteen, when I stopped hoping. Seventeen, when I buried the last photograph of her in the back of my closet.

And now, twenty-three, I was scrubbing skin that would never feel clean enough—not for her, not for the world, not for the little girl inside me who still waited at the window.

I hated that I still wanted her to hold me.

I turned off the water, and the silence crashed on me.

The mirror fogged, hiding my reflection. I didn't want to see myself. I wasn't sure who I was anymore. A daughter? A stranger? A mistake?

A knock came on the door, gentle. Her voice followed, muffled through the wood. "Your clothes are outside."

I didn't answer. I couldn't. My throat was raw with questions I didn't know how to ask.

I wrapped the towel around me, stepping out into the cold hallway. And there they were—clean clothes folded neatly, like nothing had shattered between us.

But everything had. And I didn't know if I'd ever be able to pick up the pieces.

Instead, I focused on getting dressed.

The dress was the colour of dried roses.

Not red—no, red was for lovers, for women who chose their fate with open eyes.

This was deeper. Darker. A muted, bruised crimson that bled elegance and mourning in equal parts.

Elena tugged the final seam into place. It fit too well. As if it had always belonged to me, waiting in some forgotten closet of fate. I wondered who shopped for these dresses, because they all fit me perfectly, as if taken from my measurements and then handmade from silk.

A part of me loathed Zagreus for shattering my illusion that my mother was dead. Maybe I preferred her dead if she didn't love me.

But that would be selfish of me, wouldn't it?

I hissed as Elena pulled the dress down, and I stared at the mirror.

The neckline dipped into a modest V, revealing the hollow of my collarbones like an invitation to be shattered. Long sleeves of sheer lace clung to my arms, delicate and claustrophobically suffocating. The bodice was cinched tight, boned and structured, sculpting a figure I didn't recognise. A stranger's silhouette.

"Stand, Mrs. Vitale," Elena said.

I obeyed, legs trembling beneath the silk.

She knelt to the floor and slipped the heels on—black satin stilettos, cold as knives, with an ankle strap that fastened like shackles over the anklet that still burned my skin. I hated how beautiful they looked on me. Each step I took in them would be intended. Poised. And painful.

Elena stood again, grabbed the silver brush from the vanity, and started twisting my hair. Her fingers were efficient, pinning the strands into an intricate, half-up braid that crowned the back of my head, while the rest spilt down in soft waves. It was elegant, too elegant for someone on the verge of falling apart.

"Who taught you that?" I asked quietly.

Elena paused. "My mother."

A ghost breath of memory fluttered against my ribs. Hands threading through my hair. A soft lullaby, in a voice I couldn't recall. The smell of something sweet—jasmine? Vanilla? And then silence. Always silence.

I tried to hold onto it – the memory – but it slipped like sand through my fingers. I didn't remember her face. Not really. Just the warmth. Just the absence.

"Elena," I whispered. "Does she love you?"

She didn't answer. Not right away. Her hands paused only for a second, then resumed.

"She did," she said finally. "More than anything."

I blinked, throat tightening. "Is she not here?"

Elena met my gaze in the mirror. Her eyes were steel. "No. But I remember how it felt when she was with me."

I looked away. My fingers clenched around the armrest.

There was a knock at the door. Elena's voice followed. "You don't have to go, Mrs. Vitale, if you don't feel like it."

The kindness in her voice scraped against my raw insides.

"I'll go," I said again, louder this time, because I needed to see. Because some answers are written in things too ugly to look at unless you're dressed for the funeral.

And it wasn't like Zagreus would let me stay anyway.

CHAPTER THIRTY-ONE
Breathe Me In

I sat beside him in the car, wrapped in silence so thick it felt like drowning in fog.

The night outside was merciless, as was the man beside me. Moonless sky, like the moon itself, was swallowed by the darkness, or perhaps it had destroyed its own light. Streetlamps on the window, but I didn't look at them. I didn't look at anything at all.

I hadn't uttered a single word since I stepped inside, and neither had he. Zagreus sat holding the phone in one hand and the other on my thigh, as if it was enough to tether me to this moment, to him altogether. His touch wasn't as gentle as always. It wasn't cruel, either, surprisingly.

The slit in my dress teased the pads of his thumb. Every pass, every absent-minded stroke felt deliberate. And I hated that my body noticed. Hated how my skin came alive beneath that subtle pressure. I sat perfectly still, hands folded in my lap, trying to pretend I wasn't unravelling.

He was texting someone with his free hand.

And yet, I could feel him watching me.

Even when his eyes were on the glowing screen, I felt him watching. Admiringly, if I may say. Like he was cataloguing the way the shadows kissed my skin to how the bodice hugged my ribs a little too tightly. I hated the way his gaze felt like a secret I hadn't agreed to keep.

A thousand thoughts screamed inside me, clawing to the surface, but my throat refused to open. I was terrified, utterly and literally, breathlessly terrified. Not just of him, but of everything. Of what I'd learned. Of what I hadn't.

Of her.

My mother.

Alive and breathing.

The woman I'd cried for, prayed for, mourned for in lonely silence… she wasn't dead. She had never been dead. She chose to disappear and leave me behind.

And suddenly, I didn't know who to be angry at.

Zagreus told me. With that flat, cruel honesty only he possessed. She left me. She chose to vanish. And he was right. A person forgets the one who loved them in order to protect what they loved most.

She had forgotten me.

I tried to speak, but the words crumbled before they left my tongue. I seriously didn't know where to start. Didn't know how to ask the questions that had festered in my chest for years. Didn't even know if I wanted the answers.

Was I so easy to abandon?

Was I so unlovable?

The heat of his palm was burning through the silk now, steadying me and grounding me in the most terrifying way. I could feel the tension in my spine begging to snap. I couldn't even cry. The tears were struck behind some dam I'd built long ago, some inner wall that kept me from breaking completely in front of him.

But my heart was screaming.

It wanted answers.

It wanted her.

And somewhere, it was him too. Or maybe just the dark promise that came with him. The certainty that whatever nightmare came next, he'd be in it.

Maybe that's what scared me most of all.

I was so engrossed in my own world that I didn't notice the lights from streetlamps had turned into the full-blown city ones. The car began to slow as we entered the city area.

Lights flickered past the windows in dizzying streaks, neon signs, the flashes of traffic signals, and the occasional glow of the pedestrian's phone. Civilisation. The closest I'd been to human life in… I didn't know how many days. Maybe weeks. Maybe a lifetime.

And I was panicking.

My breath hitched, and my chest tightened. It started in the pit of my stomach, the nauseating pressure crawling up my spine. I wasn't used to this anymore. I had forgotten the noise, the motion, the scent of fuel and concrete and life.

I had almost forgotten I was a painter.

An artist.

I used to love the chaos of crowds, the richness of movement, and the silent stories I'd capture in brushstrokes. But now? Now every shadow was unfamiliar. The city wasn't familiar anymore. It was a monster with too many eyes and no mercy.

The car rolled to a slow stop, and before I could process it, the doors opened, the chauffeurs in crisp white uniforms, holding umbrellas, speaking rapid Italian.

And then the flashes. So many flashes, I almost went blind.

Camera shutters burst like flames, so bright and blinding white, exploding my vision. I staggered back instinctively, eyes wide, lips parting on a silent gasp. It was all too much. Too fast for my brain to register. The world tilted on its axis, voices blurred, and I didn't recognised being shouted at.

I couldn't breathe.

A sharp ringing started in my ears. My heart thudded, slamming against my ribcage like it wanted out. My throat closed, and the edges of my vision started to dim. My lungs refused to fill.

Oh God, please, please, please, please...I can't do this. I can't breathe. I can't live. I can't... see.

When I thought I'd faint and fall, a strong hand wrapped around my waist with brutal certainty, yanking me into the solid heat of his chest. I collided with him, hands splaying across his suit, all silk and muscle and something darker underneath. Zagreus didn't say a word.

But his touch devoured the chaos and the panic.

He leaned down, his nose grazing the shell of my ear, and his warm breath danced as he inhaled deeply like he needed it. His palm at my waist slid lower, curving around my hip, pulling me tighter until not even air dared to exist between us. His other hand ghosted over my nape, fingers tangling in the loose strands at the base of my neck. Anchoring me to him.

And gods, it worked.

The panic didn't vanish, but it shifted; it became something molten, something more wicked that curled in my belly. I felt his mouth brush the side of my throat, and my hands trembled across his chest.

He held me tighter, his thumb slowly stroking along my hipbone like he was reminding me I was not going anywhere. Like he had me sorted.

And I hated that it calmed me.

Hated that I melted against him and let the warmth of his body became a sanctuary. That the tremble in my thighs wasn't entirely fear anymore. That the flush creeping up my neck was heat, and not shame.

Lust and madness behind that impossible stillness.

His grip loosened slowly, like he knew exactly how I'd fall apart if he let go too fast. His hand lingered at my waist, thumb tracing idle circles through the fabric of my dress. His mouth was still closed, and the heat of his breath brushed my cheek.

"Don't let them affect you, Dolcezza. You belong to the silence between my heartbeats, not their cameras. Let them chase your shadow, but only I... I can taste your fear and tame it."

A shiver ran down my spine, curling my toes inside my heels, and the flashes continued. A few reporters called out my name, assuming maybe I was someone else. Or someone important to him.

"Mr. Vitale! Over here!"

"Who's the girl?!"

"Is she your date?!"

But Zagreus didn't look at them. He never broke eye contact with me. His hand slid away, slow enough to burn. And just like that, the armour returned, his face became blank marble, elegant and cold. He stepped around me, letting the chauffeur open the door fully as if nothing had happened, as if he hadn't just silenced my panic with a few whispered words and a single touch.

The reporters' voices grew louder, more curious, but none dared to cross the velvet ropes.

I stepped out of the car. Legs shaking and eyes blinking against the onslaught of camera lights.

My fingers instinctively reached for him, just the air where he'd been seconds ago, and then he was there again. Walking beside me like a shadow with a pulse. Zagreus didn't offer his arm, didn't even touch me, but his presence alone pulled me to his gravity.

We entered the building, and the chaos buzzed in front of us.

Cold marble floors beneath the cathedral-high ceiling. Crystal chandeliers, dripping with light, danced above our heads. Velvet-lined walls, gold accents, and the distant sound of a cello echoing through the lobby.

And I... I was drowning all over again.

Not in panic, though, but in the sensation of not belonging.

I wasn't dressed like the women we passed. They were tall and sharply painted to perfection. I wasn't poised like them. Everything felt foreign. This wasn't my world. It was just a place made of money and menace and masks.

I'd almost forgotten I was wearing a dress.

Forgotten the slit that revealed too much of my skin. Forgotten that Zagreus picked it up for me, and he liked it.

People turned to look at us. At me. I heard the whispers again. And all I wanted was to fade.

But Zagreus? He walked like he owned every inch of this place and everyone in it. And somehow... I started to remember how to breathe again.

CHAPTER THIRTY-TWO
The Syndicate

We hadn't taken more than a few steps into the grand foyer when a tall, suited man approached. Sharp edges were carved into the bones of his face and his steps faltered slightly before he caught sight of Zagreus, and then he bowed his head in reverence. Or maybe fear.

"Mr. Vitale," he murmured.

Zagreus gave him nothing more than a slight nod, cold and disinterested as if he was a king acknowledging a peasant. The man retreated, shoulders stiff, almost relieved to be dismissed without words.

It wasn't just him.

Eyes followed us, some wide with wary recognition, others squinting with thinly veiled contempt. But not one dared approach again. Not one spoke.

Because Zagreus wasn't just a man here, he was a god. Or the devil dressed in tailored black.

He wrapped his arm around my waist with such suddenness that I gasped breathily, but it reverberated loudly in my chest. His hand slid across the curve of my hip, and he dipped his mouth once more to my ear.

"Be a good girl for me, Dolcezza. This place is full of wild."

I wanted to ask him if he was referring to himself, because right now, at this very moment, no one seemed to scare me more than him.

"Don't give me a reason to decorate this floor with blood."

Heat spread in slow pulses across my skin, and I nodded. My legs trembled at his beautiful, merciless words. He whispered in sin.

I lifted my head, looking at him through my lashes.

The scar caught the light as he turned his head slightly, and for a moment, I saw him.

All of him.

A fallen angel, carved from something unholy, something both cruel and impossibly beautiful. The scar running from his temple to his cheekbone didn't mar him, it marked him. Like he'd once fought God… and almost won.

He didn't stop to acknowledge the others. Champagne glasses raised to him. Men bowed. Women tried to smile. Some whispered behind their hands. But Zagreus walked like none of it mattered. Like he ruled the world and everyone in it was merely background noise.

I wasn't used to being looked at like this. Like I was something scandalous belonging to a man of power.

Some faces twisted when they saw me. Jealous, disapproving, and confused. I didn't blame them. I felt the same.

I wanted to vanish.

But my… husband's grip on my waist wouldn't let me. He led us down the hallway, away from the dancing and music, away from the crowd. We crossed deep red carpeting and gold-veined marble columns. The walls were lined with dim sconces, and this area was a lot more secluded. There was hardly anyone except for a few guards in black that I saw.

At the end of the corridor stood a pair of heavy, wooden doors.

Two giant men flanked them, dressed in black, built like statues. When they saw him, their heads dropped in unison. No words, no eye contact, they just kept their heads down without lifting their eyes.

As startled and terrified as I was at the realisation that Zagreus was a lot more powerful than I initially thought, it erected several goosebumps all over my flesh.

Zagreus looked down at me, and I averted my face, feeling something in the pit of my belly all of a sudden. I heard him saying something under his breath, and the guards opened the doors.

The scent hit me first, whiskey and aged wood mingled with leather and cinnamon, with something faintly smoky behind it. The air was thicker here. Heavier. Almost suffocating. Or maybe it was just me.

Maybe it was the fact that I was walking into the lion's den with the lion himself pressing a hand against the small of my back like I belonged to him. Like I was his to guide. His to own.

God, what the hell was I doing here?

Even breathing made the knot in my stomach tighten until it felt like my ribs were crushing in on it. I didn't even know if it was fear anymore. Or anticipation. Or both, tangled so tightly together I couldn't tell them apart.

The room was dimly lit, but a chandelier above with warm lights, shadows dancing on old stone walls. A massive fireplace crackled at the far end, its flames licking at the dark air like a beast hungry for more.

I shouldn't have come with him here.

I should've said no. I should've run. Or screamed. Or

pushed him away when I still had the chance.

But I didn't.

I let him touch me. I let him look at me like that, like he saw right through me, down to every ugly, trembling part of me I try to keep hidden.

And the worst part?

I wanted him to see.

"Come," Zagreus said, his voice a low command that curled around my spine like smoke. Not harsh, but not soft either. Like there was no question I'd obey.

My legs moved before I could tell them not to.

What was wrong with me? Why wasn't I fighting this?

Because deep down, in some dark, twisted place I didn't want to admit even existed, I liked the way he made me feel. Small. Seen. Dangerous. Desired. Protected.

My eyes widened.

Desired? Seen?

For fuck's sake, Celestine. He killed Adrian. Kidnapped you. Forced you into a marriage you didn't want.

Something's wrong with my head. Gods, wasn't that terrifying?

I stumbled after him, my heels clicked on the floor, but I barely heard them over the pounding in my chest.

A long, dark central table dominated the room, surrounded by men. Men who didn't look like politicians or businessmen. They looked like gods in exile. Ruthless, magnetic, and impossible to ignore. Their suits were tailored like Zagreus with sharp expressions and calculations in their eyes. There were women, too. I didn't know if I should be happy or worried for them.

I swallowed hard, already wanting to run back. Just my luck, it was already locked.

As Zagreus pulled me with him, the dim light flickered

across every angle. The curtains were open, revealing a sky littered with stars. It should've been beautiful.

But all I felt was dread.

Cards flicked across the table. A burst of curses, and someone said something in Russian before everything stilled. Everything stopped. Chairs shifted and eyes turned. And silence swallowed my pounding heart.

I froze and took a half-step back, hiding behind Zagreus like a child. His body blocked them, but I could still feel the gravity of the stares dissecting me.

I didn't belong here.

My whole body melted as Zagreus placed his hand behind him, on my thigh, just above the slit of my dress, and gave it a grounding squeeze, burning me, calming me, and claiming me in the same breath.

I looked up at the side of his face.

The scar. The brutal edge of his jaw. The way he stood tall and composed, as if nothing in this room could ever harm him, or me, not while he was breathing.

"So, the prodigal son arrives. Or are you here for the wine, Vitale?"

The voice came from the far end of the table. I snuck a glance at the man who leaned back in his chair, half-shrouded in the gold-tinted dark. He wore an ivory suit with the confidence of someone who'd killed in it before. His lips curved into something too cruel to be a smile. He held his glass with lazy elegance, as if he were toying with Zagreus.

My personal hell didn't pause. His hand found mine, and he pulled me forward.

He gave the man a nod and pulled out a chair.

"The wine bores me, Bianchi. But I hear your wife's still living with her parents? I hope the nights aren't... lonely."

The one sitting next to the man called Bianchi chuckled

under his breath. Bianchi glared at him but then turned to Zagreus and raised his brows.

Zagreus pulled me with him and moved to the nearest empty chair. He sat down, long legs folding, and he looked up at me. His eyes burned beneath his long lashes.

"Sit."

Swallowing the knot, I lowered myself onto the velvet chair beside him. The moment I sat, he reached for the chair arm and dragged it closer to him. The legs screeched faintly across the floor, and before I could process what was happening, his hand slid beneath the slit of my dress and landed on my thigh.

Heat surged as his fingers flexed on my skin as if I was his anchor... his favourite possession.

My attention wavered when someone snickered from my left.

A man leaned forward from his chair, arms crossed over his broad chest covered in tight black fabric. His buzz cut made his cheekbones look sharper, and there was a bold tattoo curling up his neck.

Three dotted lines.

Strange for a tattoo.

His eyes were dark, hooded, and his mouth twisted in something between distaste and provocation.

"Didn't know you brought souvenirs now, Vitale. That a new hobby, or just a desperate one?"

Bianchi laughed, and I suddenly wanted to strangle him for some unknown reason. What was there to laugh about? Did he tell some joke?

Zagreus's thumb stroked my inner thigh, and he didn't even look at the man. His attention stayed on me, his jaw ticked once before he finally tilted his head lazily toward the speaker.

As if the man's words had taken a long, unworthy journey

to reach his ears.

"I'd be careful if I were you, Victor."

Victor scoffed, visibly enjoying as he tipped his glass at Bianchi. "Papi's threatening now, huh?"

Zagreus turned back to me, brushing my hair away from my neck with the back of his hand. "Ignore them. They're dogs. They bark when they smell something valuable."

I nodded and looked around the room again.

They were all men of power. You didn't need to know their names to feel it. Each one sat like they were the protagonists in a movie, only they could direct. Their presence bled through the air. So arrogant, untamed, quietly chaotic, disturbing, and amused.

I scanned them, barely moving my head.

The one sitting straight across from me, with the palest blue blues I'd ever seen and dark hair slicked back. He didn't blink. Kept his pale eyes on the cards scattered around the table and played unconsciously with one in his fingers.

To be honest, he was the kind of man who would slice you a thousand times and scatter your pieces on different planets for the sport.

Beside him sat Bianchi. With phone in hand, hunched now, bored all of a sudden as he typed something furiously.

Now that the light touched his features, I realised I'd seen him before.

A magazine cover? On TV? I couldn't remember.

But I knew one thing: men like him didn't sit in rooms like this unless they were the ones who built it.

The man on my left, who hadn't said a word, had a woman draped on his lap. No, not draped. Draped would be too delicate a word. She was perched there like a queen, legs folded and one hand resting on his chest. She didn't look afraid of this room.

She owned it in her own way.

She was stunning. Her long, dark hair parted at one side, cascading like spilled ink down her back. Her skin was olive gold, like she'd been carved from an ancient sun-kissed marble, glowing under the dim light. Her eyes, deep-brown and burning, flicked across the room like daggers. She looked as if she'd set fire to this table with a flick of her wrist if anyone dared to cross her.

And her dress…

Or what looked like a dress.

It was deep red. Draped across her body in a way I hadn't seen before, flowing silk with little details, threads woven through the borders, wrapping around her waist and shoulder, one end trailing behind her like a secret. She looked like war. All blood and elegance.

And I hated how beautiful she was.

Sinfully, terrifyingly beautiful.

Then my gaze fell upon the man sitting diagonally across, toward the far right end of the table, who looked East Asian. Maybe Korean, Japanese, or Chinese? I couldn't be sure. His jawline was sharp enough to cut diamonds, black hair slicked back in a rough, low ponytail, and his dark eyes focused on the girl beside him, the one I failed to notice.

She was sitting properly in her own chair, but close. Very close. Head bowed.

Auburn hair spilt over her shoulders, framing a pale, doll-like face. She looked like she didn't belong here, frail, almost porcelain in how delicate she appeared. Petite and quiet.

But the man beside her…

He kept rubbing slow circles on the back of her hand where it rested on his thighs.

The kind of touch I was familiar with was Zagreus.

Something told me she didn't come here willingly. None

of us did. But something was chilling about how tender he was with her, as if his version of love could kill.

Everyone had someone.

Except the ice-eyed man, Bianchi, and Victor.

But looking at them, I knew they were married. At least the former two. Because both of them had rings on their ring fingers. And the pale blue-eyed one had a small tattoo on his wrist, right above his pulse. I couldn't catch it. But I recognised the initial.

S.

Written in cursive.

CHAPTER THIRTY-THREE
Whispers of Sins

I sat there, pressed closer to Zagreus as his palm burned through my thigh.

A beat passed.

Then another.

The cards on the table lay forgotten. No one spoke, but they didn't need to, not when their eyes said everything. And then, the one with palest eyes spoke.

"So, have you come to discuss the devil's toy? Or are we still pretending it's a myth?"

Zagreus sighs. "Lazarus is no myth. And Osman has it."

A collective shift through the room, and eyes narrowed, postures stiffened.

Massimo leaned forward. "You're telling me that madman got his hands on a weapon that can level countries?"

"Not just any weapon," Zagreus said. "A Russian creation, designed during the Cold War, compact, untraceable, and catastrophic."

Abel whistled. "Well, shit. That's a party favour no one should have."

Victor, as I had come to know him by that cold and deranged look in his eyes, set his glass down and adjusted his glasses. "And the Americans? They want it?"

Zagreus nodded. "Desperately. They see it as a means to tip the scales."

The man with pale eyes grunted. "And you think I'd allow my homeland to be obliterated by our so-called allies?"

"I think," Zagreus said evenly, "that if we don't act, Osman will sell it to the highest bidder. And then none of us will have a homeland left to protect."

The Asian looking man, who had been observing quietly, finally spoke. "Osman moves in shadows. He's got a kingdom to protect and his royal crown. If he's surfaced with Lazarus, it's intentional. He wants our attention."

Massimo snorted. "Well, congratulations to him. It's working."

The woman to my right shifted. The one wearing the blood red dress or whatever that was. She seemed quite interested in the conversation, unlike me and the one with the Asian looking man.

Zagreus turned to the pale-eyed man. "We need a plan, Judas. One that ensures Lazarus doesn't fall into the wrong hands."

So, his name was Judas.

Judas's jaw tightened. "And what makes you think any of us are the right hands?"

"Because," Zagreus muttered. "We're the only ones who know it exists."

The room fell silent again, and I just sat there, heart pounding and realising that I was in the midst of a conversation that could determine the fate of millions. And I was terrified.

"As much as I'd like to discuss the end of the world," I looked up to find him swirling the liquor in his glass. "I'd hate to ask you to have this conversation alone, Vitale."

All heads turned to me.

Zagreus didn't react immediately; he stared at Judas for a moment, jaw tickling faintly, and then shifted his eyes to me. His fingers slid upward just a little on my thigh, and he sighed. "Then that goes for every other presence in this room, I suppose."

Abel leaned forward to the woman in red and whispered something in her ear. Since I was sitting beside her, I heard it.

"Be a good girl, Saffron. I'd hate to paint your ass red if you make any trouble."

Okay, I didn't sign up for this.

I felt the blood leave my face. I didn't even have to speak as Zagreus pressed his lips to my temple. "Get your fix, Dolcezza," he murmured. "I'll be done soon."

I stood slowly, feeling the heaviness of every eye in the room slide off me, and walked out with Saffron and the one with red auburn hair.

The last thing I saw before the door clicked shut was Judas leaning back in his chair with a half-smile, raising his glass again.

"Now, let's talk about who is going to die first."

The door shut, and the guards outside led down a quieter hallway, dim lights and long silence. And I still couldn't shake what I just heard. Were they going to kill someone? What had I gotten myself into?

I tried to focus on my breathing as the guard opened another door ahead. A parlour-like room, spacious but cold, with tufted velvet couches, warm lighting, and tall windows overlooking the garden below. Not a prison, but it felt like one.

The guard left after I heard a click. He locked it. Of course he did; none of the men in that damn room would want their woman escaping. And yes, I somehow knew these two were also some kind of victims to their whims. I wondered what their stories were.

I watched as the red-garbed one walked in first, and she didn't even glance back, but somehow she had changed from timid one to fierce one. There's rage in her of some kind. I felt like a pervert letting my eyes rake over her waist, where the garment was missing. She was stunning, did I mention?

I heard shuffling on my side to find the other woman, a petite and fragile-looking one with auburn hair and pale skin, taking a seat, folding her hands over her lap, and fidgeting with her thumbs. She hadn't looked at anyone in the eyes yet. Not even once.

I stood awkwardly by the door, unsure whether to join her or not.

The woman in red finally turned, her mocha eyes scanning me in one long, slow, sweet look as she tilted her head. "You're new." She sighed, crossing her arms. "Looks like you've been thrown to wolves, too."

I swallowed. "I… wasn't told where to go."

The fragile one stirred on the couch; her eyes were glassy. And I took a deep breath.

"You're with Zagreus Vitale, aren't you?" she asked, and I nodded. "He's the deadliest."

No need to remind me.

I flushed and felt myself being interrogated as she poured a glass of wine and handed it to me. "He kidnapped you?"

I swallowed, not knowing how much I was allowed to tell her. If Zagreus knew, would he punish me? My tongue tied itself in knots. "I… don't know what I'm doing here."

"None of us did," she replied, sipping hers. "Mishka, by the way."

Her name was as beautiful as her.

"Celestine."

Mishka sat, crossing her legs and looking at the other woman. "Yours?"

I almost chuckled at her wide eyes, as if she wasn't expecting us to talk to her. After a heavy silence, she whispered softly. "I-I'm… Nilah."

I sipped on wine, gathering my courage, and sat opposite them. "Who were they?" I asked, though I was barely interested. I just needed to have some idea of what I was getting myself into.

"They call this a Syndicate of some kind. But it's more like a ring of devils who got bored of ruling their own kingdoms, now they want to burn others."

I stared at her, heart racing.

"And what's Lazarus?" I asked before I could stop myself. "What are they talking about in there?"

She tilted her head, studying me like I'd grown a second head. "A weapon. And a person. Depends. Built by Alexei Volkov, who thinks god is overrated," she glanced at the door, "and they want to decide who gets to wield it."

Nilah whispered, almost to herself. "And Osman Khalid has it."

"Who's he?"

Mishka sighed. "Another one of them. Though with regal blood and a real fucking crown."

I wrapped my arms around myself, a strange ache blooming in my chest. I didn't know if I belonged here or how I ended up here. Or if I'd ever belong anywhere again. I still hadn't pieced it together. Mishka and Nilah seemed to know more than I did.

I let my eyes waver at Mishka as she slowly stood and walked to the window. The draping fabric flowed as she arched her back, the hem of her red garment brushed the marble floor as she raised her hand, and without hesitating, she tore a slit clean through the length of the fabric, leaving both me and Nilah wide-eyed and gasping.

I froze.

She didn't stop, and shook off her heels, and she looked out the window. Her eyes scanned the height, the angle, and hummed to herself. "Not too high."

"What are you doing?" I whispered, only for her lips to curve into a smile, but in the most deadliest way.

"Measuring the leap."

"Leap?" Nilah repeated coming to stand beside me. She was as baffled as me as we both stared at the fearless woman in both awe and anticipation.

Mishka turned, her gaze dragging over me, then to Nilah, then back to the window. "I would love to take you two with me," she said. "But I can't risk being on their radar again. And I'm afraid… they'd only hunt you harder."

"Mishka…" She pressed her finger to her lips, hushing me.

"Sweet dreams, ladies."

Just before she climbed out fully, she reached into her strapless blouse and pulled out a lighter, and pulled out a folded handkerchief from the inner lining. I didn't have to look at the engraving on it to know who it belonged to. Abel's. She held it with two fingers over the flame until it curled, blackened, and caught fire.

"Tell Abel, I left him a kiss."

Then she dropped it in the small porcelain bowl of oils by the hearth. The fire caught fast, and the entire bowl ignited, and before I knew, she blew a kiss and jumped out the window.

I gasped, ran to the window, and grabbed the rail, panting over it as I looked down, but there was nothing. She was gone. Just like the flame, just like that.

The flames hadn't even finished licking the rim of the

bowl before I felt it. A warm throb behind my eyes. And I realised something far worse as I looked at the wine glass I left on the cabinet.

The wine.

I blinked hard, turning my head slowly over my shoulder to find Nilah slumped on the velvet divan. Her curly auburn hair fell over her eyes, and her glass was tilted.

Panic hit me in slow motion. "Fuck…"

It all made sense now. She barely drank the wine. God, why hadn't I been smart enough?

If only I could use my brain that much.

If only I hadn't been so goddamn scared.

If only I hadn't just sat there while she made her move.

CHAPTER THIRTY-FOUR
Drugged and Needy

Everything beneath me was weightless. It felt like I was floating through it like mist... unanchored and completely undone.

"Mama..."

The strange thing about this... I could see my mother. Either it was a dream of some kind, or reality, I couldn't tell. There was darkness, and a ray of light at the far end, coffins and gritty sand under my hands. My head throbbed, and I felt like choking.

Strangely, I was looking right at the very woman I was here for. My mother, her back was to me, and the familiar slope of her shoulders, the rustle of the hem of her dress as she walked away like she always did. Her hands were wrapped in someone else's. And my mind reeled like a movie... as I recognised it instantly. Adrian. My dead fiancé. My ghost.

But he wasn't looking at me either.

They weren't stopping.

"Wait... please! I... I miss you..." The words tumbled through my mouth as I tried to fight the invisible force holding me. "Why didn't you come back?"

They kept moving further, and further till the white of her dress flickered in and out of the dark like the moon behind clouds. In my head, I was chasing her into the silence and darkness. The force holding me down suddenly vanished, and I stood up on my shaky legs. I ran until my legs forgot how to carry grief.

The sky turned ink. The stars vanished, and everything became cold and biting. My fingertips were pale and trembling, and my cheeks were wet. I touched my face. Tears. Or rain. Or both. My hands weren't mine anymore. They felt foreign as they clawed at the emptiness in front of me, reaching for something I couldn't name.

But there was warmth too. Somewhere, somewhere behind me.

"Dolcezza…"

I turned sharply as the voice melted into my spine.

"Dolcezza… F…" Suddenly, there was a breath against my temple, but there was no one. I looked at where Mama and Adrian went, and that place was empty. The horizon shifted, and the ink became red.

I panicked, paranoid that this was my end. I supposed this was what real hell looked like. I stumbled and fell on my knees, clutching onto the sand under me as I closed my eyes and felt invisible hands cradling me.

And I instantly knew who it belonged to.

His warmth touched my skin before his hands did. I didn't see him, but I felt him like the heat of a fire behind closed eyes. I reached blindly, fingers curling into a chest I couldn't see. My body burned, and it was a strange kind of heat. I felt the sudden ache of need. To be held and seen. To be kept.

And he was there.

I clawed at him needily and desperately, nails scraping fabric, and my wrist was caught. My thumb circled the soft skin there, anchoring me as if I was a ship caught amidst a storm.

"I'm here, shhh," he murmured, and the darkness in his voice was welcoming. "Stop running."

"But they left me…" my voice cracked and I didn't know who I was muttering this to. Him or me. "They didn't look back."

"I did…"

His words slid down my spine along with his hands. My mouth opened and I sobbed, but it wasn't pretty. Nothing about this was. I curled into him as if I belonged there, and I felt him tremble. He smelt like smoke and something expensive.

"I'll never let you be invisible again," he whispered near my temple. "Even if I have to burn down every god."

His hands were angry, but he touched me in the most gentle way. It was foreign to me. He cursed lowly and gathered me in his embrace. And suddenly the sand under me started moving, and I opened my eyes to see metal. Raising my head, I was met with the deepest blue eyes I'd ever seen, adorned with a scar.

And I was in his arms. Almost on his lap, my body burning, and we were moving in a car. I didn't remember what happened or how we got here. I couldn't even recall my own name. All I knew was him. Not even me.

I sighed into him. Relieved, I was no longer surrounded by those coffins and sea and sand. Warmth filled my chest, between my thighs. A throbbing ache I didn't understand pulse softly like a yearning that wasn't entirely physical, but something deeper. It wasn't lustful. It was what? It didn't need any names or reasons. Just presence and breath.

"Do you feel anything?" he asked, and I took a deep breath.

"I feel… hot," I whispered, and he pressed a kiss to my forehead.

"That's just your body, Dolcezza. You were drugged, but don't worry, it'll go away. Just take deep breaths and keep remembering who you belong to."

"To you?"

He didn't answer, just held me tighter.

Everything felt half-stitched to reality, like seams between time and thought had been loosened by warm wine and whispered ghosts. My skin felt too tight and too warm now. And that ache… god… it wasn't going away. It pulsed unbearably.

I knew something was wrong. But nothing had ever felt more right.

I shouldn't want him. Not like this at least. Not when my head was spinning and my heart was water. But if he was using me… then I wanted to use him too. Wasn't that fair?

Besides, weren't we husband and wife… in sheets, if nowhere else?

I pressed my face against his chest, into the thick folds of his blazer, inhaling his scent like oxygen, smoke, and firewood. A trace of danger here and there. And something that made me want to cry.

My fingers moved of their own accord, slipping beneath the lapel, trembling as they found the buttons of his shirt. I barely managed to undo one when his hand snapped around my wrist.

"What are you doing?"

I didn't look at him, yet the ache intensified, cruel in its waking. My thighs clenched instinctively, and I twisted my wrist in his grasp.

"Using… you," I breathed.

There was a beat of silence before he chuckled.

It was a sound I hadn't expected. Not amused or cruel, it

was something else entirely. And laced with disbelief.

My lashes fluttered as I looked up. He was staring down at me. Jaw tense, mouth parted slightly, and his eyes as darkly stained obsidian. He didn't speak at first, just stared as if he was trying to solve me, or maybe trying to understand how a thing so small could unravel a man so thoroughly.

He slowly let go of my wrist, and his fingers slid away deliberately. I half-expected him to shove me off, but he leaned back, resting his head against the seat like a king bored at his own court.

"You want to use me? Then use me." I blinked at him through the haze. "Turn me into your little sin, Dolcezza."

CHAPTER THIRTY-FIVE
Need and Greed

There is a weight to want, and it's not a light or soft or fluttery kind. It drags you down by the bones, like grief wearing a dress stitched from heat and hunger.

And right now, it's sitting in my lap. Or maybe I'm the one in its lap. What a cursed cradle to be held in.

His breathing was too calm for a man of such danger. That stillness that screamed trained control as if he'd been swallowing storms his whole life and still grinned like he'd never tasted thunder.

My hands, these traitorous and trembling hands, moved again. And somehow I was touching places that I had no right to.

I didn't want to feel safe.

I wanted to feel real.

I wanted to ruin something, even if it was me.

Even if it was him.

So I leaned in.

My breath brushed against the hollow of his throat, and I watched him swallow like he'd forgotten how. The scent of him was still firewood and whiskey, sin aged like fine wine and sharpened by restraint. He was letting me do what I wanted, but I knew this was another illusion, because if he wanted to take the lead, he would.

I pressed my lips to the dip of his collarbone, and he let out the softest sound. It was low, half-choked. Curse smothered in velvet.

His fingers twitched at my waist, but he didn't stop me.

And that was the most dangerous thing of all.

He was letting me.

Like he wanted to see how far I'd go before I broke us both.

"You said I could use you," I whispered against his skin. A confession I'd never admit sober.

One button. And then another. My hands found the line of his shirt, undoing it slowly, reverently, as though each glimpse of his flesh was a scripture I needed to memorise. My mouth followed the path, tracing skin over the sternum, mapping warmth and heartbeat.

"Is this what you want, Dolcezza?" His voice cracked around my name. It was ragged, burnt around the edges, yet pristine in the core.

It was lethargically hypnotising as if his voice was manipulating me more than the drug in my system.

"I don't know what I want," I said honestly, pressing my teeth into the curve where his chest met his shoulder. "But I need something to make the ache shut up."

His head fell back against the leather seat, a sharp sigh leaving him. I felt his pulse kicking at his throat like a drum against my lips. And then... my fingers reached lower, between us.

I felt the tremble under my touch, like lightning waiting in copper wires.

I found the metal of his belt and unhooked it. My palm brushed against the hardness of him through fabric, and I felt his grip on my waist tighten, as if he was trying to anchor himself with the ghost of restraint. His hips shifted, the rough grind of his pants pressed between my aching thighs, and a sound escaped him. An unguarded, sinful moan that scorched my lungs.

He was beautiful like this.

Unravelled at the seams, thread by thread, under my hands.

He asked me to turn him into my little sin.

So I did. I kissed him like I had something to prove. Like maybe if I kissed him deep enough, I'd find a part of him that hurt me, haunted me, and the part I hated.

"You won't leave me like them, right?" I didn't know why I said that. Maybe it was the vulnerability. The ache in the chest. Or maybe I was reminded that my mother left me in the dark. I suddenly recalled the touch of sand in my palms that I couldn't contain.

He didn't speak.

Just pulled me closer.

His hands slid from my waist to my thighs, grinding me against him until the ache inside me bloomed into wicked need. He held me as if I were something breakable and burning all the once. A prayer he couldn't say out loud.

His voice came again, deeper now, with shadows in every word. He cupped my jaw, made me look into his stormy eyes, and there was this depth in them I couldn't understand.

"I can destroy everything for you, Dolcezza. I've been yours from the first time you looked at me. Even if this world disappoints you again and again, I will always be there with you. In your dreams and nightmares," he kissed my temple, "in your highs and lows," his mouth hovered over mine, maddeningly close, "and in the places no one sees. In the thoughts no one dares to touch. You breathe, and I unravel."

Then he kissed me like he wanted to ruin every version of me that existed before him.

I struggled to keep up, because he kissed me with the intention of erasing every version of me. It was slow, as if he had all the time to destroy every wall I'd ever built. His lips were warm and brutal and worshipping. And I let him. God, I wanted to let him.

A breath caught in my throat as I pulled back, and there it was, his face. That maddeningly calm exterior was cracking, like the seams of control were starting to bleed open. His jaw clenched, the veins in his neck twitching with control, eyes glassed with hunger. He looked like a man on the verge of losing control... and loving every second of it.

I could've asked him to stop. But I didn't.

Because there was a part of me – a small, shameful, and starving part – that needed this. Needed him to unravel. Not gently or softly, but in chaos.

I slid down, slowly, knees pressing into the cold metal of the car floor. I shouldn't have. I didn't even know who I was beneath the ache anymore. But my body knew what to do. My hands moved to his undone belt, and I felt him still again.

His breath hitched. And I felt him, hot and hard beneath my palm, still trapped in his boxers.

His hand came down, catching my wrist, not to stop me, but to feel me. To feel that I was really doing this. This time, I wasn't forced. This time... I was choosing to sin.

He didn't speak. He just watched me with that unreadable expression, eyes burning into my skin as if ink that would never wash off.

"Hold my hair," I whispered with the same tremble I'd been holding onto.

A breath escaped him, and something in his gaze broke.

He did it. His hand on my wrist twisted into my hair with that roughness. I wasn't trying to please him. I wasn't even trying to save myself either. Maybe… if I gave him everything, the silence inside me would finally stop screaming.

His hips bucked slightly as if he had been touched in his manhood again. The muscles in his jaw ticked, and a low curse tumbled out of his mouth. His fingers tightened in my hair, and I bit back a sound of my own. I wanted him to break me, not with violence, but with this. With worship that looked like every dangerous version of sin.

I pulled out his entire length, and I was startled that he was semi-erect. I couldn't hold it with my single hand, so I fisted his cock with both of my hands. It was thick and veiny, and I couldn't believe this had been inside me several times.

Swallowing, I looked up to meet his eyes, and they darkened as I opened my mouth and touched him with my tongue. He took a sharp breath. "Fuck…"

I loved watching him throw his head back, and my tongue tasted the salty pre-cum. In a few seconds, he was as hard as rock, swelling in my hands and standing tall like a fortress.

I didn't stop there, though. I had no reason to. His hand in my hair guided my whole mouth to his length. He was eager. But I shut my lips, and his mushroom head only met my closed lips. He let out a frustrated growl and snapped his eyes at me.

I licked my lips, blinking my hooded eyes at him, feigning every ounce of innocence I could muster.

"You said you'd let me take control," I muttered, tilting my head. "If you keep acting this way, I refuse to please you."

That got his attention, because he sighed and cursed again. "You're playing with me, Dolcezza."

I smiled. "Maybe I am," I whispered, letting my thumb stroke along the ridge of his tip, watching the way his abs clenched under the pressure. "Maybe I just like watching you fall apart."

His chest rose, sharp and shallow, like he'd forgotten how to breathe. His hand in my hair trembled—just enough for me to notice. The storm in his eyes flared.

"You're going to be the death of me," he muttered. I kissed the underside of him. Then again. Slower. Deeper. Like a promise made on holy ground. And then I took him in.

Inch by aching inch, letting him stretch past my lips, my throat opening willingly to every inch of sin he had to offer. His hips jerked, his free hand curling into a fist against the seat as a sound escaped him—raw, low, beautifully ruined.

I hummed against him, and that's when he lost it.

"Fucking hell—" he groaned, his grip in my hair tightening, but not forcing. Never forcing. Just grounding himself with the only part of me he could hold on to.

His other hand found my jaw, his thumb tracing my cheekbone with the gentleness of a man who knew he didn't deserve softness, yet begged for it anyway.

"You're mine," he growled under his breath, voice rough with reverence. "No matter what you do, no matter how sweet you pretend to be… I see the ruin in your eyes. And it looks just like mine."

I looked up at him, my lips still wrapped around him, eyes watering but unblinking. I let him see it—all of it. The ache. The loneliness. The desperate, broken worship we gave each other to keep from collapsing.

He was shaking when he finally pulled me off with a gasp, pressing our foreheads together, his breath a prayer against my lips.

"Don't do that," he whispered. "Don't want me like this. I'll never come back from it."

"I'm not trying to want you," I said quietly. "But if I do… I won't come back either."

CHAPTER THIRTY-SIX
Howls

I didn't remember the drive.

Or the mansion.

Or the way the front door slammed shut like thunder behind us.

All I knew was the wall against my spine and Zagreus.

He hit me like gravity. Hot, heavy, and inevitable. My gasp echoed down the marble hallway breathlessly, swallowed by the crash of his body into mine. His hands gripped my thighs as if he owned me, spreading me open like the space between us bothered him to the core. My legs wrapped around his hips out of instinct, not grace, and the moment I locked my ankles behind his back, he moved.

I cried out his name, shame and sanity lost somewhere in the storm of his mouth on my neck, his scent thick and wild choking me like smoke, rain, and something primal. Like a man who'd been waiting too long to sin and had finally been handed permission.

"Zagreus…" I gasped, nails clawing uselessly at the velvet wallpaper behind me as my body buckled forward.

"Say it again," he growled into my skin, voice gravel and flame. "Moan it, sweetheart."

His hips snapped up again, harder and deeper this time, his cock driving into me furiously. My back arched off the wall with a strangled sound I didn't recognise coming from me.

I didn't know where the control went.

Maybe I never had it to begin with.

His fingers were bruising at my waist, grounding me, holding me steady, but it was he who trembled. I felt it beneath his strength. There was something breaking in him, and something forming in me. Something unholy burning through him.

"You're my wife," he said, pressing his forehead to mine, voice dark and reverent and shaking with desire. "My name is carved into you, into every place, every fucking sound you make. I don't need a bed to claim you, I just need you, Dolcezza. I just fucking need you."

"I am," I whispered, nearly sobbing. I was fucking drugged, that's all I could say. "I am. I'm yours... just don't stop."

It was the moment of vulnerability. Of dependence. Of him. Of us. Of me.

He didn't stop.

He drove into me against, and my head knocked gently against the wall. His mouth caught the sound I made. Kissing me roughly and deeply, and tangled with want.

His hands came to cradle the back of my head. He knew he was breaking me open, piece by piece, and needed to soften the fall.

"I dreamt of this," he breathed into my mouth. "Every second I was away from you, this was what haunted me. You... not wanting me, not desiring me like I do. Not loving me..." I didn't know what he was saying. "You're the only thing keeping me from falling apart."

"Yes!" I moaned as he thrust animalistically.

He groaned, and it wasn't a sound of lust. It was something else. Something raw and primal.

A pain made of love too big for one body.

His pace turned frantic. He could no longer be soft, no longer wait. His hands left bruises in their wake, his mouth worshiped and devoured in the same breath.

I didn't know who I was anymore, only that I was shaking and raw and split wide open for this man who kissed my ribs, and whispered things that broke me.

"I'd burn this whole fucking world if it meant you'd keep looking at me like that," he said, trailing his lips against my jaw. "I'd kneel before God and carve my own name out of his book if he tried to take you from me ever again."

A cry escaped me.

The chandelier above us flickered. And I realised I was close to coming undone. Not just from what he was doing, but how.

He wasn't just inside me.

He was inside everything, my bones, my breath and my breaking.

He held me like a man on the verge of collapse, like I was the first and last thing he'd ever worship, and he didn't give a damn who saw us because we were still in the hallway. Doors down both sides. Wide open world behind the glass panels.

But Zagreus didn't care.

He gripped me tighter and thrust harder, and I swear, I left my body. My nails scraped down his back, desperate to anchor myself in something, but he was already everything.

He was the prayer I never said right. The punishment that tasted like mercy. The sin that made me feel alive today.

And just as the tension inside me snapped, he kissed my temple. "Come for me, wife."

And I did.

Trembling, broken, singing his name like it was the only thing I ever learned how to say.

∞

The sheets smelled like him.

Still.

Warm. Bitter salt and storm and whatever sin made me unravel against that hallway wall like a girl with no name, no shame, and no future.

I stared at the ceiling for what could've been seconds. Could've been hours. My thighs ached, and my ribs ached. My mouth tasted like regret and roses.

Still, when I shifted my legs and felt the slick sting of where he'd once been, something inside me pulsed. Throbbed.

God.

I hated myself.

He married me without asking.

He killed Adrian.

He used me.

He took what I didn't offer, and then last night, I asked him for more. Moaned for it. Whispered his name like I'd die without it. How do you hate a man properly… when your body doesn't seem to want to?

I sat up. The bed was cold on his side.

Of course, he wasn't here.

Coward.

I slipped out of bed, knees weak, balance unstable, and the bruises between my thighs hummed shamefully.

The curtains were draped, and there was no sign of Elena anywhere.

I brushed my teeth, took a bath, and went to the closet and found another dress like the ones he'd filled it with.

All soft and revealing and sexy. He dressed me like a doll. Or a wife. Or someone he wanted to pretend had chosen this.

This one was blush pink. A two-piece co-ord set, high-waisted skirt, and cropped blouse with small pearl buttons down the front. It looked like something out of someone else's life.

I wore it anyway.

My hands shook as I buckled the ankle strap of my nude heels. And then, without meaning to, my fingers brushed the anklet.

That anklet.

A diamond-studded chain with a small, pale, opal that shimmered when the light hit just right. His gift for me. His mark.

I stared at it for too long. Swallowed the bile and the ache.

What the fuck was I doing?

I should've burned everything he gave me. I should've screamed and fought, and demanded answers.

But instead, I stood in his clothes. In his house. In the prison, he called marriage.

And my body still wanted him.

I pressed my palm to the mirror and closed my eyes.

This isn't me.

I'm not this girl.

I won't become her.

He said I'd see my mother last night. But last night... last night changed something. I could see it in his eyes just before he buried himself inside me like a man too far gone. Like he didn't expect that to happen. Like he didn't mean for it to mean anything.

Liar.

Manipulator.

God, I hated him.

I left the room to look for him. He'd have to give me answers. If not, I'd starve myself.

CHAPTER THIRTY-SEVEN
Being Unable to Love

"What is hell? I maintain it is the suffering of being unable to love." - Fyodor Dostoevsky

There are prisons built from stone, and then there are the ones you wear like skin.

Those ones taste like your own fucking name on someone else's tongue. That ache like bruises between your thighs and whispered lullabies while tearing your ribs apart to see what's inside them. Was it the heart? Or just an organ that had no right to feel.

I didn't know what I was anymore. A victim or a wife, or even a woman. I was something in between. A half-burned psalm, trying to remember which god she used to belong to.

Or was there any god at all for ones like me?

The hallways were too quiet as I walked, and the mansion itself was holding its breath, waiting to see what I'd become. The vaster it was, the scarier it was.

I wasn't sure I could face myself in a mirror again if I passed by one. But I could face him even if I had to swallow glass to do it.

The kitchen smelled of rosemary and heat when I entered. Elena stood at the counter, slicing ripe figs with her usual calm, that unsettling grace of a woman who had long since accepted the monstrous as mundane. I wondered what her story was, or if she had one to begin with.

She looked up when I entered, but didn't smile. Nothing like I was expecting her to.

"Where is he?" I asked, barely holding back the storm.

Elena wiped her hands on a linen cloth, unbothered, and didn't spare me a glance. "Outside."

I blinked. "Outside?"

Outside made no sense. The mansion was encased in sea from the south and hills with forest from the north.

What the hell was he doing outside?

She didn't offer more, and that maddening silence dared me.

I walked out of the kitchen to the main doors I often stared at. Elena didn't stop or follow me. I walked a bit more, and no guards stopped me. No locked doors clicked shut, and no shadows whispered warnings.

I stepped out barefoot, taking off my heels because outside was a bit stony and I didn't want to fall face-first. The skirt of the co-ord set I wore brushed against the floor as I walked. Wind slapped against my face, and for the first time since I'd arrived, or been kidnapped, here, I breathed, not like a survivor but like a woman remembering what air used to taste like before it was filtered through someone else's lungs.

Freedom is not the absence of walls. But is the moment your body forgets it was ever caged.

I stood at the edge of the Cliffside, wind screaming and the sea below roared.

And for a moment, I was infinite.

Before I felt the last digit of infinity on my waist.

I jumped, startled, heart lurching into my throat, and eyes wild. I turned with a jumpy squeal only to find my destroyer.

Zagreus Vitale.

Bare-chested, hair ruffled as if he'd just woken up from war. My eyes lowered to find him wearing slippers instead of the leather boots he normally wore. Slouching grey joggers hanging sinfully low, giving a lewd view of the V-line that disappeared into his joggers. There were some scars on his torso and chest, yet they beautifully enhanced his allure.

A lazy trail of hair disappeared below, mocking gravity with the way it begged the eyes to trace further. I'd never seen him like this. His abs were sharp and toned, sculpted like a sin he never had stone for. Broad shoulders and a hard chest. I couldn't decide where to look because every part of him demanded attention.

Veins curled down his arms like lightning frozen mid-strike; long, strong, and calloused fingers dug lightly into the dip of my waist, possessive without permission.

And his stormy grey eyes, glinting with shattered ice, scanned me as if I was a prey he was too tired to chase, but still wouldn't let escape.

Zagreus Vitale didn't need armour to look like a weapon. He just needed to wake up.

And the fucking scar on his face, a clean, brutal gash across his cheek, just below the eye. He always hid it with his tailored perfection. Now, it made him look less like the devil in thousand-dollar suits and more like an angel punished for loving too recklessly.

I looked away. God, I looked away because his gaze was too much to hold.

My cheeks flushed with memory of last night.

"Don't act shy now, Dolcezza," he murmured with that

familiar venom-sweet drawl. "You've had me inside you more times than I can count. And I've heard you beg for it, remember?"

He tilted his head, mouth twitching like a wolf half-amused. "No need to blush over seeing your husband half-naked."

I said nothing. My spine stiffened, and my eyes burned and focused on something else entirely. Two shotguns behind him. On a stool. And there were some linen cloth and oil.

He turned and crouched by a wooden bench and began cleaning the guns. Slowly and methodically. Like violence calmed him more than prayer.

To be honest, he was hard to read.

His back arched, muscles flexed, and I swallowed, watching his bruised knuckles, tensed shoulders, and I hated how my eyes drank it all in like a sacrament.

"Why?" I finally said. "Why are you out here playing with guns while I rot inside your gilded hell?"

He didn't look up. Didn't even bother to regard me.

"Peace looks different to everyone, Dolcezza."

My breath caught. The way he said it. Like he meant it, and I strangely felt it deep in my bones.

"You said I'd see her. My mother."

That made him pause. The silence was loaded like the gun in his hand. He finally looked up, cold or resigned.

"You will."

"When?"

He stood abruptly. And I instinctively took a step back. "When you're ready."

"I am ready."

"No, you're not." His voice turned steel. "You're still breakable. I saw it last night and she... won't be what you expect."

"You don't get to decide what I can handle!" I snapped, stepping toward him. The wind howled louder.

"I'm not deciding. I'm protecting you."

"From what? Yourself? I don't need your protection, Zagreus. I need the fucking truth."

He stepped in closer. Shotguns were tossed onto the bench, and now he was inches from me.

"No," he growled. "You need someone to blame for your tears and ache. And I'll be that. I'll be the villain. But I won't let you meet her until I decide that."

My hands trembled. "I'm not weak. I can handle her."

It came out as a whisper rather than a statement. He looked at me as if I had just proven his point. And then, like a man undoing centuries of restraint, he grabbed me by the waist and pulled me to his chest. My palms found his naked chest, and I looked up at him wide-eyed. His hand gripped my jaw, the other buried in my waist, and he was so tall my neck strained.

"Ask me for anything, Dolcezza," he murmured, so close his breath danced over my lips. "Jewels? I'll pour oceans of diamonds at your feet. You want silk dresses? I'll drape you in sin and satin. You want stars? I'll pluck them from the sky and make them beg to orbit you."

His thumb dragged across my bottom lip, slow and dirty.

"But don't ask me for the truth. You'll choke on it."

My breath hitched.

He tilted his head, eyes flicking down to my mouth with a hunger that was both reverent and ravenous.

"You think you're ready to bleed with answers? You flinch when I breathe too close." His voice dipped lower, filthier. "Your body betrays you, little wife. You say you hate me, while your thighs clench when I touch you. You want the truth?" His hand splayed across my spine, dragging me flush against him. I could feel him. All of him.

He leaned closer, lips brushing the shell of my ear.

"The truth is... I dream about ruining you. Slowly. Thoroughly. In every way your precious little soul thinks it can survive."

My heart stuttered.

His mouth ghosted down my cheek, not kissing but branding.

"I'll be the villain in every fairy tale you were ever told, if it means I get to keep you breathing. I'll lie, I'll cage, I'll withhold. But I won't let you break just to satisfy your curiosity."

I swallowed hard. My legs trembled.

"And until I say you're ready... You don't get to see her." His lips finally pressed to mine. A threat. A promise. A vow sealed in heat and silence.

"Ask for anything else, Dolcezza," he whispered. "But don't ask me to let you burn before I've even taught you how to rise from ash."

I panted and shook my head. "Anything, you say?"

His eyes twitched and I realised he regretted saying anything, because what I was about to say would make him regret everything. But for some reason, he licked his lips, bit them, and caressed my cheek. "Anything."

I took a deep breath, swallowed, and opened my mouth. "Then let me paint again."

CHAPTER THIRTY-EIGHT
Wounds That Don't Bleed

He stared at me.

There was nothing pure in his eyes. He never stared at me like a man staring at a woman, but like a god staring at something he created in a fit of rage and then couldn't stop worshipping—that kind of stillness, that kind of thunderous silence.

The air around us stiffened, coiled like a predator in waiting. I shifted my weight, unsure whether to speak or scream. But Zagreus didn't blink or breathe. His eyes did the talking.

His gaze held me hostage in ways the gilded mansion never could.

There was no kindness in that stare. Just possession and certainty. That unbearable intimacy of a man memorised every inch of my weakness, and was now quietly daring me to try and run.

I turned slightly, as if to walk away. As if to escape that unbearable stillness burning through my skin.

But I felt it.

That slow step forward. That low hum of power. Several

thunderbolts ran down my spine as his two fingers traced the edge of my wrist with such devastating gentleness, as if I were made of silk he didn't yet deserve to tear.

"You tremble," he murmured, voice dipped in warmth that should've been outlawed.

I didn't reply. I didn't trust my voice. My throat had sealed itself in shame and something far more dangerous... its desire.

His hand slid up my arm, leaving behind heat and holy dread. Stopping at the crook of my elbow, where the pulse betrayed me the loudest.

"Stay with me."

My heart thudded.

"I didn't run," I whispered.

He leaned in, forehead almost brushing mine. 'But you want to."

My silence was confirmation enough.

"Then don't," he said. "Don't run. Don't try. Don't even think of leaving me, Dolcezza."

"And if I say no?" I asked, chin tilting in defiance that barely masked my shiver.

A long pause, then a cruel, slow smile graced his lips. "Then I'll have to make you say yes."

My breath caught.

"But," he added, tone light as velvet yet tight like rope, "if you promise not to run, I'll let you paint again... I'll reward you."

My eyes snapped to him. "With what?"

"Anything."

He released me then. Wiped his hands and chest with a linen towel. Methodically and unhurried, as if time bent to his will.

I watched as he lifted the gun he had been cleaning earlier and held it toward me.

"Do you know how to use it?"

I blinked. The steel looked colder than the sea.

"No," I whispered, throat dry, fingers curling slightly.

He stepped behind me, heat radiating off his body, licking at my frozen skin. His palm found my waist, and the breath knocked out of me as he pulled me back against his chest.

"You'll learn," he murmured.

I shuddered.

His hands wrapped around mine, positioning my fingers along the barrel, the stock, the trigger. Every touch was a symphony of restraint, instructive but laced with obscenity.

"Relax your shoulders," he said into the shell of my ear, breath hot. "It's not going to bite you."

"I'm not good with... weapons."

He chuckled lowly. "You've been living with one, little wife."

My heart stumbled. My body remembered every time he touched me like prayer and punishment.

"Hold it steady," he said, adjusting my grip against. My fingers twitched on the trigger the moment his lips found the back of my neck, a single, searing kiss that made my knees falter and breath abandon me.

"Now," he whispered. "Shoot."

I did.

The bullet kissed the sea with a scream, and I felt the recoil jolt through me; or maybe it was just him, the gravity of his body at my back, the hands still wrapped around mine, mouth dragging down to the base of my neck as if the echo of the gunshot had awakened something primal in him.

My breathing was ragged.

The heat of his naked chest against my back did something to me.

It was something hidden and buried that suddenly needed

to be unleashed.

I dropped the gun.

It clattered against the wood.

I turned, my hands found his chest, still bare and warm. I looked up at him, lips parted in a gasp I hadn't fully taken yet. And I kissed him. It was instinctive and sudden. It shocked me too.

I felt like I'd implode if I didn't kiss him.

At first, he didn't move.

As if shocked or unsure or resisting something monstrous inside him.

Then I reached higher, tiptoed to deepen the kiss, fisting his hair, and that's when I felt him growl. From his chest. From his gut. From hell.

He crushed me to him, hands gripped my hips, sliding down and pulling me up, hoisting me slightly so our mouths could crash together with rawer, messier precision. His tongue traced the outline of my lower lip before plunging in like he'd waited centuries.

My hands clutched his shoulder, nails digging in, and he didn't stop. He only deepened it. Kissing me and devouring me.

I let him.

Because whatever cage this was, it had started to feel like mine too.

∞

There are things a woman should never forgive. But the body, traitorous and trembling, often kneels before the very hands that broke her.

I kissed him.

I kissed Zagreus Vitale like he was mine to kiss, like I hadn't wept for days in the corner of his mansion, like he hadn't pulled me from the wreckage of my own life only to reassemble me with shackles. Like he hadn't murdered Adrian with the same hands that now held me.

I kissed him.

And now I stood alone, barefoot in a room filled with everything I thought I wanted, and none of it made sense anymore.

In less than an hour. He fulfilled my wish.

There they were.

The brushes I had begged for laid out, and the canvases, tall, white, blank like fresh tombstones waiting to be ruined by memory. And the colours.

God, those colours. So many hues I used to worship. Ochres and oxblood. Azure and burnt sienna. Crimson that reminded me of bleeding knees and berry-stained summers. Viridian which once mimicked Adrian's laugh in a garden. I used to know these colours intimately. I knew how they breathed on canvas, how they bled into one another, how they told stories my mouth never dared to speak.

But now?

Now they stared back at me like strangers I had once danced with, but no longer remembered the rhythm.

I sat on the stool; it creaked beneath my weight.

My hands shook as I picked up the brush. The bristles felt too soft. My skin felt too raw. I touched the palette, dipped it in blue, watched it pool into the well of white like it was trying to become something truer. But it didn't matter.

I was colourless.

I was muted.

A ghost of a girl who used to feel too much and now begged to feel nothing at all.

What was happening to me?

God, what had I become?

I kissed him.

I kissed him.

I kissed the man who killed Adrian.

Tell me again, lord. Remind me why I hated him. Please.

Because somewhere between the sea air and the weight of his hands and the tremble he chased down my spine, I forgot. Somewhere between the gunshot and the way his mouth devoured mine, I lost the thread of rage I had been weaving for weeks into a noose around my own hope.

He murdered Adrian.

There. That's the truth.

He shot him. Took his life. Erased him from every day I was meant to live with him. Zagreus Vitale rewrote the entire second half of my life, his violence, and handed it to me as a forced marriage.

So what, then? What reason, what possible reason, could outshine that fact?

The fact that he ruined me?

The fact that I never chose this?

The fact that every breath I took under this roof tasted like my own funeral?

The fact that I was his wife, not by love, not by faith or accident, but by force?

There was no reason. There couldn't be.

And yet… when his lips found mine, something ancient inside me stirred. Something that should've stayed dead.

It wasn't love.

It wasn't forgiveness.

It wasn't even desire in the way women often understood it.

It was recognition.

Of pain.

Of loneliness.

Of a mirror I never wanted but now couldn't look away from.

Maybe it wasn't that I wanted him.

Maybe it was that I wanted to want anything at all.

Because for days now, I'd been drifting in this house. Eating food I couldn't taste. Sleeping in sheets that smelt like him but offered no warmth. Staring at the door that never opened. Breathing in a world that no longer had oxygen.

Maybe I kissed him because he was the only thing real in my world.

And that terrified me.

I looked at the canvas again, still blank and waiting and pure.

My fingers hovered above it. The brush was weightless.

Could a woman paint without colour?

Could I speak in this new language of grief?

Could I still make something after everything was taken from me?

I dipped the brush into crimson. It bled like a wound. The first stroke trembled. It didn't look like anything. But it was there.

A beginning.

Or ending.

I didn't know.

A monster had given me back the one thing no one else could, the desire to feel something again.

Even if it meant bleeding across every canvas until I remembered who I was before he put a ring on my fingers and a bruise on my soul.

CHAPTER THIRTY-NINE
The Art of Unbecoming

I ruined everything.

Not intentionally, or violently, but quietly. Festering rot of inability.

I had sat here for hours – maybe more, I didn't recall – surrounded by the tools that once bowed to my fingers. And yet, all I created was a goddamn mess. A chaos of colours with no voice. A battlefield of bleeding hues, and none of them brave enough to mean anything.

My knees ached from kneeling on the hardwood. My pulse trembled with the sticky guilt of wasted paint. And my throat... was thick with grief that didn't sob. It curdled.

I stared at the canvas before me. No, wreckage of one. I tried. God, I tried. Dipped the brush, stroked the white, dragged colour after colour, and nothing came of it. No faces. No story. No ache poured onto the surface.

Just noises in my head.

Blues crashing into reds that looked more like bile than passion. A slash of ochre that meant nothing to me anymore. Smudges of viridian that taunted me with memories of Adrian's laughter. It all stared back at me like strangers. And I? I felt like a fraud sitting among them.

I once sold a painting for twenty thousand dollars. I remembered the number because it made me vomit. Not from joy, however, but from the terrifying truth that I was no longer anonymous. I was wanted. Coveted and feared me.

And now? Now I couldn't even paint a single thing without hating every second of it.

I was weak.

Pathetic.

A husk of a woman who once made colours weep on command. I used to paint with pain, and people called it genius. Now, all I had was pain, and it just made me still. Silenced and useless.

My fingers tightened around the edge of the canvas. And then something inside me snapped.

I tore the canvas in half.

The sound of it tore through the silence along with my frustrated grunts. My breath caught in my throat. With all the fury and shame and self-hatred I could muster, I threw it all at the door.

The moment it hit wood, the door opened.

And there she stood.

Elena.

Her expressions didn't flinch. But I saw it. That small flicker of surprise. The tray in her hand trembled only slightly. On it, a tall glass of orange juice and perfectly sliced fruits.

Of course.

Everything here was perfect, except me.

I wiped my face. I refused to let her see the tears, even if they were still drying on my cheeks.

"I'll clean it," I muttered.

Elena stepped forward, calm as always. She set the tray

down, watching me without judgment. Or maybe she did judge me. But she did it in silence.

"Master awaits you in his study," she said softly.

My jaw clenched. I hated the way she said master, like I belonged to him. Like this was normal. Like I hadn't desecrated a piece of myself in this room.

I didn't answer. I just gathered the broken wood and mangled fabric. Hands stinging with splinters. My soul felt splintered, too.

Elena waited a few seconds longer, then added. "You should freshen up."

I glared at her. Briefly. With the kind of contempt that had no real target. She was just doing her job. And I? I was the girl who couldn't even do what she was born for.

∞

The bathroom mirror was cruel.

It showed me a woman stained with colour she didn't understand. Blue on her collarbone. Crimson down her forearm. Green smeared across her throat like ivy trying to strangle her.

I cleaned myself slowly. Methodically. Trying to erase evidence of who I'd become. I scrubbed the dried paint from my neck, my chest, and under my nails until my skin reddened and stung. But nothing worked. I was stained beneath the skin now.

I changed.

One of the dresses he'd brought. Of course it was revealing. Dark red. Silky. I was trying to do neither. But I wore it anyway.

Like a prisoner in uniform.

I didn't touch the fruits or the juice. I didn't deserve the softness.

I stormed down the hall, my feet silent against marble. Fury tucked behind every controlled breath. I didn't wait for

Elena. I didn't even knock.

I pushed the door open and froze.

There were three people in the room.

Two women. And one man.

The man I recognised. The lawyer who brought the wedding papers. Sleazy smile, expensive watch, and looking uncomfortable for some reason.

But the women?

One was young, too young to be here. Slender, stylish, and lips painted the shade of coral.

The other... she was older. Beautiful in a quiet, aristocratic way, her features were sharp, but there was something so achingly familiar in the arch of her cheekbones. The shape of her mouth.

And then it hit me.

She looked like me.

Older. Hardened. And polished by the years I hadn't yet lived.

I stood awkwardly, breath caught in my chest. I opened my mouth to apologise and step back, but his voice stopped me.

"Come in."

Rough. Gravelly and absolute.

I lifted my head.

And saw him.

Zagreus Vitale, behind his mahogany desk like a monarch carved from dusk. Sleeves rolled up, revealing those forearms, tanned, veined, and marked by living. His powder blue shirt made his skin look darker, more severe. The scar on his cheek caught the light, and my insides churned for all the wrong reasons.

His eyes met mine. Grey. Smouldering and commanding. Daring me.

I got the message.
Behave. Or bleed.
So I did what I always did lately.
I obeyed.
I stepped inside. Quiet as winter and small as guilt.
But my heart was beating loudly in my ears.
Because something was happening in that room.
And I wasn't ready.

CHAPTER FORTY
Silence Talks

There was a chair waiting for me.

Of course there was. A silent throne with its back perfectly straight and its upholstery too pristine for someone like me to sit on. I hesitated briefly, but that second cost me the power. I felt it drain out of me.

"Sit," Zagreus commanded.

So I did.

My legs carried me forward with the grace of a condemned woman. I lowered myself onto the seat, back too stiff, knees too close together. My fingers found one another in my lap and began their ritual of nervous fidgeting.

Silence settled, the air shifted.

The older woman cleared her throat. "I'm Isadora," she said. Her voice was sharp but not unkind. "And this is my daughter, Leona."

Leona gave a small, polite nod. It looked like she didn't really care to be here. She was wearing a vintage dress, but with a modern touch, a deep neck, and flowing fabric, which made her breasts bounce out. Her long legs crossed, and the mini skirt she wore barely did anything to hide the pink underlining of her panties.

I averted my gaze from her display of body, realising I was wearing something similar.

Isadora, though, looked sophisticated and conservative. A beautiful shade of pink complemented her pale skin, and her eyes were a rich shade of brown.

Her eyes stayed fixated on mine. And I didn't know what to say except mumbling, "I'm Celestine."

She nodded.

Someone sighed, and I realised it was my husband, who pushed the chair back and rose. My breath hitched. I still recalled that I kissed him back. I could still feel his hands upon me, his lips upon me. And the impact he had left upon my soul.

I averted my eyes, looking anywhere but at him. Because I knew, the more I'd look, the more I'd hate myself.

But ignoring him didn't do me any good. I could feel him.

The floor beneath me seemed to brace itself as his steps cut through the air, measured and slow, as if a predator was circling its prey, it didn't intend to eat just yet. I didn't dare move, but my spine tightened with each sound of his polished shoes against marble.

The couch dipped beside me, and his hand was on me.

A broad palm cupped my waist, heat searing through the fabric of the red silk dress. His arm coiled around me in a quiet calm, anchoring me amidst this storm. He sat beside me, not on another chair, no, on the same one. Pressed close. Overbearing and possessive.

My breath caught, and my body froze.

The chair was made for one, but now it held two, and not equally. I was swallowed into his side, anchored by his body and heat. His fingers settled just beneath my ribs, thumb stroking the fabric slowly.

And strangely, I didn't feel claustrophobic anymore.

It was almost as if his touch calmed me.

"You should listen, Dolcezza," he murmured in my ear. "You're about to learn some truth."

I flinched at the intimacy.

Isadora didn't blink, as if this wasn't new to her. She waited, hands folded neatly in her lap. Dignified. Like a woman who knew how to survive humiliation without flinching.

Zagreus tilted his head slightly and said, "This woman... Isadora. She is your mother's sister."

I blinked.

"My mother doesn't have a sister."

The moment I said it, I knew it wasn't just a refusal. It was certain. A certainty I didn't know I had until it left my mouth.

Zagreus's grip on my waist tightened.

Isadora smiled, if you could call it that. It was a sad, bitter tilt of her lips that made her look older than she did a moment ago.

"Your mother would have preferred you believe that," she said softly.

"You're lying," I whispered.

"No," she said. "I'm telling you a story you were never allowed to hear."

"She never mentioned you. I didn't remember you," I shot back, shaking my head. "Not once. Not in any photo. Not in any letter. Nothing. You were never there."

"Because I was erased," she whispered, eyes gleaming. "Because I was the black sheep of the family. The disappointment. I married a man I wasn't supposed to, and your grandfather disowned me. We were close, once, your mother and I, before everything turned to ash."

I wanted to scream. To accuse her of delusion. But something held me back. Something in her tone. In the gravity of it.

"Then why don't I remember you?" I asked. "If you were family once, if you were real, why don't I remember anything?"

"Maybe there are more things you don't remember, Celestine."

My world paused.

My lungs forgot how to breathe.

Because something in me knew she wasn't lying.

I didn't remember my childhood clearly.

Just flashes. Scraps. My mother's perfume, jasmine and dust, a piano in the sunroom. A birthday with no candles, and Adrian.

Always Adrian.

He was the beginning of everything I remembered clearly. Four years of him and me. My memory began where he began, and before that? White noise.

Faded walls.

A child's drawing crumpled in a drawer.

I stared at Isadora.

She stared back.

"You're lying…" I whispered in disbelief.

"I wish I were."

"I don't believe you!"

"You don't have to," she said. "But the truth doesn't need your belief to exist."

Zagreus said nothing, even when my eyes burned and I held back my tears.

"Why now?" I whispered. "Why are you here now?"

Isadora's gaze softened. Her daughter was almost embarrassed.

"Because you're in danger," Isadora said.

And suddenly the room got colder.

The flames in the hearth seemed to dim.

Zagreus tensed beside me. I felt his hold tightening.

I turned to him, and then back to her. "From whom?"

"From the people who buried the first half of your life," she continued. "And from the man sitting next to you."

Zagreus let out a low breath, something between amusement and menace. "Careful, Isadora."

'I've been careful my whole life," she said. "And look where it got me."

My vision swam. I wanted to run and hide, but I did neither. I sat there, crushed into the side of the man who murdered the boy I loved, staring into the eyes of a woman who claimed to be blood. And for the very first time, I realised I didn't know where I came from.

Or who I really was.

Or what Zagreus Vitale had done to get me here.

But I knew one thing.

Something had been stolen from me.

And whatever it was, it had a heartbeat.

CHAPTER FORTY-ONE
Memory

"Your mother wasn't what she seemed," Isadora said. "You don't get to say that," I snapped, voice rising slightly. "You don't know her."

Isadora's gaze didn't shift, her hands remained folded in her lap, as calm as a nun before execution. "Don't I?"

"Don't talk about her like that," I hissed. "You show up after decades, after abandoning her, and now you want to play oracle?"

"I didn't abandon anyone. She abandoned you. She exiled me."

"I don't care! She raised me! She fed me, loved me, protected me…"

"From what?"

My mouth opened, but the answer never came. What had she protected me from? I remembered scraped knees and soup when I had a fever. I remembered her cold hands brushing my hair. But I didn't remember why we were always moving. Why did we never stay anywhere longer than a season? Why I never had friends. Why birthdays often felt like funerals until she remarried my father.

I remembered her love in fragments.

I remembered her fear in full.

"That's enough," Zagreus said.

Isadora turned to me slowly, expression unchanged. "You can't control what's coming, Celestine. You can't change the outcomes of your mother's doings."

"No," he said on my behalf. "But I can."

And that… sent a shiver down my spine.

She looked at me one last time. Her expression haunted, defeated, urgent.

"Remember our deal," Zagreus added.

Isadora nodded once. The lawyer stood, gesturing politely for her and Leona to follow. They did. The door closed behind them with a quiet finality, as if the truth itself had just been escorted out of the room along with them.

And I was left with him.

Breathing heavily. In disbelief and desperation.

"You are going to tell me what that meant," I said with broken voice. Because he was the only man who knew everything. He knew more about me than he knew about himself.

When he didn't say anything, I added with desperation. "Right now, please."

Zagreus leaned against the edge of his desk, the slow poise of a man who'd walked through centuries of storms and come out dry. "No."

My fingernails bit into my palms.

"Why not?" I demanded, stepping toward him. "Why do you always get to play god with my life? Why am I the only one left blind?"

His eyes flickered toward me, glinting steel and unreadable tempests.

"You're asking the wrong questions, Dolcezza."

I wanted to scream.

"What the fuck does that even mean?!"

He only smiled. That infuriating half-curve of a smile that always arrived before some cryptic truth, or kiss I didn't ask for.

So I threw something. A paperweight from the table. It shattered near his feet with a beautiful, delicate crash. But it didn't affect him one bit.

"Tell me what she meant," I growled. "What did Isadora mean about my mother? About me?"

"She was the shadow of your mother's sun. What do shadows know but the secrets the light hides?"

"You speak in riddles again. Tell me, please, Zagreus. I can't... I can't live like this... It's too much for me... It's messing with my head and I..."

"I speak in riddles because the truth would tear you limb from limb."

"I'd rather be torn than fed lies!"

Another object flew, this time a glass tumbler. He dodged it with an ease that made my rage burn hotter. My chest heaved faster and heavier.

In two swift strides, he was in front of me. Grabbing me by the wrists and pulling me to his hard chest.

"Enough," he growled. And I struggled. Writhed against his grip, chest heaving and breath shallow with fury and despair and need. The pressure on my chest grew unbearable, like my body didn't know how to contain the grief spiralling through it.

"Let go of me!" I spat, venom curling on my tongue. "You smug, sick, manipulative bastard, let go or I swear I'll..."

"You'll what?" he hissed, stepping closer, eyes dark with something perilous. "Curse me again? Bite the only hands keeping you from falling into the abyss? Go ahead, Celestine.

Prove to me you still have fire."

"I hate you."

He slammed me against the table. Books toppled, and my back met the cold wood. His hands braced beside my head, caging me in. The space between us disappeared.

"You don't get to hate me," he growled. "Not when you're still wearing my name on your finger. Not when you crave me more than you claim."

I opened my mouth to curse him, to tell him he didn't mean anything to me, but was quickly silenced by his mouth. Fierce, brutal, and desperate. Teeth clashed, lips bled. I bit him hard enough to taste the copper on my tongue, and he groaned into my mouth like I gave him pleasure. His hands gripped my waist, then my throat, then slid down to my hips.

I kissed him back because I didn't know how else to scream.

I let him kiss me because everything else had already been taken.

But when he pulled back to look at me, his breath ragged, eyes blown wide with want, I whispered the only thing I still knew to beg for. Vision blurry with tears, and chest heavy.

"Don't just fuck me," I choked. "Please… make love to me."

His jaw tensed. Something shifted in his eyes. "Dolcezza…"

"I need to forget," I whispered, trembling now. My hands gripped his shirt, anchoring myself to him like the edge of a cliff. "Please… make me forget everything… I can't take it… I can't…"

A sob broke loose. I hadn't meant for it. I hadn't meant to fall apart like that, not beneath him. But my body betrayed me, and so did my heart. Tears slid silently down my cheeks as I stared up at him.

231

"Make me forget," I repeated. "Even if it's just for to-night... please..."

His mouth met mine again, but slower this time. Less rage, more ruin. More reverence.

He kissed me as if he hated himself for needing me too deeply like someone who'd buried his love in a tomb and found it clawing its way back out.

"Say it again," he whispered against my lips.

"Make love to me."

His hands were slow and almost trembling when they slipped beneath my dress. His mouth left a trail down my neck, my collarbone, pausing at each place where pain had lived in silence. He didn't speak, he simply touched me.

I arched into him.

To feel something real when everything else felt like smoke and mirrors and half-buried lies.

My fingers tangled in his hair. My tears wet his shoulder. He kissed them on my cheeks like absolution.

And I prayed to the lord to let me find salvation, if I was considered eligible for it.

CHAPTER FORTY-TWO
Reaching Salvation

His hands were still on my neck. Firmly controlling. The way a storm pins a tree in place before it decides whether to uproot it. He was deracinating me in the same manner.

The edge of the table bit into my spine, cold wood searing through the thin barrier of fabric that was no longer entirely whole. My breath came in sharp, unsteady bursts; every exhale and inhale seemed to tangle in the fist he had buried in my hair.

I was shivering, though my skin burned.

Tears streaked down my face, carving black rivers through the ruins of my mascara. I didn't care how I looked, only how it felt to be held like this. To be broken open by someone who had studied the architecture of my defences long enough to know exactly where to strike.

He was my enigma.

"More," I choked out, though I couldn't name what I meant. More of what? I wanted to ask myself. More of who? I didn't know. "Hurt me. Destroy me. Don't stop until you've emptied every last piece of me…"

His eyes caught the light. If steel could burn, it would

burn like that. My tormentor didn't speak a word. He didn't need to. The air between us was enough. It'd been loaded for some time, and now it was detonating.

He moved against me like a never-ending war. Like every motion was a siege and every pause a test of whether I'd surrender or burn. My body answered before my mind could think. My voice cracked hymn to ruin.

I clung to him as though holding him tighter would make him crueller. I wanted cruelty. I wanted him to be the blade and me the skin. I wanted pain that rewrote me.

Relief hit me. Lighting splitting the tree open. My vision blurred, my body buckled, and I bit back a cry that still escaped, ragged and too human.

But in the same breath, he was gone.

Not gone entirely; his hands were still there, steadying me, but the war had stopped. The storm had passed. My body, still caught in the aftershock, searched for the rest of him, confused and empty.

I looked for him, and then at him. Lips parted to ask why, but he was already adjusting the cuffs of his shirt, fastening himself back into the pristine calm that always came after his tempests. His movements were deliberate, measured and maddening.

Before I could speak, he bent and swept my brokenness into his arms. I should have fought it, demanded answers, clawed at the silence, but my limbs betrayed me. He fucked me like a madman. Rearranged my guts. Sucked my soul.

My head found its place against his shoulder, and the scent of him seeped into my lungs like a drug I didn't want to recover from.

The room spun, not from dizziness, but from the whiplash of him; how he could strip me to bone and then cradle me as though I were the last holy thing in his keeping.

I closed my eyes. The world narrowed to his steady heartbeat beneath my ear, the faint rasp of his breath above my head. Somewhere between waking and the dark pull of sleep, I felt cool water against my skin, the ghost of his touch as he wiped away the evidence of my ruin.

Fabric whispered around me as he dressed me in something soft. My mind was too heavy to hold questions anymore. His warmth pressed against my back, the gravity of his arm securing me against his chest, staking a claim in my dreams as well as my waking life.

Just before I slipped under, his soft, low, and rough voice brushed my ear subtly.

"Sleep, Dolcezza. Your husband will chase away your demons."

I believed myself. But how would he chase away the demon I was most scared of? The demon wrapped his arms around me. The demon called me Dolcezza and called himself my husband.

∞

Darkness was never still in my dreams. It had never been ever since I met Zagreus Vitale. Or was it before that? Was I always doomed to darkness ever since forever?

It moved within me, breathed inside me. Pressed its palms over my eyes and whispered my name like a curse meant to be broken.

"Stina…"

A voice crooned in that darkness. My mother's voice. Lilting and slow. Haunting and melodical. Familiar and unfamiliar. "Sleep, Stina, sleep. You're safest when you don't open your eyes."

I tried to obey, but the dark kept pulling me backwards, through hallways smelling of smoke, through rooms with no walls, only shadows choking me. Somewhere, a door slammed again and again, the echo bleeding into my bones.

I was small in this dream. My knees bare. My feet were cold on a floor that seemed to pulse with a heartbeat rhythmic with my own. There was no furniture, only corners shifting when I looked away. And the faint scent of iron in the air.

"Where are you?" I asked, though I didn't know who I was speaking to. I was desperate. I wanted my mother. "Mama…"

"Shh…" she said again. But her voice was wrong this time. It wasn't warm like I used to feel. Or safe when the thunder roared outside. "If you're quiet, they won't find you, little Stina."

I wanted to ask her who she was talking about. But I couldn't comprehend anything.

My hands were wet, stinky, and my chest ached like I'd been running forever. In the distance, I heard footsteps. But I couldn't see anything. Only feel.

"Don't move," she warned. But her hand, when it touched mine, was ice. The sudden light from across her struck her bare face. The warm mocha eyes that used to comfort me stared at me blankly. I expected the welcoming features my mother always adorned.

Only it wasn't her face anymore. It was hollow. Skin stretched too tight over bones. Older and weaker. Her eyes were wide, soulless, and her pupils were gone. Her lips cracked as she smiled at me. "Sleep, Stina. Sleep forever."

My heart lurched as a gut-wrenching scream tore through my lips. Something grabbed my ankle, and I fell down, rolled over and over through nothing, through her voice still calling after me, and my screams. The smell of ash and something burning through the echo of my own cries.

Just when I felt like I was falling off a cliff, I woke up choking on air.

My eyes snapped open, and my chest tightened. It took me

several minutes to realise I was in a room; it wasn't dark. My heart jackhammered against my ribs, my nails digging crescent moons into my palms. My breath came in short, sharp bursts, and I was already screaming before I knew what I was saying.

Cold hands grabbed me, and my wails grew louder.

"No, no… get off… stop!"

Arms wrapped around me from behind. Iron-strong and warm for some reason. My body thrashed against them until the scent hit me. Cedar and smoke. Zagreus.

"Dolcezza, hey, hey… look at me." His voice was low but edged. As if he was standing too close to the cliff I rolled down from. His hand came to my jaw, turning my face toward him, but I couldn't stop trembling. My skin was clammy, and my hair a damp, tangled mess.

"I…" My throat closed. My chest hurt. "I don't…"

"You're safe," he whispered into my ear, forcing me to meet his stormy eyes. "It's me. Zagreus. You're safe. I'll keep you safe."

The word safe broke something in me. I collapsed forward into him, fists gripping his shirt so tightly I could hear the stitches strain. My sobs were violently messy and raw.

"I don't remember, Zagreus," I gasped against him. My voice was shaking so badly I barely recognised it. "Why don't I remember my childhood? Why don't I remember my mother?"

His arms tightened. "Dolcezza…"

"Don't… don't call me that unless you're going to tell me the truth." My nails scraped at his shoulders, desperate for an anchor. "Do you know? Do you know what happened to my mother? I don't know if what I know is true or not. It's killing me. I can't… I can't live like this. I can't live with the lies."

His eyes held something he had no intention of exposing me to.

"Yes," he said finally.

I froze. Everything tilted. My tears blurred him, but I could still feel the intensity of his gaze.

"Then tell me," I whispered. "Please. Please, Zagreus... I can't live with this fog in my head. I feel like I'm missing pieces of my own soul and..."

He shook his head, jaw tightening. "It's not time."

"I don't care about time..."

"You will." His rough voice cut through mine. "There are truths that don't free you, Celestine. They bury you like they buried me. And I will not hand you a shovel and watch you dig your own grave."

Celestine.

My sob caught in my throat, half-anger, half-grief. "You don't get to decide..."

"I do." He leaned closer, pulling me closer on his lap, pressing against mine. His breath was warm, steady, and deliberately heavy as if he was fighting something far darker than my darkness. "Because I promised someone I would keep you breathing. Even if you hate me for it."

I wanted to fight and scream. But my body betrayed me again, collapsing into the solid wall of him, letting his warmth bleed into my cold skin. His hand was in my hair, untangling the mess, stroking slow and sure as if he could smooth the nightmare out of me.

"I hate this," I whispered into his chest. "I hate not knowing."

"I know."

He didn't let go of me until my breath slowed and my sobs dulled to tremors. Even then, he kept one arm around me, his thumb tracing slow circles against my spine.

In the quiet, the words came back. Her words.

Sleep, Stina. Sleep forever.

CHAPTER FORTY-THREE
Purple Morning

I had started wearing silence. It was comforting, and something I could control.

It had been three days since Zagreus refused me the truth, and three days since I left my voice to rot quietly in my throat. It felt better that way. My words had curled up like dead petals of a dead flower. Littering the floor of a mind I no longer wanted to clean.

The morning unfolded with the same rituals. I awoke. Elena arrived without knocking; she never did, and swept into the room with a dress draped over her arms, a deep, rich purple today. Colours of mourning veils and royal coffins. I sat there obediently and vacantly, while she fused with zippers and fabrics, humming something light as though my life was not a mausoleum she visited daily.

I did not speak to Zagreus. Zagreus did not speak to me. He was less at home now, a phantom with a name only, spending his hours elsewhere, in a room I would never see. In a world I was not a part of with people who would never know my face.

I thought my silence did not touch him. It had all the weight of a moth's wing against his armour. I had stopped trying to measure my worth against his attention. I knew the answer already. I was a shadow painted on a wall he had long since stopped looking at.

He did care for me in his own twisted way. But it was not enough for me.

But the nightmares remained. They came and went. Clung to my damp clothes, dripping into my mornings, choking the air I breathed. I still woke screaming, still feeling the phantom cold of my mother's hand in my dreams. I no longer asked him for comfort, for answers, for anything.

I also tried to paint. Every day. Every hour and every second, I was alone. I desperately gripped the brushes, but all I birthed were corpses on canvases. Lifeless shade. Lines that trembled with my unsteady hands. Paint spilling like blood onto the floor. The sound of my sobbing mingling with the wet slap of ruined art. My heart tore a little more with each failed attempt.

I wanted salvation. I reached for it, clawed at it, prayed to it in the language of colours, but my hands came back empty every time. Eventually, I stopped reaching.

I was dead, both inside and out.

When the rage finally came, it was not volcanic. I slammed the edge of a canvas against the floor. Wanting to hurt the world in the way it had hurt me. The sharp thud rattled into the air. My fists followed, punching the marble until the sting burned my arms. I slammed my hand again, and a muted creak filled the air.

I froze, tears streaking my face in salty rivers, my breath shuddering. I pressed my palm flat to the spot. What was that sound? Marble did not creak.

That small, almost shy groan of movement beneath the

surface. I tested the other tiles around it; they were cold and hard. But this one… this one creaked.

My pulse began to pound with a rhythm that did not feel my own.

I staggered to my feet, wiping the mess from my cheeks with the back of my paint-stained hand. My gaze darted to the door. Elena could return any moment.

I found my painting spatula and wedged the metal bit into the hairline seam of the tile. My hands shook so violently that I almost dropped it. Ten minutes bled away in grunts and gasps, in fingernails scraping stone, until finally, the tile lifted.

Beneath it was darkness. And in that darkness, a small wooden box laced with dust. It looked like something meant to be forgotten.

I pulled it out. My hands were coated in powder, my lungs drinking in the musty scent of things that had not seen light in a decade. My heart rattled in its cage. What was this? Why would anyone put it here? Did Zagreus put it here?

The box was warm where my fingers gripped it.

I carried it to my vanity, locked the bedroom door, and sat.

It opened without a whisper of resistance. Inside were photographs. A smaller jewellery box. And the shock could choke a woman before she'd even drawn her next breath.

It did to me.

The first photograph was Zagreus. Younger by four, maybe five years. Black tuxedo, no scar cutting across his features. The scar I traced in the dark so many times was absent. He was… lighter, not smiling, but there was a curve at the corner of his lips that suggested something dangerously close to joy. His arm was wrapped around a woman in a white wedding dress. Her face had been scratched out; not blurred, not torn but violently erased.

I turned the picture over in my hands, the dust smearing

across my fingertips.

Two more photographs. The first was an ultrasound of a foetus. And the second was Zagreus again. Shirtless, laughing at the camera, his head thrown back, the picture catching him in that fleeting, dangerous moment where men forget they are men and become simply human.

My hands trembled so violently that the images almost slipped from my grasp. I set them down before I could damage them, my breath slicing the air in uneven shards.

The jewellery box was velvety, and my fingers brushed over its surface as though I were touching something sacred and forbidden.

Inside lay a diamond ring.

The initial engraved inside was C.

The truth fell on me like a world collapsing.

Zagreus had been married.

Before me, before the day he forced ne into vows I had never chosen. He had loved... or at least bound himself... to another woman. A woman who had worn white beside him. A woman who had carried his child, or the possibility of it.

I could not move. My breath was gone.

My world was not mine. Perhaps it never had been.

And for the first time, I wondered if I was not a wife at all, but simply the ghost who had been stitched into the dress of another woman's life.

CHAPTER FORTY-FOUR
What I Cannot Unknow

I thought grief was more than screams and whispers, a soundless convulsion in the marrow, gnawing through silences and leaving its bones rattling inside your chest. It was not always death that birthed it; sometimes it was discovery. A photograph. A ring. Or a box in the floor where marble ought to be eternal.

My hands still trembled, raw with dust and paint, and something fouler... the stickiness of truth half-swallowed. The images seared into my skull would not leave me. Zagreus, younger, lighter, and unscarred. I did not know why looking at his scarless face disgusted me more than his scars.

He was laughing.... With a faceless woman, promised in white, pressed against him. One he loved.

I told myself I had misread, misseen, misremembered. But no... the evidence sat too real in my lap. I had been an interloper in a life already written. A counterfeit bride stitched into another woman's veil.

I didn't even know it affected me so much. It shouldn't matter. I shouldn't care. Why the fuck did I give a damn if he was married or not? I didn't love him. I didn't love him at all.

I scrambled. The box was clutched to my chest like a life-line and a curse. My fingers fumbled frantically as dust streaked my knuckles when I pressed the panel down, my heart hammering a drumbeat loud enough to summon ghosts. I wiped my face with the heel of my palm, smudging tears into grey shadows, grabbed a brush, and sat before the blank canvas. Pretending I didn't hear the footsteps outside.

Just as I wiped the tears, the door opened with a click. And I quickly felt his presence. It was diabolical how he was here when I didn't want him to be here.

I knew before I lifted my eyes that he was not himself. Because he hadn't visited me these last three days. Avoided me, if I put it in female language. So, his untimely arrival was odd. I lifted my eyes slightly, catching the sight of his tie hanging undone around his throat like a noose loosened at last. His storm-grey eyes were hooded, glazed down with something darker than fatigue. Lust. Wine. The scar on his face looked sharper beneath the dim light, crueller, as though it had deepened in my absence.

My heart clenched. My gaze fled, and I bent my head to the brush in my hand as if colours could shield me from him.

The sound of his shoes softened as he crossed the room. Then a pause. My body knew before my mind did. I felt the heat of him at my back. A shadow folded over me, and he crouched, lowering himself until I could feel his breath stir the stray strands of hair against my temple.

"Dolcezza…" he purred, softened by intoxication, almost childish as his arms wrapped and slipped around me, and in one sudden pull and a gasp, I was lifted and rearranged onto his lap.

I stiffened. My limbs screamed to resist, but my body betrayed me, sagging into him as though I were stitched from the same fabric as his need. He buried his face against my neck, murmuring against my skin. "I missed you."

My throat closed. I swallowed the knife of my anger. "Where were you?"

His chest rose against my back; he was breathing slow, inhaling whatever I had to offer. "Out."

"Out," I repeated with a scoff. My nails dug into my palm, carving half-moons. "Out where? Business or…" I let my words falter because I wanted to know where he was. With whom? Was there a woman? Or was it just my imagination? It shouldn't matter, but why was I so restless? "Or was it someone else?"

He stilled. A silence before it breaks. His face lifted from my shoulder, and when I dared glance sideways, his expression was nonchalant, stoic, almost cruel in its refusal to be moved.

"Do you want me to lie?"

I shook my head, tears dancing in my eyes as my heart buckled beneath the weight of it. "Why lie? Is it that easy for you to lie every time?"

"Because lies don't hurt you." As if lies wouldn't hurt?

My mind clawed at words but found only jagged questions, and I turned around subtly, masking my tears.

"Why did you marry me, Zagreus?" My voice cracked as I tried to gather myself. "Why did you kill Adrian? Why do you know more about me than I know about myself?"

He shifted, pulling me tighter against him. His body was heavy and suffocating around mine. His half-lidded eyes burned and met mine. "Dolcezza…" Trembling lips ghosted the shell of my ear as if he was trying to gather himself too. "I decide what belongs to me. And I keep it. Whether you beg, bleed, or burn. All of you is mine. And I'm yours."

I didn't believe him. The photographs I saw said something else. He was married prior to me, and that burned something in me. I was ash, I was fire, and moreover, I was just air. Invisible and everywhere. He wouldn't care about me. Why would he? I was just another woman, but he was the only man I let claim me. I was his claim. His dark claim.

My throat trembled, but I pressed on. Rage clawing through despair. Anger was something I couldn't control. I felt like losing myself entirely. There was so much going on and I had no idea where I was, or what I truly was. Everything felt like a lie and I wondered if I was ever real.

Being done with my emotions, I swallowed hard. "Have you ever... loved someone, Zagreus? Ever... ever once felt something that wasn't ownership, wasn't this endless cycle of ruin you drag me through?"

Something shifted, and I felt it in my bones. I slightly turned my head only to find his jaw clenched tight and breath hissed between his teeth. His eyes flickered, stormy greys turned into pits of darkness. Guilt, anger, despair, frustration, loss... and gain.

But the emotions disappeared as soon as they came, and his hold tightened painfully. "Don't do this."

I hissed through the discomfort. But I could not stop. I wanted to wound him, to dig until he bled. To pull out the buried box and make him watch those photos. "You don't deserve love, anyway. Never will. And I hope... god, I hope..." I swallowed the tears as I held his gaze. "I hope you never get that person, Zagreus. I hope they tear free from your grasp and leave you rotting with the truth of what you are."

The storm broke. His calm shattered, rage lighting the hollow spaces of his face. His hands tightened around me as he turned me to face him, and his eyes reflected raw and shuddering pain, burning against fury that could gut a world.

He gripped me hard enough that I gasped, his voice ragged, almost breaking, and furious. "Don't."

But I already had. I realised I had never been closer to his heart, or to my ruin.

I was never afraid of storms, though. Maybe I never encountered them. But the one in front of me was deadlier than any. And I was foolish enough to stand at the centre of him.

He reduced my world to him only. But I wouldn't let him have his way with my thoughts and head. So, I did the only thing I was capable of. I pushed him. And surprisingly, with him intoxicated, I easily pulled away from his grip and crawled away from him to the door.

But like I said, I was foolish.

His hand shot out, rough fingers circled my ankle, and I was dragged back beneath him as the air punched out of my lungs in a startled gasp. My body betrayed me, part surrender, part resistance.

"I don't deserve love?" he snarled, his breath hot and whiskey-laced. "You're my fucking wife, Celestine." His Italian accent was as thick as smoke and curled around vowels. This was the first time he ever called me by my name. "You belong to me. Your love belongs to me."

I wanted to spit at him, to claw my way free, but his grip on my jaw left me trapped, his calloused fingers digging crescents into my soft skin. Anger flared in me, but beneath it, treacherous warmth ignited. The warmth of recognition of his touch, of being held captive by his gaze, even in cruelty.

"Stop this fucking nonsense." I twisted in his hold, but he wouldn't budge. He pressed his body unapologetically closer.

"Stop this fucking nonsense, huh?" he snarled. "This is not nonsense. This is my way of claiming you. You hate me, don't you? You'll hate me more today."

I hated him for it, hated him because some part of me did want it. My chest burned with humiliation of my own heartbeat.

"You don't own me," I spat. "You can't claim what I don't give."

Something dangerous flickered in his eyes. He swallowed the fury. He slammed me closer, his forehead brushing mine as his lips trembled with words unspoken before he crushed them out.

"You are mine, Dolcezza, in every way. I'll never.." his voice cracked imperceptibly, "…let anyone tear you from me. Even if I have to chain you to my shadow."

Who would tell him his words were chains themselves? That he was terrifying, suffocating, and my anchor.

His hands gripped my hips, bruising and forcing me against him until every inch of me was mapped by his violence. My mind screamed resistance, but my body betrayed me.

Shivers raced under his touch. I wondered if he could feel that too. If he was feeling me too.

My breath caught as he licked his lips, and there was no tenderness in them. Just hunger, frustration, a desperation he didn't have language for.

There was no religion that could save me now, and I realised that the moment he leaned down and his lips devoured mine in a kiss too brutal to be called a kiss.

I closed my eyes and opened my mouth, inviting him in, and simultaneously, my eyes shed tears. What was I doing? It was not lucid. But did it even matter?

I was beyond the point of rationalism. Beyond the cogency. Beyond sanity. He groaned into my mouth and I bit his lips hard, drawing out blood, tasting it on my tongue, but he didn't pull away. If anything, the bulge between his legs grew bigger.

"You think I don't know how to love?" he growled against my mouth. "I only know how to ruin, how to burn. And still…" his voice softened, painfully human for a fraction of a second, "… still, I would burn the world just to keep you warm."

My nails dragged down his arms. "You're pathetic," I whispered. "You call this love? You only know how to cage what terrifies you. Admit it, Zagreus. I terrify you."

He chuckled as his hand slid into my hair, yanking my head back, forcing my eyes to the mirror as he pressed me against the cold floor. My reflection stared back. Wild-eyed, torn between fury and darkness, something shamefully hungry.

"Look at you," he breathed, manhandling me to stand, and his arms found my waist. His thumb brushed my lower lip before he bit his own. "You hate me, don't you? Hate me all you want. But don't you dare look away. You'll remember this, every breath and mark I give you."

"Say it," he demanded. "Say you're mine."

I swallowed, my reflection fractured in the mirror, and my heart thundered with every question I never wanted answered. Was it madness to crave the very thing I despised? Was it sickness to find beauty in the hands that shackled me?

My lips parted. "I am not yours…" I breathed out.

He shook his head in disbelief. "You're very stubborn. Don't worry, I'll fuck the resistance out of you and by the end of this night, either you'll forget your own name or… become mine."

He grabbed a fistful of my hair, yanking my head back as he dragged me towards the full-length mirror in the corner of the room. With his other hand, he tore at my clothes, crystals flying everywhere as he exposed my soft, creamy skin to the cool air.

"Watch, Dolcezza," he demanded, voice a low, dangerous growl. "Watch as I claim what's mine. Watch as I fucking ruin you for yourself."

He shoved me against the mirror, the cold glass a stark contrast to the heat of my skin. His hands roamed my body, squeezing, kneading, leaving bruises in their wake. He kicked my legs apart, spreading me open for him.

Zagreus undid his belt and pants, freeing his large, thick cock. It jutted out, hard and angry, the tip flushing a deep, angry red. He stroked himself once, twice, before gripping my hips hard enough to leave marks.

With one brutal thrust, he slammed into me, burying himself to the hilt. He didn't give me time to adjust, just started fucking me hard and fast, the obscene sound of skin slapping against skin echoing in the room.

"Fuck, you're so goddamn tight," he snarled, hips pistoning in and out, his cock sliding in and out of my dripping womanhood as I moaned. "Watch, little wife. Watch as my cock moves in and out."

One hand snaked up to my throat, squeezing lightly, while the other reached down to rub at my clit, pinching and tugging the sensitive nub. He leaned down, biting at my neck hard, sucking a dark bruise into my skin.

"This cunt belongs to me," he growled, giving a particularly hard thrust. "This body belongs to me. You belong to me, you understand? Say you fucking get it. Say you're mine."

CHAPTER FORTY-FIVE
Husband and Wife

My body jolted with each savage thrust, my back slamming against the cold mirror as he took me with a ferocity that stole my breath. I watched, transfixed and horrified, as his hips pistoned in and out, his thick cock disappearing into my stretched, glistening folds only to emerge slick and throbbing.

Tears were streaming down my face. It was so rough, so cruel... but why did it feel... good?

His hand tightened around my throat, squeezing, as he leaned in to growl in my ear. "This is what you fucking wanted, isn't it, Dolcezza? To be used, to be claimed, to forget yourself?

I could only whimper in response, my nails scrabbling at his muscular forearms. He was everywhere, surrounding me, consuming me, until I couldn't tell where I ended and he began.

My tormentor chuckled darkly, a sinister sound that sent shivers down my spine. "Such a good little wife, taking her husband's cock so well. Watch how your greedy cunt swallows me, Dolcezza."

His other hand, slick with my arousal, pinched and tugged

at my clit, sending sparks of agonized bliss through my core. I clenched down around him, my inner walls fluttering and gripping his plundering cock.

"Fuck, you feel... ungh... so fucking good," he snarled, hips slamming into me harder, faster, the obscene sound of flesh meeting flesh filling the room. "Never forget this, wife. Never forget who you belong to."

My mind reeled, drowning in sensation, in the brutal, beautiful words dripping from his lips like dark honey.

I was losing myself... drowning in his touch, his scent, his all-consuming presence. He was ruining me, breaking me... and god help me, I thought I was starting to like it.

I met his gaze in the mirror, stormy grey eyes colliding with my tear-filled ones. In that moment, I saw the truth of his words, the dark, twisted love that drove him to claim me so ruthlessly.

It terrified me, thrilled me, broke me... and in that shattered moment, I felt a twisted sense of power.

"I'm yours..." I whispered, voice breaking on a sob as he hilted inside me, his pelvis grinding against my sensitive clit. "I'm yours, Zagreus. All yours."

The admission seemed to unleash something primal in him. He kissed me with a brutal, dominating press of lips that stole my breath and swallowed my cry. His tongue invaded my mouth, claiming every inch, conquering me utterly.

"That's right, little wife," he growled as he broke the kiss, lips brushing against mine. "You're mine. This body, this cunt, this soul... it's all fucking mine."

He punctuated his words with a series of sharp, brutal thrusts that had me seeing stars. I clung to him, nails digging into his shoulders, as he used me, took me.

"Never forget this, wife," he commanded, voice a dark, dangerous rumble. "Never forget how good it feels to be claimed, to be owned, to be... Zagreus Vitale's wife."

My mind shattered as my orgasm crashed over me like a tidal wave. I screamed, a sound of agony and ecstasy, as my cunt clamped down around him like a vice. He roared, a sound of triumph and dark satisfaction, as he slammed into me one last time and stilled.

We remained like that for what felt like an eternity, chests heaving, sweat-slicked skin pressed together, reflections locked in the mirror - a brutally beautiful portrait of a husband claiming his wife, a woman shattering in the face of his obsession.

Zagreus scooped my limp, satiated body into his strong arms, carrying me towards the opulent bathroom. He set me down gently in the large, sunken tub, the warm, scented water lapping at my skin like a lover's caress.

He stripped off his shirt, revealing the intricate tattoos that covered his muscular torso, before stepping into the tub behind me. The water sloshed as he settled, pulling me back to lean against his broad chest.

Large, calloused hands, still slightly unsteady from the vodka he'd consumed, began to wash me. They glided over my skin, soaping me up, rinsing away the evidence of their brutal fucking.

There were so many things in my head, but he just took them all. His touch was so lethal. And now I was tired and exhausted. Emotionally and physically.

"Shh, Dolcezza, let me take care of you," he murmured, voice a low, drunken rumble. His fingers lingered on my breasts, kneading the soft flesh, before pinching and rolling my nipples between them. "Such perfect little tits."

I whimpered, back arching as he teased my sensitive peaks. I could feel his cock, already hardening again, nudging against my lower back. He was insatiable, this husband of mine. Insatiable and possessive, always hungry for more.

One hand drifted lower, over my stomach, before cupping my mound possessively. "I want to breed you, Dolcezza. So fucking bad. I've never wanted anything but you," he growled, fingers delving between my folds, stroking my renewed arousal.

It must have been the alcohol, because Zagreus never voiced his wants and desires like this.

"And..." His voice dropped an octave, rougher, dirtier. "Every part of you. I want to claim it a thousand times."

I gasped as a finger, slick with soap and water, pressed against my puckered hole. I clenched instinctively, trying to keep him out, but he was relentless. He pushed in, breaching me, claiming my most intimate place.

"Such a tease, trying to deny your husband what's rightfully his," he scolded, finger pumping in and out of my virgin ass. His other hand came up, gripping my jaw, forcing me to meet his intense, drunken gaze. "Open your mouth, wife," he demanded in a low, dangerous growl. "Open it and take what's coming to you."

Before I could react, he was spinning me around, gripping my hair, and crashing his lips against mine in a brutal, dominating kiss. His tongue invaded my mouth, claiming it, conquering it, as his finger plunged deeper into my unwilling ass.

"No, please..." I whimpered as the invasion became painful.

I choked on his kiss, on his taste, as he fucked my mouth with his tongue and my ass with his finger. Tears sprang to my eyes as he took me, as he conquered me, as he made good on his promise to ruin me utterly.

He broke the kiss abruptly, both of us panting. His cock, rock hard and throbbing, nestled between my ass cheeks. I could feel it pulsing, twitching, as if eager to claim the last untouched part of me.

"Beg for it," he rasped, eyes blazing into mine. "Beg your husband to take your ass, to make it his. Beg me to ruin you completely."

His finger pumped faster, harder, stretching me, preparing me for his inevitable invasion. His other hand gripped the base of his cock, stroking it, teasing me with the promise of what's to come.

"Beg, wife," he growled, voice rough and demanding. "Beg me to fucking claim you."

My mind reeled, drowning in sensation, in the brutal, beautiful violation of my body and the dark, twisted pleasure it brings. I knew I should resist, should fight against this, but... god help me, I couldn't. I needed him to make me forget everything.

I opened my mouth, voice breaking on a sob. "It's…. itchy…."

With a sound of dark, male satisfaction, Zagreus removed his finger, gripping my hips hard enough to bruise. And then he was pushing forward, the thick head of his cock breaching my womanhood. "I won't hurt you. But I'll make this little hole mine."

CHAPTER FORTY-SIX
Pain and Lies

I woke up to the ache. Not in my chest, though that too was restless, thudding uneven, guilty for having betrayed itself, but lower, where my body still remembered him. I was aware too of his hands mapping out my body last night, sore in hollow places where he pressed himself into me. I hated the way it felt honestly, and I hated myself more for craving the honesty of his body when his mouth gave me nothing.

The sheets smelt of him, and yet he was gone.

I pulled the robe over my shoulders as if it could hide the shame stitched into my flesh, cinched the belt so tight I almost wanted to choke myself with it. I told myself repeatedly that this was the last time, the last lapse, and yet the lie cracked before it formed. My mind repeated questions and lies I believed in.

But what more did I expect?

Of course he'd leave. I was not the woman he loved. Not the one he considered human. I was just his toy, a doll he could play with whenever he wanted. Toy with my emotions, and leave me to fend for myself.

Who was I to him? Why did he keep me close yet never let me touch the marrow of his truth when he knew everything about me? Why did I feel as though I was living in a borrowed body, a stranger's shadow?

And the depth of my thoughts mocked me. My body hurt, but not half as much as the darkness where answers should have been.

I stepped into the corridor, adjusting the hooks of the long, partially sheer lingerie robe he probably left beside the bed, and found Elena polishing silver in the anteroom, her face serene as if she didn't care what was happening to me in this house.

"Where is he?" My throat pained as words left my mouth.

Elena slowly looked up and let her eyes take me in. If she was surprised seeing all the red marks all over my visible skin, she didn't show.

"Master had business. It was urgent, and he left before dawn."

Business.

"Elena," I pressed, folding my arms to keep them from trembling. "How long have you served him?"

Her eyes lifted. "Long enough to know he doesn't forgive easily."

"That isn't what I asked," I snapped, surprising even myself. Desperation slithered out of me. "What are you to him? A confidante? A keeper of his sins? You know him more than I do, don't you? Tell me, Elena, who is he really?"

There was a pause, and she inhaled sharply. "I'm just his servant."

The simplicity of her tone enraged me. "And before that? Before you became this shadow in his halls? Did he... did he love someone? Did someone leave him broken enough to carve that scar into his face?"

There was a tiniest flicker, and her hand froze on the silver tray. "The scar…" she said softly. "Came from his loved one."

"Loved one?" My pulse jumped. "Who? Who was she?"

Elena's lips tilted. "Sometimes, the truth is hidden not because it's cruel, but because it is too tender to survive your touch. You don't need to know everything, Mrs. Vitale. If he wanted you to know, he'd tell you himself."

The air left from my lungs, and I swallowed hard. "What does that mean? What truth?"

But Elena dipped her head. "Forgive me, Mrs. Vitale, I must prepare luncheon. The master expects several guests this afternoon. I suggest you also get ready. He wouldn't like seeing you roaming around wearing this."

I looked down at myself. The clothes I wore were indeed revealing, but I didn't care.

"Guests?" I frowned. "Who?"

"Important ones." That was all she gave me before she got up and swept away to the kitchen. Alone, I stood anchored by my own fury. If he thought I would wait for him to tell me something, he was wrong.

If there were answers, they would be buried in his study, where he never let anyone in.

I turned around, making sure Elena was busy cutting the vegetables. I had exactly three hours before the afternoon. If I was right, the guests would start coming by half past one. I had to get ready too. Give or take, two hours.

I jogged to his study barefoot and twisted the knob. It was open. Maybe it was his arrogance, or certainty, that I would never dare. I entered, took a deep breath, and avoided looking at the desk where he fucked me last time I was in here.

I rifled through drawers with my trembling hands. Rifling through sheaves of documents that gave me nothing but dust, transactions, letters to faceless names. In between the documents, my eyes landed on one with a very familiar name on it.

Celestine.

My heart raced as I pulled out the file with trembling hands. Swallowing hard, I flipped it open only to find several photos of me. In art exhibitions, with Adrian, and among my loved ones. There were several pictures of Grace, too, along with other colleagues. My heart stopped beating, and I read the words written over some pictures.

Mine.

Oh Lord....

How long had he been stalking me for? These pictures... I flipped one of them and my eyes widened. It was of me and Adrian, on a date, where he first gave me flowers. The white daisies. It was our first date.

Chills ran down my spine.

Four years. Four years ago, daisies clutched in my hands, Adrian smiling, my hair falling over my cheek, captured, frozen. Was he there that night? In the shadows of the street? In the crowd? Had he followed me home afterward?

Every memory I thought belonged to me suddenly felt poisoned.

How many times did I laugh, unguarded, thinking I was free?

How many times did I undress in my own room, believing the walls were mine alone?

The photos of Grace... why Grace? Was she collateral? A warning? Did he follow her too, the way he followed me? Was she in danger simply because she existed in my orbit?

My hands trembled so violently that the papers rattled, like bones clinking together. I wanted to drop them, burn them, rip them apart, but I couldn't stop looking. My face. My smile. My vulnerability lay bare in glossy ink.

Did he keep count of my steps, the cadence of my breath,

the way I tilted my head when listening? Did he watch me sleep?

I swallowed hard, bile rising in my throat. He had called me his. But what did that mean? Possession? Obsession? Protection twisted into something grotesque?

What else did he know? About Adrian? About my family? About every secret I thought was safely buried?

I hastily looked for more pictures. And to no surprise, I found my father's. Aunt Brenda. And Adrian's side of the family. Strangely, there were some bills attached to my father's picture.

Ten thousand dollars.

Fifty thousand dollars.

And a hand-written note.

Moved to Bulgaria to a private hospital.

The room spun and the walls seemed to close in. The study wasn't a room anymore, it was a shrine. A mausoleum of my life, dissected and catalogued by someone who had claimed me without my consent.

He moved my father somewhere else when all the while I kept thinking he was in Italy. Why was he taking care of him? Moved him to another private hospital and spent so much money on his treatment?

It didn't make sense. One minute he was ruining my life, hurting the people I loved, and the second he was... being this version of him I couldn't recognise.

And the most terrifying thought of all crept in, uninvited, ruthless: if he had been watching for four years, if he had always been there... What else had he done that I hadn't noticed yet?

Frustration rose like bile, and I quickly put the pictures back and tugged at my hair.

I needed to know more about him. Him, and not me. Where did he keep his past? Where did he keep the piece of himself? Obviously, it wouldn't be so easy to know about him, but I wouldn't stop even if death knocked at my door.

My eyes snapped to the bookshelf. The red room. He knew I wouldn't return after what I discovered there. And what could be a better place.

I got up on my shaky legs and shook as I pulled out the volume from the shelf. The mechanism sighed, and wood slid, stone groaned. And there it was, the hidden room.

I stepped into a cathedral of perversion. Restraints glimmered like cold jewellery, and the ankle I wore burned against my skin. I was suddenly reminded of it. There were leather whips, cuffs, sticks, and some perverted-looking toys.

I swallowed. My heart bruised itself against my ribs. This is not who I was. And yet I couldn't look away.

But I didn't have time for this. I needed to find something, to make me feel less insane.

CHAPTER FORTY-SEVEN
His Past or Mine

I told myself I would only look for a moment, only to quiet the noise inside my head. But twenty minutes passed with nothing but frustration. Drawers yielded dust, telling me he didn't use this room very much. I didn't know if I should be relieved or not. But the ledgers and books I could not decipher. I tore through the artefacts of his secrets until exhaustion claimed me, until my body sagged against the bed with the bitter taste of defeat.

Maybe I was looking in the wrong place. Or maybe he didn't leave any proof of his past anywhere in this mansion. Tired and defeated, I got up and looked around once again, finding nothing and was about to leave when my eyes landed on a half-hidden object, pushed behind the frame of an old mirror; a plain wooden box, unremarkable to the world. Yet before I touched it, my blood recoiled, as though my very bones knew what waited within. My fingers trembled, the hinge groaned open, and my world collapsed.

Photographs. More photos.

Not recent. Old. Older than the weather. Weather-worn,

fragile at the edges. A boy, solemn and sharp-featured, his eyes carrying shadows older than his years. And beside him, there was a girl. Brown haired, dark-eyed, and wearing a pastel blue dress, princess-style with a wide smile on her lips as she looked at the person clicking the photos. Mischief or tenderness painted on her face. But it was not her presence that struck me; it was his gaze.

The boy looked at her as if she were the only thing worth looking at.

He was taller than her by a few inches, wearing shorts and a matching shirt. I didn't have to investigate to know who that boy was. I could recognise those stormy-grey eyes even if I lost my memories.

Every photograph, every angle, his eyes were fixated on her, drowning in her. Love unhidden, devotion raw, as though his young bones had already been carved for her alone.

My throat closed. Air became heavy. Was this her... his first wife? The first and true one? His childhood love and his chosen soul? The one he loved dearly?

I pressed my palm against my mouth to keep from sobbing aloud. It was ridiculous, was it not? I had no right to this ache, to this hollowing pain. I was nothing but an interloper in his story, and still, my heart fractured.

Why did I care? He loved another. He was someone else's.

He was there. In those photos. Even younger, yes, but those storm-grey eyes had not changed. They were the same eyes that looked through me now, cutting, scorching, unravelling. Except here, in these frozen pieces of time, they weren't stormy at all. They were soft. Open. Alive with something terrifying in its purity... love.

Not lust. Not possession. Not hunger disguised as desire. Love.

The kind of love that swallows you whole and remakes

you from the inside out. The kind of love I had never tasted from him, not once, not even in those rare, fleeting moments when he held me like I mattered.

Did he whisper her name when the world was silent? Did he dream of her when I lay beside him, foolish enough to believe the weight of his arm meant anything? Did he keep me close because I reminded him of her, or because I was convenient enough to ruin without consequence?

I pressed my palm against my mouth to keep the sound inside, but the sob clawed anyway, desperate, relentless. My ribs ached from holding it in. My eyes burned, but I couldn't look away.

The way she leaned toward him. The way his gaze never wavered, as though she was gravity and he was helpless to resist her pull. The way time itself seemed to bow to them, as though the universe had chosen them long before I ever existed.

I was nothing but a trespasser. An intruder. A name written in the margins of a story that had already been told.

And yet, why did I care? Why did it feel like something inside me was tearing, splitting into jagged halves that could never be stitched back?

I had no right. No claim. He had never been mine to lose. And still, the hollowness spread, blooming wide and merciless in my chest.

Would he ever look at me like that? Would he ever breathe my name like a prayer instead of a command? Would he ever drown in me the way his boyish eyes drowned in her?

No. The answer was no. And I hated myself for asking.

I hated the jealousy burning through me, ugly and desperate. I hated the envy I felt for a girl I didn't know, a girl who had already been immortalized in his memories while I… What was I?

A fleeting distraction.

A shadow pressed against his walls.

A secret he could throw away whenever he pleased.

The photographs blurred as tears finally slid, hot and merciless down my cheeks. I wanted to tear them apart, to shred them until her smile was gone and his gaze erased. I wanted to destroy her, erase her existence from his story so there could be space left for me.

But even in that desire, the truth suffocated me.

He had already chosen once. And it hadn't been me.

I wiped my tears furiously, scolding myself, whispering foolish girl in my head. So very foolish. I pushed the photographs back into their coffin of wood and closed the lid as though it might silence the wound inside me too. I gathered myself, stood on my shaky legs and stared at the box.

Was this my end? Was I not... enough? But why did I want to be enough for him? He killed Adrian, so why?

I turned, desperate to escape before my shame drowned me completely and a scream escaped me instead.

All air left my lungs as I stumbled back and stared wide-eyed at the door.

Leaning casually against the frame, arms folded across his chest, dressed in a dark grey suit with a lighter shirt beneath. The scar bisected his expressions, hiding him as it always did. Making him unreadable. But the weight of his gaze, I felt it pierce straight through me.

My knees went weak. Words tumbled out. "I... I didn't mean to... I was just looking for... I got lost, I swear, I didn't know..."

He straightened. My pulse thundered.

"Are you satisfied?"

Silence cracked open between us. My lips trembled. "I.. I was searching for..."

"You were," he stepped closer and I took one back.

"You've been scratching at doors that were never meant for your world."

My mouth dried. "I didn't mean to pry."

I knew he'd punish me. How was he home so much sooner than I expected? Why didn't I hear his footsteps?

"You meant," he cut in. his tone was strangely calmer. "Do not insult me with your stammering."

Heat surged in my cheeks, shame curling my spine. I wanted to vanish into the floor, to erase the evidence of my trespass. "I was only curious…"

"Curiosity," he said, now close enough that I could smell the faint trace of sandalwood and steel on his suit, "is the first betrayal. You forget whose house you walk through. Whose silence feeds you. You think there are no consequences?"

I swallowed hard. "Will you punish me?"

His eyes narrowed. Before I could take a step back, he reached out, caught my wrist, and dragged me closer. My body crashed against the wall of his chest. My breath stuttered, his hand tilted my chin upward, forcing my eyes into his as his raked down my flimsy sheer robe.

"I should," he murmured as my breasts pressed against him, and the fabric faltered. His eyes caught the motion, and they darkened. "I should teach you what happens to those who dig where they do not belong."

Tears burned the corners of my eyes. I could not speak. His gaze held me captive, burning with something I could not decipher.

"But I won't."

His hands dropped away, leaving me weightless. The abrupt absence of his touch was worse than his grip. He stepped back, smoothed the front of his suit, and in the same measured tone said. "Get ready. My guests are here."

I didn't need to be told twice. I ran from there to our room, panting and sobbing. When I reached the room, I locked the door and stood alone in the middle of the room. Why hadn't he punished me? Why had he spared me, when cruelty would have been easier? The absence of wrath felt more terrifying than its presence.

My hands shook as I pressed them against my chest. Trying to hold myself together. Hyperventilation tore through me, and suddenly I couldn't breathe.

Why had he let me go? Why did mercy feel so much sharper than violence?

And why, despite everything I had seen, did the hollow ache in me only grow deeper?

CHAPTER FORTY-EIGHT
Selene

It is a terrible thing to dress oneself for strangers while the mind begins to unravel, as if I'd lose mine any moment. The mirror held no kindness whatsoever, only a fractured reflection of myself and a woman draped in a gown of deep crimson, her throat burdened with jewels that glimmered like small, merciless eyes. My hands shook when I fastened the necklace, they betrayed me when I reached for the anklet I wanted to take off. That cursed trinket clung more to my skin as though it was fused with my flesh. I tugged until the skin burned red, until my breath rasped short and shallow. Still it did not move, as if the metal knew something I didn't.

I laughed in disbelief. I was losing my mind, wasn't I?

My lungs tightened, air refusing to stay. For a heartbeat, I thought I might claw the dress off my body and run barefoot into the day.

But the knock on the door startled me. Dragged me back from wherever I was heading.

"Mrs. Vitale?" It was Elena.

I swallowed. "I'll be there in a minute." I hoped she heard

my voice because even to my own ears it sounded distant.

I heard footsteps retreating and took a deep breath. I needed to go downstairs. If not, someone would come again.

Gathering myself, though I wasn't sure if I was doing the right thing, I opened the door and headed to the stairs. I could already hear the soft violin music and chattering. I wondered how many people were there.

Just as I reached the stairs, my throat clogged. The hall was no longer a hall but a theatre where I was the main event. Murmurs clung to the air, laughter too brittle to be honest. Men with eyes like predators. Women adorned in silks that whispered of concealed arsenals. None of them was familiar, and yet... two faces sliced through the fog of unknowing.

Isadora. The woman who claimed to be my mother's sister. She stood in deep emerald satin, posture erect, smile unfaltering as though she owned not only the room but my very breath. And beside her, her daughter looked radiant, a polished and younger version of her mother, standing with a wine glass. Too perfect, so much so that it made me swallow hard. My blood recoiled as if it recognised her before my mind did.

Every step down the staircase felt heavier than the last. Their eyes clawed over me, weighing and measuring. Whispering to themselves. My arms folded over my chest. Suddenly feeling too exposed and uncomfortable.

Why was I even here? Why did he tell me this was happening? That there would be so many people?

I hated the thought that followed. Where was he? Zagreus. My reluctant anchor, my shadow and torment. My eyes hunted the crowd, desperate for the sharp outline of his presence. I despised myself for needing it.

The clink of glass startled me. And I looked to my left to see a man in his mid-twenties approaching me.

He lifted his glass and winked. "Well," he said, lips curving into a snake's smile. "If it isn't the dead."

My body stiffened as the room rippled with stifled laughter. I couldn't decipher anything. This place was too crowded. My mind caught the single word. Dead.

He stood taller than most, shoulders broad but not brutish, his frame honed, and his hair was dark, swept back with the casual arrogance of someone who knew he needn't try. A faint scar cut through his brow, lending him a charm that was as cruel as it was deliberate. And those eyes were filled with mischief and cunning, yet swept in something that smelled of rot, of secrets and burials of truths.

I forced my voice out. "What do you mean?"

He tilted his head, feigning innocence, his smile deepening. "Mean? I don't know. What did I mean, Selene?"

"I'm not Selene. My name is Celestine."

He chuckled at that. "Is it now?"

I swallowed. "Who…" my voice cracked, but I forced it to steady. "Who is Selene?"

"Don't you know?" he leaned closer, his breath warm against the rim of his glass. "Or did he never tell you?"

A silence fell between us, and the crowd leaned in, though pretended not to. My palms dampened, my pulse thundered against my ribs. My throat ached with the intensity of all those watching eyes.

I wanted to run. I wanted Zagreus to appear and rip this man apart. But all I had was the sound of his laughter echoing inside me.

Who was he? Who was this stranger who spoke my name, or not my name, but something close, something foreign to my tongue yet familiar in its rhythm, as if he were plucking threads from a tapestry I did not remember weaving?

"Who are you?" The words left me dry, sandpaper against the roof of my mouth, betraying my trembling hands even though I tried to steady them against the railing.

The man smiled. Not kindly, but it was a smile that did not stretch to the eyes, a predator's curve carved onto his lips, the kind of smile that made the air curdle in my lungs. His hair was dark, a lustre of coal under the candlelight, combed back too neatly to be trusted. His suit was severe, every line tailored to perfection, but it was his gaze, sharp, cutting, laced with mockery, that seemed to make me uncomfortable without touch.

"Who am I?" He tilted his glass, the amber liquid within it catching the light like trapped fire. "Maybe a friend." His voice was velvet, but woven through with barbs, as if each syllable was meant to pierce.

"I don't know you." My voice cracked. "And you... you called me..." My throat locked. "Selene."

His smile widened. "Did I?" He feigned thoughtfulness, sipping lazily from his glass, his eyes never leaving my face. "Perhaps it was a slip of the tongue. Or perhaps not. Names are peculiar things, don't you think, tesoro? They can be both prisons and keys."

The words crawled into my ears, lodging there like parasites. Prison. Key. Selene.

Who was Selene? Why did it feel as though the sound of it stirred something in me, something faint and buried, a whisper pressing against locked doors?

"You're mistaken," I forced out, clutching at the folds of my crimson dress, as though its fabric might ground me. "That is not my name."

"Ah," he said smoothly, stepping closer until the space between us shrank, the scent of his cologne wrapping itself around me. "Then what is your name? Celestine?" He said it with a kind of cruel emphasis, as though he were testing its shape on his tongue. "Do you even know?"

My stomach plunged. His words were not mere taunts;

they were needles, pulling at seams I did not even know existed within me.

"Why are you saying these things?" I whispered. My voice shook, desperate and defensive.

His grin widened, wicked, triumphant. "Because truth has a way of finding you, tesoro. You can bury it, you can smother it, but it does not die. It waits. And when it resurfaces, oh, it devours."

My knees weakened. I staggered back a step, every nerve screaming, every breath tangled in panic. "Stay away from me."

He chuckled, low and insidious, as if my fear delighted him. "Oh, but why would I? You're the most fascinating ghost I've ever seen. A woman is dead, yet breathing. A bride, yet not a wife. A name, yet not a self." His head tilted, his eyes glinting. "Tell me, do you bleed the same? Or did he strip even that from you?"

I froze, unable to breathe, the words splintering into me until I thought my bones would crack beneath them.

A shadow fell across me, taller, darker, heavier than any I had known. The stranger's smirk faltered for the barest fraction of a second, his eyes cutting past me.

"Step away from her."

Zagreus's voice. Low, lethal, the kind of tone that promised ruin. His presence consumed the room before my eyes even lifted to him. He moved through the crowd like a storm made flesh, every line of his frame coiled with restraint and fury. He did not look at me, but at the man before me, as though his entire being narrowed into one singular, merciless focus.

Strong arms wrapped around me before I could even react, pulling me flush against him. His cologne, dark and grounding, drowned out the stench of fear that had clung to me. The world shrank into the circle of his grip, and shame burned through me for how much I leaned into it—for how much I had longed for him to appear, to anchor me, to remind me I was not alone in this nightmare.

"Stay away from her." His words came again, sharpened steel now. His chin lifted slightly, his scar catching the light, his eyes burning with unspoken violence.

The stranger only smirked, unfazed, swirling his drink in lazy defiance. "Ah, Zagreus. Always so possessive." His eyes darted to me, wicked amusement dancing there. "But tell me… does she even know what she is to you? Or who she was?"

Zagreus's jaw flexed, a silent warning, a promise of blood. His grip on me tightened.

I couldn't breathe. Couldn't think. The walls closed in, the voices of the guests drowned into muffled static, and all I could hear was the echo of that name—Selene, Selene, Selene—hammering at the inside of my skull.

And I hated myself most of all for the tremor of relief that coursed through me at his touch, at his protection, even though I did not understand what I needed protection from.

CHAPTER FORTY-NINE
First Wife

Threats usually come with a sound, but Zagreus had learned to make them without any sound, taught by nights when silence had been the only currency that mattered. He did not raise his voice. He moved a fraction, the smallest correction of his posture, and the room tightened as though someone had turned the key on an invisible lock.

"Temper your curiosity," he said, and the words were not for the man before him so much as a blade sheathed under a velvet glove. He kept his tone even; cruelty had long ago learned the usefulness of ease.

The other man answered with a smile that had nothing of humour in it. He stepped closer, the press of movement deliberate and the motion of one who relished testing limits. Up close, his eyes were clever, like a hazard contained in glass. "Would you risk killing your only family, Zagreus?" he murmured. "You would not."

My world shuddered.

Only family?

My chest thudded, a frantic beating in there. Zagreus had

a family. He had roots. I had thought I lived in a house of one man's absolutes; instead, there were others, lines of blood I had not seen.

I turned, stupidly certain that my mind would supply proof of error, some explanation that would stitch the quicksand beneath my feet. The man who had spoken loosened his suit cuff.

I looked between him and Zagreus. There was a resemblance between them, but it was a subtler inheritance of expression, a mirror altered by time.

All the questions in my head, all the emotions I felt, were very strange. As if reading my confused expressions, the man chuckled and nodded.

"Yes," he answered before Zagreus could. "We have no parents to call. No cousins or extended family who come with casseroles and small talk. We buried what remained of that world and learned how to be the only thing left." He watched me as if measuring whether my face would crack from the truth. "They… did not survive her."

"Enough, Corvin," Zagreus warned. But Corvin only stepped closer.

"Why? She's your wife. She deserves to know your past. That's how you make your relationship strong, isn't it? By living in the past."

"Corvin."

Corvin scoffed. "I don't listen to you, big brother. You left the family four years ago, so don't pretend you have any right over me."

I swallowed hard, feeling Zagreus's hold tightening on my waist. He was pissed. But he had done excellently in masking his anger. Instead, he took a deep breath. "You will stop," he grumbled. "You will step back and hold your tongue where it belongs. I will not have my home turned into a theatre for your entertainment."

Corvin shrugged, more insolent than fearful. "And if I don't?" he asked, curious as if the world had been made to display provocation. And strangely it did.

I looked between them, aware of the tension and wanting to escape it anyhow.

Zagreus's hand slid from my waist to his side; for a second, his face softened with an emotion I could not name – pity would be the wrong word, anger would be insufficient. There was a danger in him now that had edges I did not want to be near.

"We do not speak in riddles here," Corvin said quietly. He looked to his brother. "You have always guarded what is yours. We know why. I remember the days before ash. Very clearly. The woman you loved… she took more than a heart, Zagreus. I am not watching the past repeat again."

I wanted to step forward and squeeze the truth out of their mouths until the bones of my questions showed. Instead, my limbs obeyed some older, more frightened counsel. I made a small, ridiculous attempt at composure and spoke where any sane silence would have been wiser. "I… I have no right to be in your affairs. I apologise for intruding."

Corvin's gaze slid to me, and I placed the weight of all my questions against my ribcage and hoped they would not make me cough up what I had found.

Zagreus's look snapped from Corvin back to me. His brows lowered until they met the top of his nose, and the room contracted again. I felt suffocated.

"You are his wife. You have every right to know, Selene."

"Enough, Corvin," Zagreus muttered.

I shook my head. "Why? Why are you telling all this now? It doesn't make sense. You don't know me. Why are you calling me Selene? I am not her, I'm Celestine."

Corvin chuckled. "Maybe I like calling you that."

"I will kill you," Zagreus growled while taking a step forward, before I pushed myself in between them and stared wide-eyed at him.

Behind me, Corvin laughed. "You forget," he whispered, "that there are debts that blood cannot pay. You would not risk destroying your only family. You wouldn't risk losing a brother. After your first wife killed our parents, I wouldn't risk losing my brother to others."

I tried to steady myself. "I should go," I whispered. Before I could move, Zagreus's hand slid out to capture me.

"You are not to wander by yourself," he said softly, and that softness suffocated me more.

There was a rawness in my chest. Zagreus's first wife killed his parents...

For a moment, I thought he would catch me when I snatched my wrist from his grip. And before he could hold me again, I found myself moving away from the heat of his body and out through the doors, propelled by an animal impulse to breathe.

I ran.

The corridor opened into the porch without deliberation. There was a need to ransack the night for something that resembled truth. The sky was a hard blue that was not kind to the eyes. Below, the ocean drew its long breath and exhaled against the cliff. The wind took my hair and braided it into panic, and still I couldn't breathe.

Zagreus had a brother. And his first wife killed his parents.

I stood at the edge where the land gave itself up to the water, and felt my whole life unspool. The sound of the tide was not comforting at all. It was accusatory. I pressed my palms to my face until my heartbeat steadied or until I imagined it might.

What had I touched in that box? The photographs were tender and proof of everlasting love, one that contradicted the cold man who owned this place. He had mourned someone. He had been bound before I arrived. Did that binding explain his cruelty? Did his first wife make him this way? Did it justify his possessiveness and madness? No. No justification could be scraped across what he had done to Adrian, how he had forced into my life without asking.

And Corvin. He said so many things in riddles. But I was no fool to not understand. He loathed Zagreus's first wife. And in the process, he was sceptical of me too. I could understand him, I would've been too if I was in his shoes.

But if Zagreus had a brother and a history of being bound to remnants of family, where did I stand? In what ledger had I been recorded? Wife? Usurper? Pawn?

The air stung. Salt penetrated my breath. I felt cruelly small and absurd.

I was not a person; I was an accumulation of other people's consequences. My ankles ached from the anklet more than the heels, and still I could not remove it. My dress clung to my skin. My lungs flamed with the need to run further away, to bury myself in movement until the name Selene and the shadows hunting me were blunt from the motion.

I pressed my forehead against the cold railing and tried, for the first time all evening, to count the beats of my heart. Each one uncertain. Each one held a question that would not be soothed by numbers.

CHAPTER FIFTY
Death of Us

D eath was not dying. Often times, it was the silence between two people. Secrets between them that destroyed
everything revolving around their little world. And at that moment, I felt the same.

It pressed against my ribs harder than the crashing waves,
harder than the spray of salt that hung in the air. I stood on
the edge of the cliff, trembling, my palms damp, my throat raw
with unsaid words, and yet, I could not breathe. I could not
breathe with him behind me, his presence so close it might as
well have been my shadow, his gaze so heavy it burned through
my skin.

I didn't know how long he had been standing there. But I
knew he had been there for some time now. I wondered if he
found me pitiable or vulnerable. Was I desirable to him now?
When I looked and felt like dying?

I turned slightly, catching him in the corner of my eye. He
stood a step away, sculpted in the dusk, his face carrying that
scar that seemed to tell more stories than his tongue ever did.
But his unyielding, stormy-grey eyes watched me with some-

thing I could not name. Pity? Rage? Longing? What was it, Zagreus? No word in my limited mouth could catch it.

I jerked my head away, refusing to drown in that stare.

The waves below roared, wild and untamed. "What am I, Zagreus?" The words slipped from me before I could stop it, like a whisper made of my broken heart, not knowing if I meant him or myself.

There was only silence that greeted me. What was I expecting anyway? He'd rather stay quiet, watch me burn or drown, but would never give me answers.

I laughed bitterly. My chest ached. "I don't even deserve your words now?"

The air grew heavier. My knees buckled, but I forced myself to stand, to pretend I wasn't crumbling from the inside out. My mind screamed the words my mouth wouldn't whisper.

I wanted to die.

Would he care more if I jumped? Would he care if I vanished into the waves, swallowed whole by the ocean? Would his hand reach for me? Would my absence carve a hole in him, or would he fill it with another bride, another woman... another body... to chain beside his heart?

He once had a wife. A wife who killed his parents. A wife he must have loved once, to keep her pictures. Would he keep my pictures too? Would he mourn me?

What was I truly?

"Speak, Zagreus..." I choked, my tears burned down my cheeks. I turned around slowly. His figure blurred through the veil of saltwater that left my eyes swollen red. "Or please... let me go."

I wanted to run. My body begged to collapse, to disappear, to be erased. "I cannot live in this hell."

'This is not hell, Dolcezza."

I stumbled backward as he advanced, my spine pressing against the rail. He did not stop. He came closer until his breath slid over my lips, until his body caged mine, his hands pressing to the metal beside my waist, trapping me. His eyes were no longer patient but consuming.

"Every moment I spend with you," he said, "whether in pain or peace…" his face lowered until the heat of his breath seared me. His gaze pierced through me. "Hell will be without you."

The world stopped. My lungs forgot their work. I stared at him, at the shadows pooling in the hollows of his face. "And what about me? Do you realise you've created a personal hell for me?"

His jaw clenched. "Then endure it," he murmured. "Endure it because this hell has me. Because I cannot give you freedom, Dolcezza. You are mine. Mine to fight with, mine to suffer with, mine to keep breathing beside me."

My chest caved, heat rising through my veins. "And if I don't want to be yours?"

A flicker crossed his eyes, gone too quickly. He leaned closer, lowering his mouth to my ear. "Then I will chain the air itself to make sure it never leaves your lungs. You will remain even if it destroys you. Even if it destroys me."

My breath hitched, and my body sagged against the rail and him. His nearness was too much, his words like a cage made of silk and steel. He had not said the word, but I knew he'd never let me go. He would never name it, yet he lived in it.

I wanted to die from the weight of it.

My vision darkened, flecks of light scattering at the edges. The sea's roar faded into a muffled hum, and my knees gave out. All the skipping meals came crashing down on me. I was hoping to fall, but I did not. I hated that it was his arms that caught me, strong and locking me against him. I hated that I clutched him unconsciously, my fists twisting in his suit, holding on even as my mind screamed to let go.

I fainted in his arms.

And for a one merciful moment, before the dark swallowed me whole, I thought... perhaps hell was softer than I had imagined.

∞

When I opened my eyes, the world was wrong and black, the ceiling above was cloaked in shadows and the candles long extinguished. My skin was sticky with sweat, my body was as cold as stone. The last thing I remembered was the sea and his hands, his suffocating closeness. And now... silence and darkness.

My chest tightened. The party was over. I had been asleep for hours now. And he was not here again. I looked at the table where a glass of juice was placed, as well as frozen berries with some kind of medicine. He cared enough for me not to die, but he didn't care to soothe my aching heart?

Something inside me snapped. I threw the blanket off, my legs tangling and my breath choking in my throat. So he changed me too? To this flimsy sheer lingerie, but couldn't stay with me?

Rage and terror bled together as I clawed at the clothes. My hands crashed into the lamps, shattering them across the floor. The books stacked neatly by the nightstand, I sent flying. The mirror crashed as my palm slammed into it, my reflection splintering into dozens of wild-eyed strangers.

Where was he? What have you done to me?

I stumbled backwards. The lingerie he dressed me in was crimson. And I wanted him to bleed the same way. Grabbing the piece of the shattered mirror, I advanced towards the door. He would die with me. I slammed open the door and froze.

The whole mansion was dark, no lights on, and there was

no sound. Strange, because I was accustomed to guards roaming during the night. The air pressed against me with a suffocating stillness, and I stood there another minute.

I swallowed hard as the jagged piece slipped from my fingers onto the ground.

Was this my chance? My only chance...

My pulse thrashed in my throat as I hurtled down the staircase barefoot, the rim of the lingerie gathered in my fists. The front doors loomed, and I was somehow expecting them to be closed shut, but as I shoved at them, my breath shattered in my chest. They opened.

There were no guards or shadows. My heart lurched. Where was everyone? But did it matter? It didn't.

I didn't think for another second... I ran.

Bare feet struck cold stone, then the jagged dirt path leading towards the cliffs. My breath came ragged, tearing through my throat, but I didn't stop. I couldn't stop. The world stretched out before me, the moon high and pale. The sea roared below as if mocking my desperation.

Every step cut into my soles. Pebbles bit into my skin. My lungs burned, and my hair stuck to my face. But I ran, and ran, through the cliffs and into the dark embrace of the forest.

The trees closed around me, and the branches scratched my arms, tore my dress. My chest ached, but I welcomed the pain... it reminded me I was still alive. Still moving and still free.

But was I?

Every rustle made me flinch. Every shadow stretched too long. My heartbeat became a war drum in my ears. He was behind me. He must have been behind me. This couldn't be this easy. Zagreus would always find me, always bind me to him in some way.

"Please..." The word slipped out as I stumbled over a

root, falling to my knees and clawing at the dirt to push myself up again. My nails tore, and blood slicked my skin. Still, I ran.

The forest seemed endless. My breaths were short and uneven. Hours could have passed, or mere seconds, I no longer knew. Only the terror remained, pumping through my veins, consuming me whole.

Just as I saw the clearing, I heard a sound from behind. I froze. My back colliding with a tree, my chest heaving, and my eyes darted through the shadows. Did he find me?

"Zagreus?" I whispered as my heart twisted. I hated myself for hoping it was him, for craving the prison of his arms when I had just fought to escape them. Because if it would've been someone else, I didn't know how I'd survive.

I turned, barely took a step forward when a hand clamped against my mouth. The sharp sting of cloth pressed over my lips and nose, damp and suffocating. The sweet, sickening burn of chloroform invaded my lungs and I thrashed, clawed, tried to scream, but the sound died in my throat.

It was not Zagreus.

The panic flared, and I tried to kick him, but he invaded my advances and chuckled. My world collapsed at the familiar voice. Just as the white dots danced in front of my eyes, I heard him whisper in my ear.

"You were better off dead, sister-in-law."

CHAPTER FIFTY-ONE
Zagreus Vitale

I've always believed the world was a carcass. Rotting and useless. A playground for men too weak to crawl and too afraid to burn. But I... I was different. People talk about destiny and justice and kindness when all that saccharine bullshit is meant to tame the masses. But I was never tamed. I was never born to kneel.

I slit my uncle's throat when I was six for disrespecting my mother's name. His blood baptized me, and I didn't even flinch. All it took was a knife and a heart that wanted this world to burn. I was built for destruction, and I proudly wore it like a second skin. Violence was in my nature. The world gave me nothing but reasons to hate it, so I hated it back harder. And I fucking thrived.

Until her.

Selene Visconti.

The little girl with two crooked ponytails, scraped knees, and a smile too bright for a place as black as this earth. An angel, if angels bled. Her heart was pure gold, uncorrupted by this darkness that made the rest of us look like ashes on her stone. She didn't belong here, not in this filthy graveyard of men and monsters. And yet... she walked straight into it, barefoot, fearless as if she could cleanse the rot with nothing but her tiny hands.

And me? The bastard born of fire and ruin? Bowed at her altar.

She was the only proof I ever had that maybe hell could wear the mask of heaven. That even a man like me could feel something holy.

Selene Visconti. My curse, my prayer, and my undoing all in one.

Even her name still tasted of marrow and fire when it slipped through my head. I shouldn't remember it this vividly, and yet I did. Every curve of her letters was etched into me like scripture carved in bone.

She was the only thing I didn't poison. For her, I stripped myself bare of blood and knives. For her, I swore I'd be more than the devil they raised me to be. I never killed a man in her presence. I begged on my knees for her. Zagreus Vitale, the prodigy, the untouchable, and the fucking nightmare of men, begged for a woman to stay. And she did. She let me make her my wife.

For a moment, I thought I had cheated fate. I thought I'd stolen something pure and pressed it into my rotten chest until I could feel it beat again. But fate is cruel. Crueller than any blade.

I lost her.

I lost the only goddamn thing worth bleeding for. Buried her with my own hands, laid her down in the grave I carved out of my chest, and shoved my heart in with her. Her carcass. Our unborn child. My devotion and my ruin. Gone. In one second. In one heartbeat.

I promised her I'd follow her into whatever afterlife dared

to claim her. That no god, no man, no grave could keep me from her. I made a vow, and I never fucking broke vows.

The note on my desk mocked me now. And I knew I fucked up. A little slip. Overwhelming emotions, I let them take over earlier.

Ghosts and brides shouldn't exist together.

My jaw locked. It was a bad idea to host the party here. I shouldn't have done it, knowing what the consequences would be. But it was mandatory. Diana Visconti needed to leave her den. She needed to make an appearance. Though she didn't, her minion did. And for now, everything is going according to plan.

I knew my little wife would take the bait. She loved her freedom more than her life. I left the doors unguarded on purpose, let her run on her pretty bare feet until she tasted the illusion of escape. I wanted to see which vulture would swoop first. And he did. Corvin always took the bait when the prize was her.

It was never about the party, never about the guests or the charade of crystal glasses and silks. It was about smoking out the rats who thought they could use my wife as their pawn. They thought they're clever, but they forgot who built the fucking game.

Though some things went unplanned, I'd have my fun soon.

But why did it feel so empty? My temple throbbed, and my pulse clawed at my throat. I raked a hand through my hair, tugging hard enough to tear the roots from my skull. Corvin. The bastard. The leech.

He touched her.

He laid his filthy claim on what's mine. And the world expected me to remain still? To remain calm?

I mashed the edge of the desk with my fist, and the wood

cracked beneath my knuckles. I tasted the iron on my tongue, and it took me a second to realise I'd bitten through my lip. Blood reminded me I was still flesh, still mortal. Not the god-damn ghost they all whispered I was.

But my bride… was flesh too. Warm and frightened, prob-ably. Running through the dark with her heart rattling against her ribs. And in her terror, she will mistake the arms that catch her for sanctuary.

I was fifteen when I inherited the underworld. I've burned empires less than this. And now they want to gamble with my goddamn soul? They forget I already buried one wife. And I'll be damned before I bury her twice.

Selene. Celestine. Angel. Bride or ghost. Whatever name she bears, she is mine. She will always be mine. And I will raze the world until the smoke spells her name in the sky if I have to.

I crumpled the note.

I married her once, she was my wife once, and I lost her. I found her again, married her, but this time, I won't lose her. Not again. Not until she remembers me. Not until she calls me hers again.

If fate wants war, I'll give it hell. My own hell.

Author's Note

Dear Reader,

When I first started writing His Dark Claim, I didn't set out to write a simple love story. I set out to write the kind of story that unsettles you, tempts you, and makes you question where the line between ruin and redemption really lies.

Zagreus and Celestine are not perfect, and neither are we. They are broken, twisted and flawed; their love is not simple or gentle. It's cruel and all-consuming. And yet, within that chaos, I wanted to explore something achingly human, how even the darkest of hearts can still long for connection, and how love can bloom in places where it has no right to exist.

This book is not for me, it's for you. About surrender and not fairy-tale romance, but about obsession, hunger and devotion that can destroy you just as easily as it saves you.

If you've ever been drawn to shadows, if you've ever craved the forbidden, if you've ever wanted a love that terrifies you as much as it consumes you, then this book was written for you.

Thank you for opening your heart to Zagreus and Celestine's world.

Acknowledgment

To the voices in my head that never let me sleep. To the late nights and the heartbreak playlists, and the endless cups of tea that kept me alive.

To my friends and readers who reminded me that even in darkness, stories matter.

And most of all... to you, holding this book in your hands. You made my dream real. Thank you for letting me share my monsters with you.